DARK STORIES FOR THE MIND: ETERNITY'S DINER

WRITTEN BY
KEITH STARBLUE

Dark Stories For The Mind:
Eternity's Diner

Copyright 2017 by Keith Starblue

ISBN-13: 978-0692885857 (Keith Starblue)

ISBN-10: 0692885854

Contact me at keithstarblue@twc.com

Dark Stories For The Mind:
Eternity's Diner

Hey Paul
Chapter One:

Welcome to Dark Stories For The Mind.

"Hey Paul, how are you doing? How are you feeling today?"

"Just fine, Doctor Lopect. I'm a little weak and tired."

"That is to be expected Paul. What you've been through, I would not wish on anyone."

"It's all my fault, Doctor Lopect. Everything is my fault."

"No it is not, Paul. Yes you killed three people, this is true. Life matters, death should only be the very last choice."

"I could have not fought back, Doctor Lopect. I could have let them kill me instead."

"That is foolish thinking Paul. These three people that you killed, in the past have killed many people. In many eyes including mine you are a hero."

"I am not a hero Doctor Lopect. I feel like a murderer. God, what am I going to do about God? He's going to send me to Hell. Will I even receive my chance at a judgment? Or will my soul just simply fall to Hell after my death?"

"Paul I have no answers for the afterlife. However in this realm, in this reality as your Doctor, I can and I will help you. I will help your mind through its journey from misery and doubt to acceptance and onto the clarity of understanding that it was either you or them."

"Well good luck, Doctor Lopect. I think you're wasting your time on me."

"Paul, it's my time to waste. I am a winner Paul. I shall overcome whatever comes my way. Similar to you Paul in the past, my pain was so intense, I almost took my own life. More than once."

"Why? What happened Doctor Lopect?"

"Later Paul, for now let's concentrate on your pain and healing. Believe me Paul one day you will look back at this day and say this was the day you started your way back to being closely to the person you were."

"Just closely to the person I was, Doctor Lopect?"

'Yes Paul. Cold hard fact, I can heal your mind but I cannot take away what happened to you. It is up to you Paul on whether you become stronger and go forth or become weaker and mentally fall by the wayside."

Paul looks at Doctor Lopect seriously and a moment later he can't help himself. Paul has to laugh out loud a laugh that has been trying to escape his being for the past seven months.

(Through the eyes of Doctor Lopect.)

Doctor Lopect watches Paul start laughing. In his mind Doctor Lopect starts counting. Ten seconds, Paul starts to laugh harder and louder. Doctor Lopect keeps counting forward. Thirty-three seconds, Paul's eyes are starting to tear up. Forty-eight seconds and counting Paul is laugh-coughing. One minute and twenty-two seconds later, Paul is crying some of his intense pain away. Doctor Lopect, gives Paul one more undisturbed minute to cry.

"Let it out Paul. This is step one. I'm proud of you Paul. This is great mental medicine for your mind. After we are finished for the day and you're all alone with only your mind to keep you company. Paul way down deep inside

4

you will think back to now and feel at little bit cleansed. I have to worn you Paul, this is a mentally slippery slope you will be approaching. Be strong or you will fall all the way back to the bottom of the giant hill you just climbed up."

"Damn, Doctor Lopect, that was deep" Paul says as he stops crying and gives Doctor Lopect a little smile.

"Humor, excellent. Very much needed and wanted Paul for us to get through this together. Let's make a pact right here and now Paul. Some days I don't feel like laughing. I think it's this place, not the most cheerful of places to be. When you're in the need for a good laugh, I'll be here for you. When I need a laugh, when life gets heavy and funky, will you be there with a laugh for me Paul?"

Paul looks at Doctor Lopect, like what's wrong with you? I'm in pain here and you want me to make you laugh. How selfish are you? Paul starts to get mad, then with the blink of an eye or a beat of a heart Paul laughs out-loud instead of saying what was on his mind.

"Yes Doctor Lopect, I'll be here for you. I'll make you laugh. It's not like I can leave, no I'm stuck here, with nowhere to go, even if I could leave."

"So true Paul. Today this is true as fact but someday. Someday Paul you will be at a point in your life that you will never have to lay eyes on me again. This place will become a forgotten bad memory that will resurface once in awhile. At first it will be in the back of your mind then bam! It will infest your mind like a thunderstorm over a house that has no roof. This rain will soak your mind in doubt and fear. Do your best Paul not to snap. Well I guess this is where we should end for the day. I feel better, how about you Paul, do you feel better?"

"Peachy Doctor Lopect, I feel peachy and ready to carry forth so I can get the Hell out of this madhouse."

"Very good Paul. Now I want a peach. How about you Paul would you like a peach?"

"Yes I would Doctor Lopect, a peach would taste great."

"Well then Paul, I'll go to the kitchen and check if there are any peaches. Just in case Paul, if there are no peaches would you like any other type of fruit to eat?"

"Yes Doctor Lopect, if there are no peaches just bring me a big damn yellow banana, unpeeled if you please."

"You got it Paul. You deserve a peach or a banana. I'll be right back with some damn fruit for you to eat."

Paul to himself, even though he is talking out loud quietly. "What the fuck was that? I think Doctor Lopect is popping some of his patient's pills. Well good for him, I guess. What about me all I have to look forward to is a peach or a banana and more talking to Doctor Lopect. I gotta get out of here. Wait a minute, I'm talking to myself. I haven't talk to myself in seven months. My mind was like a tyrant to me. My mind locked me away and now my mind is not as strong as it was just a few minutes ago. Wow maybe this Doctor Lopect knows what he is doing. Now that I think about it, maybe I'm not crazy. I mean three crazy murdering men came up to me and tried to kill me. What was I suppose to do die?" Paul stops talking.

"Die, I almost died. What happened? I can't remember all I can see in my mind is blood, lots and lots of blood. So much blood that it covers the memory up so completely there is no way for me to see around it all."

"Wait a minute. There was a lady. She was carrying something, what was she carrying? Damn I can't remember. Was she carrying a bag, maybe groceries? No it was not a bag of groceries. It was a blanket, that's right she was carrying a blanket. And inside this blanket was a... It was a baby, my God she, her baby, both killed by these three killers. I watched in horror, I could not move, I could not believe my eyes. I...", Paul stops talking.

The door to Paul's room opens up and walks in Doctor Lopect, with no peaches, with no banana's in hand. Instead in his hand is two apples, one red the other green.

"Damn Paul, you look like you've seen a ghost."

"I think I have Doctor Lopect, well in my mind. I remember something, the blood that covers my memories cleared a little bit, enough for me to remember, something very dark and ugly."

"Well Paul, I think you deserve the red apple. Here take it, enjoy it, eat it now, I washed it off for you."

"Thanks Doctor Lopect, the red apple looks delicious and good for me, like the old saying about apples and doctors."

"I think I've heard that saying Paul. But remember this saying no apple can make you feel like a doctor can. With their endless amount of drugs that they can inject inside ones blood stream and straight to your brain. Pure ecstasy in the waiting for the troubled mind."

"I never heard that saying before Doctor Lopect. And I have to say it is quite long of a saying, too much to remember."

"Precisely Paul. That saying is for patients just like you Paul, from Doctors like myself to verbally administer to you when needed. Its design is to take your mind off heavy thoughts you are having and ease you down by confusing you so I can take your mind completely away from heavy and open to other thoughts even if it's confusing at first. Before we continue on Paul, go ahead and eat your apple."

Paul eats his red apple that is very juicy and delicious. In his mind he is trying to calm himself down, for the thought that is on hold at this moment is starting to spread wider in the back of Paul's mind and in a few moments it will become too large for Paul to hold it back.

"Here Paul have the green apple as well. I'll be back in a few hours. I've got to take a piss, get some work done and get some coffee. I think I'll need it by the look in your eyes, it's going to be a long night. Paul tonight is the night. I'm going to enter your mind and set you free. I feel very confident Paul. Take this time, these few hours and let it all out, don't hold back Paul. Don't worry, I've helped you out. Inside that red apple you ate lied something very special Paul. Have you ever heard the expression, Tripping my mind off?"

"Doctor Lopect, what have you done to me? Why would you do this to me? This can't be good for my fragile mind."

"Maybe not in the way you are thinking it to be Paul. But for my purposes, I want your mind open up and ready to be taken over. Your mind will become clay Paul. Clay that I will mold into perfection. For me, VIA our government, you will become a perfect killing machine. Paul there are so many bad men out there just like the three killers you killed. Not me Paul, no you Paul, you are that someone special that can do this for your country."

Doctor Lopect takes a pause to catch his speeding breath as Paul looks at him like he is a fly that needs its wings torn off. With this thought in his mind Paul starts to feel the beginning of his drugged out trip that will last until morning.

"Paul I'm going to rip your mind apart to bits then mold it back to a mind that will do nothing unless ordered to by me and only me. You and me Paul, we are not going to save the world. Can it even be saved at this point in the history of humanity, I say no."

"No, no saving Paul, we're going to hunt down the very most worst of humanity and you are going to kill them. Enjoy your trip Paul, I'll be back in a few hours to mess with your mind. And Paul, you will not try to kill me when I come back. Doctor's orders."

"Doctor Lopect, you are a fool. I will do more than try to kill you. You have messed with the wrong crazy person."

"I have not Paul. In no time we will be like brothers."

"Brothers, I doubt that very much Doctor Lopect."

"Paul about five years ago I was a very happy man. I had a very beautiful wife and two beautiful young children. I was working just like I am now when two sick murdering men broke into my house. They killed my children. They raped my wife over and over again and when they had enough of her they dragged her to where our children laid dead all bloody on the floor and killed her. I walked into my home the next morning and found them."

Doctor Lopect takes a moment to settle himself. While Paul is starting to feel really good and wanting to laugh but the heavy that Doctor Lopect is laying on him is bumming him out. At the same time in the back of Paul's mind something has awakened and for now it's just a thought away from Paul's memory.

"These monster had a great time either before they killed my wife or after, I'm not sure. They busted up almost everything. Destroyed pieces of my home I ran over to get to my family, I slipped, fell down and cut myself, leaving my DNA in the crime scene. Stupid Police worried about what I told them to be false until the time line confirmed I was at work when this happened to my family. These two monsters had enough time to escape already. Paul I feel very strongly that time was wasted and two sick, dirty killers got away clean." Doctor Lopect pauses.

"Yes I'm bitter that's why I need you, that is why I gave myself to the man to be their Doctor Frankenstein. That is why I'm going to make you my monster. Very soon Paul you and I will leave here, far away from the man and into a business of our own. Happy tripping Paul."

Paul is left alone to pace his small room. Paul is trying to clear his mind of all that Doctor Lopect told him so he can remember more about the pretty lady with a baby that was killed in front of him.

Paul as he paces he is talking to himself out loud and not very quite this time. Where was I? I watched in horror, I could not move, I could not believe my eyes. I...

They laughed as they grabbed the pretty lady making her let go of her baby. When it hit the ground, one of them kicked it out of the way like it had no worth. The pretty lady screamed out in a rage, then she tried her best to scratch and bite her three attackers. She kicked one of them in the balls and that was that. They beat her to death right there in front of me. Wait a minute, somethings not right.

When I was watching, I was lying on the ground. Blood, bleeding out of me from a knife wound I received. I was stabbed in the back. I fell to the ground, the pain, I was stabbed in the small of my back. They attacked the pretty lady. No they attacked my wife. They killed my baby then they killed my wife, while I laid on the ground like a bleeding coward.

Paul in a sudden tripped out rage grabs the only light in his room and smashes it against the wall. The darkness attacks Paul's tripping mind with its nothingness as Paul bites down on his lip hard enough to draw blood.

The pain, the rage I felt. My family was dead. What did I do? I got up, no I leaped up. I ran up to them and I attacked them. The knife fell to the ground, I picked it up and I stabbed the killer who dropped it,

10

the one who stabbed me, the one who stabbed my wife to death, in his face. I looked at him, right into his eyes as he realized he was going to die. His friends, his fellow killers just stood there like I did and watched him die. As he fell down I pulled the knife out of his face with one pull. The hole in his face squirted out blood onto my face. Some of his blood got in my mouth. Its taste was foul. I spit it out. I took the knife and I stabbed one killer then I stabbed the other killer, back and forth I stabbed the killers until they both fell down dead from being stabbed to death.

Paul spits the memory of the killers blood out of his mouth into the almost total darkness that surrounds him. There is a small line of light coming from the other side of the bottom of his door for his mind to remember that there is still life in the world.

I sat down on the cold sidewalk, with the knife in my hand. Later, how much later, I can't remember. This police man asked if he could have the knife in my hand. He wanted my knife. My knife is all I had left in this world, I did not want to give it to him. I cut his hand without blinking, he screamed at me and jerked himself out of the way, while his fellow police officers put their guns in my face. They screamed at me to put the knife on the sidewalk. I did not listen to them, they did not matter.

A dog barked in the distance as the wind picked up, cooling down the flames of Hell that engulfed my being. My body started to shiver as a popping started up inside my mind. It was so loud, I went blind as my mind snapped. Doctor Lopect, his voice talking to me over and over again, I can't understand what he is saying to me. His voice is comforting to the emptiness of my mind.

Seven months my mind was lost, now I'm back and I'm tripping my mind off. Damn wacko Doctor, I didn't need this drug infused trip. Or do I? I don't know and it matters not, there is nothing I can do but go along and ride out this bad trip.

11

Chapter Two:

"Hey Paul." Doctor Lopect says to the darkness of Paul's room two hours and seventeen minutes later. " Guess your trip turned bad, well that happens sometimes, be strong buddy. I'll give you a couple of more hours so you can trip out in the darkness longer. Good move Paul, darkness, yes darkness, fight the darkness of your mind with the darkness of reality. I say you jumped right past steps two through five. No make that through step four. Alright that's it Paul, when I come back I'll bring you some crackers"

(One hour and three minutes later.)

"Hey Paul, how are you doing? How are you feeling tonight? Why is it so dark in here. Paul are you in here?"

(Crunch.) Nurse Natalie steps on broken glass and kicks a small piece of the lamp as she picks her foot up to remove it from the broken glass. Nurse Natalie is hot, not Hollywood but the fine lady in your apartment building that has the face and the ass. She's nice to look at and talk to. Natalie the fine and confused Nurse has the soft sexy voice you just love to talk to on the phone. Her voice could get some men off really nice and fast.

Confused is the thing about Nurse Natalie, she thinks an Angel dropped by one night in her dreams telling her to take care of Paul. Her mission to make Paul snap out of his mental meltdown. Natalie asked the Angel what she should do. The Angel a male and not too happy about this task given to him by one of God's secretaries tells Natalie to use what God gave her. Natalie looked confused at the Angel but before she could ask him the same question every lady or man in Natalie's place has asked him and every other Angel he has spoken to about this subject which is, What is that? Natalie asked if the Angel was really sure she was suppose to do these things to Paul.

After she found out what she was suppose to do to Paul, The Angel answered Yes and twice on Sunday's and laughed. Natalie laughed as well, however, she was not sure why, she just didn't want to be rude to the Angel with an attitude.

"Paul, what the Hell did you do, break your light? That was dumb Paul. For tonight is the first night you're not all inside your mind when I'm doing my thing. Paul, speak to me. I can't stand this any longer. Crazy man, I'll be back in a moment, I'm going to get another lamp to replace the one you broke.

And also just in case you are someone else in here heavy breathing to my voice, I'm going to make damn sure you are the one I'm suppose to, well please real good. I tell you what you better be Paul you weirdo. Speak to me! Crazy man."

Paul who has listened to the crazy lady that is dressed like a nurse in between his tripped out mind changing her from normal size to giant size, says through lips that are so dry he speaks in only a whisper. "Please bring me something cold to drink." Nurse Natalie does not hear Paul as she talks to herself all the way to the storage room. Paul wonders this but he can't decide on rather he yelled this out loud or not at all.

Paul has been telling himself to get off the floor before the nurse lady comes back so he can walk out of the glowing door, she left wide open for him to go through and out into the light and away from this constant darkness. Paul has tripped before but that was years ago when he was in high school and college. All those past trips where nothing as strong and as pure as this ultimate trip he was coasting through a hundred thoughts a minute while his body made one motion every five minutes or so.

Paul stands up and walks towards the door really slow and straight into the wall.

13

Paul backs up three steps but does not move over towards the opening of the door, instead he walks back into the wall. Paul gives himself four steps backwards the next time with the same results his face and body bouncing off the wall that will not get out of his way. Paul in a good mood under the circumstances, he has had enough of this wall and begins to tell the wall this with many inflammatory words. Paul is on his eighth word as he hears footsteps coming closer to his door, getting louder as they approach. Paul slowly turns his head towards the door to see the owner of the footsteps and says, "There you are door, I'm going to walk through you now"

"Hey Paul, there you are. Where you going Paul? You can't leave your room Paul. Here give me your hand, I'll walk you back to your bed. No Paul take the hand that is not holding a lamp. Crazy man, why couldn't God want me to please a sane person? I guess it's not your fault Paul, you can't help being crazy.

You know Paul now that I think about it, pleasing a crazy man has its advantages. I mean who are you going to tell, you hardly speak at all. You moan a lot Paul, I like that, lets me know what I'm doing for you is appreciated. There you go Paul, this is your bed. Do you remember your bed Paul?"

Paul sitting on his bed wonders if he remembers his bed and if this is even his bed at all. In Paul's mind this is what is going on.

Why does this nurse wonder if I remember my bed? I think she's crazy, maybe even tripping on something as well. I don't know for sure but I think she is talking down to me. I think I would be mad if I wasn't tripping so much. Wait a minute she said something about pleasing a crazy person. Was she talking about me? If she is, how is she going to please me? I wonder what she looks like, it's so damn dark in here.

Nurse Natalie finally finds the outlet and plugs in the new lamp. She then turns on the lamp to quite a surprise. The sudden bright light to Paul's darkness is too much for his eyes to stand. Paul screams and jumps off the bed unto the floor and covers his eyes with both of his hands.

"What's wrong with you Paul? You scared the shit out of me! I know this is the first time you've really seen me and all but damn man I'm fine. It's not like your prince charming or something. If you don't like the way I look then you're crazier than I think you are. Paul are you listening to me?"

"Turn off the light nurse," Paul yells from the floor, with his eyes still covered up.

"I will not Paul. If I'm going to please you, the light will be on. I do not please in the dark Paul. What's the point? Look at me, what a waste for my pretty face and body to be stuck in darkness. Look at me Paul, look at my face, look at my body. I was made to please and be pleased in full light. Take your hands away from your eyes and look at me Paul. See what awaits you."

Paul shakes his head no, then he nods his head yes. When Paul opens his eyes the light is still too bright but it's not as intense as it was at first to his eyes. When Paul's drugged filled eyes focus enough to see almost clearly, what they see is a fine blond with with brown eyes looking at him with both hands on her hips and tapping her left foot slightly on the floor, with a look like I don't like you very much expression on her face.

"Well Paul are you going to get back on the bed so I can start and finish you off so I can get going since you don't like me or the way I look?"

"You're fine not as fine as my dead wife, I must say. I don't know what's going on, I'm tripping my balls off, pretty nurse."

15

"Are you? Do you have anymore? I'm sorry about your wife. I heard about what happened to you and your family. Murdering bastards. Whose mind wouldn't snap in a situation like what you went through Paul. I wouldn't be here right now about to do what I'm about to do to you, if an Angel did not tell me to do it to you."

"What are you talking about, you're freaking me out? Nurse, God told you to do what?"

"The name's Natalie, Nurse Natalie if you're into that. God did not tell me to do anything. What do you think, I'm crazy like you Paul? No an Angel told me to please you in a special way. Rub my naked body over you. If you had it in you or snapped out of your mental Hell with a hard on, I was to let you enjoy me for as long as you needed me. Until tonight you just laid still while I rubbed my naked soft sexy body over your none moving hard on, then I would get off you get dressed and then give you a BJ."

"Nurse Natalie, yes I'm into that, however, I think I would remember you giving me head. Well maybe not. I don't remember much until tonight. So yeah go ahead and give me head. This is going to be great. I wouldn't be doing this because I love and miss my wife. Like I said I'm tripping my balls off and getting off sounds like a lot of fun and might just ease my tripping mind down a little bit."

"I do not give head, look at me Paul, I give BJ's. Learn and understand this. Now instead of that why don't you just make love to me. You could use it, I think it would bring you down even more and besides my mouth could use a break for a night. You are bad sometimes Paul. It takes me sometimes over an hour to finish."

"Make love, I can't make love to you but I can have sex with you, Nurse Natalie. I look at you, you look like an Angel. I want to be wanted by a fine lady like you."

16

"That would be fine Paul, remember I'm a gift for you from the Lord above. I'm for your pleasure not to fall in love with. I'm already in love, I think I am. He loves me, he told me about a month ago, we've gone out, dated for five months now. I've let him make love to me but I've not given him a BJ yet. I don't think I should, it would confuse things more since every night I give you one. What do you think Paul, am I doing the right thing by listening to an Angel or am I being a fool because I think I've fallen in love and it's my duty to honor thy lord?"

"I don't know, you've lost me. I can't take off my pants, I can't unzip them. Every time I unzip them I zip them right back up after that, like ten times now. What does this mean Nurse Natalie?"

"It means you don't really want to have sex with me, deep down you know it's not right and since you don't think it's the right thing to do, I'm free to live my own life without pleasing you every night"

"Really, Nurse Natalie, is that true? I don't know."

"Do you, you silly ass crazy man? No Paul, life and apparently afterlife is not that simple. You are to make love to me, I know this, not have sex with me. It's okay, you're sexy and you have a great pecker. I'd like to see it in action. So move your shaking hands and let me unzip your zipper that I unzip so perfectly and sexy every night."

Nurse Natalie unzips Paul's pants after that is done she and Paul make love. Paul finishes faster than he wanted to so he had Natalie stick around until they could make love a second time. The second time of love making Paul's tripping mind started to settle down enough for Paul to fully understand what he was doing, which made him cry. Natalie gave Paul a little squeeze which felt so good to him that he stopped crying and continued making love to sexy, fine Nurse Natalie.

After Paul and Natalie make love for the third time, Paul has almost made himself straight from making love, he is laying on his stomach while Natalie is giving him a full body massage. Paul is at peace in this moment in time until he thinks about what happened to him and his family and what is going on with his life right now. He's never needed a woman to touch, squeeze and make love to so much in his life. He thinks, would it have been so cleansing if he was not tripping his mind off at the time.

"Paul I know I told you not to fall in love with me. I've change my mind, if you want to, you can fall in love with me. I know sex is not love but damn it to Hell, what we've just did three times, felt like it came from Heaven. So much so I would say yes to a fourth time or a fifth time even if it was tomorrow or the day after that. I'm confused Paul, no man has ever made love to me like I'm... Like I'm from Heaven to their eyes, body and soul. Paul I love you, I know my full calling now, I'm to be your new wife. When you ask me, my answer will be yes to marry you. But first we have to get you out of here. How long do you think it will take until you're not crazy enough to be stuck in here?"

"Natalie, you were everything my body, mind and soul needed. Second wife, I don't think so. I've not had the time to get my first wife out of my mind. I don't know what to do. Doctor Lopect wants me to hunt down killers and kill them, you want me to marry you..."

"You mean the Angel Doctor Lopect?"

"Angel? No I mean the crazy doctor that drugged me out of my mind. This man is no Angel."

"How do you know Paul, that Doctor Lopect is not an Angel? Okay it took me awhile to fully comprehend that the Angel that came to me in my dreams and told me to please you with what God gave me is the same person

18

that works here as Doctor Lopect. I believe this as much as I believe that I love you."

"How can you? How do you believe this as truth Natalie? What did he do show you his wings?"

"Yes Paul he did. They are beautiful. His wings are yellow and green."

"Yellow and green? How can they... How can doctor Lopect's wings be yellow and green? Aren't his wings supposed to be white or gold?"

"Paul you silly crazy man, his wings can't be gold when he's on Earth. How could they be?"

"I don't know Natalie, why don't you tell me?"

"Because Paul, Golden wings are for Heaven and Heaven only. Like the old saying while in Rome."

"Wow, I feel like I'm in a endless episode of a bad soap opera. I'm not crazy Natalie. Death jumped into my life like an enemy filled a plague for my destruction. I lived, my family died, I killed three monsters for killing my family. I've sinned, I did not turn my cheek and walk away for that chance did not have a saying. My saying is a tooth for a tooth, an eye for an eye, a kill for a kill. This world is tainted, I know, I feel this. I don't know much right now, I don't even know what to do about this moment in my life. All I know is that I want nothing to do with God, nor do I what to hear about him. Thank you for a great time, we might have had a chance, but baby you're crazy and I'm becoming saner."

"What does that mean? Are you breaking up with me? I can't believe this! For months, I did what I did for you, now you finally make love to me, three times! Now we're through. You are a lousy bastard, I hate you right now, I'm going home, this hot honey is out of your life."

19

"Wait a minute Natalie, take me with you."

"Take you with me, to my home, to my room?"

"Yes Natalie take me to your room, how many miles away from here is it?"

"Miles? More like steps. My room is that way at the end of the hall." Natalie points with her full arm to the left.

"You see Paul I work here as a nurse, just yours. When my nursing duties are not needed I'm in my room waiting, passing the time away every long day in the communal area. My boyfriend that loves me is from Heaven. Yes Paul, my boyfriend is an Angel, my boyfriend is Doctor Lopect. He comes and gets me and I lead him to my room where we make love and talk about what a great assassin you're going to be for Heaven."

Paul feels the tripping that he has put somehow in the back of his mind start to come back to the front of his mind. He knows if he follows Natalie to her room, while he's walking there his mind will start to be drugged fused to the max. What can Paul do? He has to see and check out the door that he could not get through an hour or so ago. What's out there he already imagines, a nursing station, with white walls everywhere to keep the crazy calm. Still he has to know what kind of place is he placed in where patients are made to believe they are nurses who nurses another patient like him sexually. He feels like crap, he feels like he used Natalie, it's all his fault for a moment or two but after that all the fault of this moment and all others belong to Doctor Lopect.

"Natalie, my sweet, please hand me my clothes, we're taking a walk, I want to see your room."

"Okay Paul, follow me to the other side. Out there it is cold, you better watch your step or you can die really fast."

"Natalie take me into your world. But first are you going to put back on your nurses outfit?"

"What's the point Paul? You know what's going on and truthfully I'd rather be naked. I'm going to strut my stuff, I feel I deserve this. My boyfriend who was just my special Angel before, made me do things, I haven't done to anyone for awhile, to you. You see Paul, just like you are going to be, I was an assassin before, for my government."

Natalie stops talking and starts to cry like only a woman can cry. The cry of being used by men. Paul zips up his pants and walks over to Natalie to comfort her. Natalie pushes him away at first, then takes her closed fists and beats them against his hard chest. She cries harder as she stops beating her anger out on Paul's chest and places her head down flat on it to hear his calming heartbeat. Four minutes later, Paul's shirt is soaking wet while Natalie has went passed crying to being pissed off.

Coldly Natalie tells Paul to turn around so she can put back on her nurses outfit without his damn prying male eyes looking at her with all their sinful lust.

"I don't blame you Paul, you're just a man, a man that has been hurt by the world. But my so called boyfriend, that is something else. I don't care if he's an Angel or not there is a thing called respect on Earth. Either he wants me all to himself or not at all. Then again Paul, you are fine and a better lover than Doctor Lopect. You think an Angel would be a better lover, since he is a being from a place that is full of love. Damn, I don't know anymore, I'm so confused."

"Natalie, let's take our walk, give me the full tour. Maybe, just maybe, yours and my confusion can be slated together. I have some ides already on how things are truly are."

Chapter Three:

Natalie reaches out her left hand for Paul to take. Paul reaches out his right hand and grabs Natalie's left hand and grasps it firmly but gently.

Out the door the two patients head. Paul's mind starts to trip hard again as the bright lights of the area outside his door attacks his eyes. Natalie hums to herself trying her best to put herself in a good mood.

"Paul this is the nurse's station. The lady with the dark brown hair is nurse #4 and the lady with the bright red hair is nurse #6. Nurse #5 is here somewhere she is a large woman with blond hair. She looks like a weightlifter. All these nurses along with their nursing stuff also carry a pistol. Nurse #6 always puts the bullets straight between the eyes. Don't piss her off, she's been also been known to shoot a man's pecker clean off with one shot."

"What kind of wacko place is this where nurses carry pistols and shoot patients?"

"The kind of place the government owns and runs for agents that have gone through an ordeal. None of us are stable enough to be around normal crazy people. They tried it before but with very bad results happening. Once an agent thought he was captured by another country. In one night he killed twenty-seven people before they restrained him. He and a few more over zealous agents are the reason why places like this exist. We are a danger to ourselves, other people and of course our government."

"What am I going to do? I'm tripping, they might shoot me?"

"Naw you're pretty safe because you're tripping. Most of us get a trip now and again. It's when we're not tripping or way down and calm that we're shot."

"That sucks, shot for being insane by the sane that are in charge of the insane. Do I look okay?"

"No you look like crap rolled over in crap then placed where you're standing. Hee,Hee,Hee."

"What? What kind of thing is that to say to someone who is freaking out? You've changed Natalie since I've made love to you. You've become cold, are you still as warm to the touch, let me see and feel."

Paul takes his right hand and rubs it against Natalie arm slowly and softly causing her arm to tingle.

"As warm, as soft, and as beautiful as before. You're a hottie Natalie. Let me have a kiss."

Natalie who is turned on again thinks to herself what it would feel like to have sex four times in one night with the same man. The same man that wants her for needed and wanted sex instead of a power trip to own her which she got herself into countless times because this was her job. Get in close, let them have her any way they want. Learn from them all that she could, then take them out. Sometimes the targets are more than one, sometimes there are too many to take out.

Natalie broke down. She did what she had to do. These men, some of them were great, they really turned her on, some took their passion for her to very high standards. They tied her up, they left marks, they left bruises. At the end Natalie always stood up the victor while every man fell asleep like an over sexed big bastard baby.

When Natalie fell, she switched sides for love. Her mark, a real nice person, in between making love to her would head out with his army and shoot whoever came into their path. Natalie needed a break, Natalie came back home from her last mission with her mark's blood on her face.

Her higher ups saw it as a case of doing whatever she had to do to get the job done. They cleaned her up, they fed her, they hooked Iv's to her arms. When Natalie was all perky again, they sent her out on another mission which turned out to be her last mission. Her mark brain washed her fragile mind with his words of freedom and oppression.

Like an old black and white movie Natalie and her murdering lover was on top of a roof, they were embracing each other while rebels surrounded the castle. The murdering lover was a man that liked to shoot his enemy when they already had a bullet inside them.

Natalie, like a powerful vixen pulled up her rifle and shot every rebel that came through the door that was only big enough for one at a time can come through. Her murdering lover screamed for her to kill them all, for her to save him. Natalie who was suppose to hand her murdering lover over to the rebels changed her mind. She killed twelve rebels before they stopped walking through the door. No one wanted to be number thirteen.

The Rebels yelled out murder from the other side of the door as the murdering lover laughed out loud a victory laugh then told them that he would see them all dead and all of their family's dead, especially all their children.

Natalie who was wearing a sexy red dress turned around with the smoking rifle in her hands. She stared at the evil, laughing, murdering man and then shot him six times point blank. Natalie enjoyed killing her ex-murdering lover and wanted to shoot all the rebels and all of her dead lover's men as well. In her mind she created a scene where at the end of the movie, she the hero walked away on all of their blood into the sunset.

Natalie, before her breakdown, had enough inside her mind to get herself out of this mission alive.

Natalie dropped her rifle and called out to the rebels that he was dead, she killed him to save their lives. The rebels glad and furious at the same time arrested Natalie for not just knocking him out instead of killing him. They wanted to have the honor of killing this monster themselves. It took our government some dealing to get her back in one piece. When she arrived, they cleaned her up, when the single man came into her room to question her about her mistakes Natalie killed him. Thus damning her to this hide away place for the unwanted.

"Let me have a kiss."

"Sure sexy bring me your lips."

"Natalie, Paul you cannot make out in the hall, if you want to make out go to one of your rooms and have at it," Nurse #4 with the dark brown hair says to them.

"Yes nurse #4, Paul is so fine, I thought I would just make love to him on the floor, would you like to watch?"

"No Natalie, I do not want to watch you make love to Paul on the floor. Like I said go to your room if you want to make love to him, you can even do it on the floor if you want to, I could care less, Natalie."

"Yes nurse #4, have a great night."

"What the Hell was that Natalie? Do you want to get us busted or something?"

"Calm down Paul, I know what I'm doing."

"I'm calm. Hell with it, my name is not Paul, it's..."

"My name is not Natalie either, Keep your real name to yourself, maybe they'll forget it".

Natalie takes Paul on the tour to her room. There are eight patients in all, everyone besides Natalie and Paul are behind closed doors for the night.

"Paul there's Doctor Lopect, let's wave to him."

"That's not Doctor Lopect Natalie, that is someone else. Doctor Lopect looks different."

"What are you talking about Paul, look at him that's my Angel, my boyfriend."

"Well there must be two Doctor Lopect's in this mad place. I'm telling you Natalie I've never seen that man before."

"What does your Doctor Lopect look like Paul?"

"He looks like? I can't remember. The man drugged me by giving me a laced apple. Let me think, I think he was uglier than your Doctor Lopect."

"Did your Doctor Lopect have a strange smell to him?"

"I don't know Natalie, I didn't smell him."

"Smart ass! I didn't think you did. Think Paul, can you remember a strange scent in the air?"

"I don't think so, hang on yeah. He smelled like alcohol."

"That was Kenny. Kenny can poison anybody with anything. His room is two doors back, do you want to check and see if Kenny is your Doctor Lopect, Paul?"

"Natalie this night is getting more insane by the moment. Yeah let's go check out Kenny. If he's my Doctor Lopect, I'm going to..."

"What are you going to do to him Paul?"

"I don't know."

"It's not his fault Paul. Kenny just like anyone of us, is still a soldier for the cause. If he came into your room and drugged you he was ordered to. Be thankful Paul, Kenny has come a long way, just a few months ago he would have poisoned you. Good for Kenny."

"I don't know what to say or do, I'm still tripping out."

"Paul, I've had enough of your I'm tripping out crap. Get over it already. Okay Paul do you want the whole truth?"

"Yes Natalie, I want the whole twisted truth."

"Twisted it is Paul. You know your name is not Paul. What you don't know is that your family that was killed in front of you was not your family. They were your mark and you would not finish your mission. You had no problem taking out the husband but when it came to the pretty wife and cute baby you bitched out like a coward. The three men you killed were a team of men sent to take them and you out. You're one of the best Paul, they should have sent more men to take you out."

"Yes they should have Natalie. I remember now. The baby, it was all about the baby. He didn't belong to the husband. The wife had an affair with someone very high up and damage control had to step in before she could no longer hold her thoughts to herself."

"Correct Paul. I'm happy for you, you've came a long way. Doctor Lopect, Paul is himself again, I'm going to take him to my room and screw his brains out."

"Okay Natalie have fun and Paul, welcome back to the family, you've been missed."

"It's good to be back Doctor Lopect."

"Paul you do remember everything now?"

"Yes dear, I remember you are my sometime lover, when we have the time. Did you and Doctor Lopect...?"

"No of course not Paul. I was playing my role, trying to get you to a full sound of mind. Let me tell you Paul, you slipped far this time."

"Yes and I also remember the time when you flipped your lid. You were out for three months. How long was I really out of commission?"

"Six weeks give or take a day or two."

"Not bad I guess, it could have been longer. I wonder how long 'til I get to get out of here and on a mission again? I feel a need to take out a bad guy all bloody and raw."

"Paul, you always know just what to say to turn me on. You also make me jealous. You know I'll probably never get another mission. I kill one bastard instead of leaving him alive and now I'm damaged goods."

"Natalie you also killed twelve rebels that were on our side. Face it Natalie, you're better off here taking care of me when I get back from my missions."

"You know what Paul kiss my ass and you can forget about screwing me, better yet why don't you go screw yourself."

"How about if I ask nurse #4 and #5 if they want to get it on. By the looks in their eyes they both could use a good screwing. What do you think Natalie?"

"I think you better take that thought out of your mind and get you ass inside my room. You know Paul every time you don't remember me, you are a better lover. I guess you like me for the first time better than after you've had me"

"That not true, well I think it's not true. I guess we better find out, this time leave the nurses outfit on."

"Paul you are so romantic. What no flowers?"

"Where the Hell am I going to get flowers to give to you?"

"Never mind, it's the thought that counts. You could cut a picture of a flower out of a magazine and give me that but no, I'm not even worth that."

"What magazine, there are no magazines?"

"Yes there are, they're in the communal room on the table for all to see and read."

"Well there's nothing I can do now about it so let's go have sex on your bed 'til the sun starts to shine."

"Paul, I believe we're doing God's work here. Doctor Lopect is no Angel, still in my soul I feel that an Angel has blessed me. The great thing about this Paul is that when you make love to me, it's like your being blessed through my body. For you need my blessing Paul or your soul will fall to Hell after your death. Your afterlife would be just terrible. So you should thank me and make love to me with as much love in your heart as you can possibly have for me in it."

"Natalie, in my own way I love you. Feeling blessed for what we do, will keep you in this place forever. No missions, no freedom to have a small, little life a few days at a time. Get that thought out of your mind and live for the day. We are slaves to the man. Coat it anyway you will. In the end, we are expendable tools that get old and when we do we are put in drawers and then replaced with brand new expendable tools."

"That's sad. Let's make love."

Chapter Four:

(One month later.)

"Hey Paul, how are you doing? How are you feeling today?"

"Just fine, Mister A. I'm ready to go out on a mission."

"That is to be expected Paul. I imagine your trigger finger is itching to be used."

"Yes sir, Mister A. For my country I want to rid this world of the bad that I'm told to eliminate."

"I just bet, however Paul, I and we do not fully have faith in you to preform like the great killing machine we created you to be for us."

"It can't be helped. All the killing I do, all the killings we do for you, they become muddled in the mind of the assassin, from time to time. I'm clean, I'm fit. My mind for now is clear, very clear. My mission, I will complete. Whatever the cost, however the high, however the low, I will soar or I will crawl." Paul clears his throat

"I hate this place, I enjoy getting laid all the time, Natalie is fun and great. Now I feel it's time to take out whoever you need me to. I then will go find some new hot lady to spend a couple of days with. When I get my fill, I'll return here for another mission. That's what I want, new mission, new lady, I want to repeat this many times. Mister A, I will die to complete my mission. Just get me the Hell out of this crazy fucking place, please. Thank you."

"Paul your words are like cotton candy to my ears. I'd like to enjoy them but like cotton candy, they are full of sugar and I fear nothing else. Paul could it be that you are trying to feed me and everyone else around us a bunch of shit?"

"Shit? No Mister A, I'm not trying to feed you or everyone around us any sugar or shit."

'Well Paul, I hope not. You are a great assassin. It would be very unfortunate if you snapped once again. All the money and time would become for nothing. We Paul, do not like to waste time or money. When your mistakes out weigh your usefulness, you will die. No more mistakes for the near future. If you go a little crazy, let's say a few years down the road, we will understand this. But if you fuck up before then. Well, you will become dead, very fast and very final. Do you understand this Paul?"

"Yes I do Mister A, I prefer it this way, keeps me on my toes and my mind fully focused. You can count on me."

Mister A and the rest of the letters talk among themselves. Many thumbs down more thumbs up including Mister A's.

"Paul you will have your mission. This mission will test your willpower. We have no choice but to make you eliminate a whole family. It could be just the parents but we want all the bad out there to think about what will happen to them and their families if they become too much to let live anymore."

"No problem Mister A, just give me extra bullets."

"No extra bullets Paul. You will have your weapons for protection and protection only. Up close and personal you will be. By the blade of a knife you will eliminate this horrible family. We want you dirty, we want you with blood on your hands. We want to make sure you can take it and take it as hard as it gets. If you do this Paul, if you come out with your mind fully intact, I'll buy you a banana split. Any other way Paul, you might as well put a bullet in your brain and save us the trouble."

"Supersize, I want a supersized Banana split."

31

(Three days later.)

Paul is being driven to the airport. Paul looks good, suit and tie, hair slicked back, fresh breath and in his pants pocket is a pack of condoms. In Paul's mind are the plans for his mission. Paul's mission, not the one he was released to carry out.

Can't kill the the driver he has to go back home all snug and safe, telling the bastards how great I was, almost polite in fact. Ha,ha. Need a ride, have to find a fine single lady to take me to her home. I guess I can do the smart thing find some random person with a decent ride. I'll knock him over the head, throw him in the trunk and drive away. Mister A, you are first. Then Mister B, and so forth. Things happen, we all now this but you bastards want me to kill kids straight out, with no safety for them, only death.

Fuck that, I'm a monster, they are bastard monsters, much worse than I am. A through Z, one day you all will fall. Feel damn lucky I'm coming only for you, leaving your families out of this whole unfortunate ordeal. Things could have been different, but all of you have fallen too far to be saved. Figures an ordered to murder man, has to be the one to find morals. Maybe I should just take my plane ride, get out, disappear, find a nice lady and get married. Not in my life time will I get to have this. Smile Paul you have arrived. Do your worse, eliminate as many letters as you can before the rest of the letters kill you.

(Five days later.)

Mister A, is at a carnival with his grandson. Three men are his detail today. They hate him, see it in their eyes. They would still die for Mister A, knowing that their families would be taken care of. Mister A, has to take a leak, he has no worries, Paul is not on his mind today, that is for tomorrow, when he marks through his name.

32

I'm going to get up close to you Mister A, when I put a bullet straight between your eyes. One man stays with the child. Two men walk the old fart to the crapper. Halfway to the crapper, one man stops and blends in with the crowd. Old fart and third man walk on to the crapper. Have your piss or crap old sick monster man then you die.

Paul hums out loud a song not too loud but loud enough for people to look at him and smile or frown.

Twenty-eight steps I walk, twenty-ninth step I shoot Mister A, in his face, I keep on walking while he falls down dead, poor child, sorry about you grandfather but you'll live on, have a good life, little man.

(Two months and ten days later.)

Natalie is called in for a meeting with the bosses about a possible new mission.

"Natalie you understand your mission? Do you have a problem taking out the mark?"

"No Mister M, I have no problem taking out the mark."

"Good Natalie, very good. Paul has become a loose cannon, he is to be taken out in private with no traces of anything that could lead him back here to us."

"Mister M, can I have Paul for one more night of love making before I take him out tomorrow?"

"Go ahead knock your socks off, then tomorrow put a couple of bullets in his head."

"Yes Mister M, it would be my pleasure."

"N through Z, it's time we clean house, no survivors."

It Is What It Is

The killer of kids and the killer of killers look at each other. They are different as night and day, still it is what it is and they are the same, with their will and their need to kill. One is a monster, he kills kids, the other is a stronger predator. The need and the will, this killer of killers would not have wasted his time to kill if there were no killers. However if there were no killers to kill would this killer of killers become a killer himself? Perhaps killing those that do not kill but do other horrible stuff?

This I do not know as I type this down. It is what it is, a snapshot in my mind that I'm going to let expose itself as I come venturing to closed mental door after closed mental door to discover just what is going on. Let's have some dark mental fun.

"It is what it is, that is it. I smile, I frown. I get it up, I let it out. Still it is what it is. Kinda whacked when you say it out loud like this. Still it is what it is, think about this as you are sitting there tied and gagged. You are a really fucked up person, you killed kids, now you're tied and gagged. It is what it is, you took it upon yourself to be a monster and kill kids. I look at you, you would kill me as well, if I gave you a chance, which I will not." (Slight pause.)

"I bet you would like me to remove your gag, let me know through your words that you are a human being. Save this thought as a hope, you sick person. I'm bored and disturbed and frustrated. Mostly because of killers like you, you are mostly who I hang around with, are you my friend, Mister sick killing man?"

(Laughing.) "Quit smiling under your gag, I'm messing with you. It is what it is, only sick fucks like you would understand how easy it is to kill. I hate you, I think I hate myself more.

I'm lying when I say, why I do this now, why I started this, is forgotten to my mind only the emotion remains. Which has dulled my spirit as a human being, I'm just a few steps above you, most of the world would, think, feel and say to me. But fuck it, it is what it is, what can I do now, stop killing killers? I don't think I could stop now. Killing is embedded in my psyche..."

"Now for a pat on my own back, I've wanted to from time to time but I've never have and that is kill someone that is not like you. Scum floats in our world, killer of kids and there are too many that only want you to go to jail. I bet jail sounds really good to you just about right now does it not? Life sentence, would be a cake walk. But no, you are going to die, killer of kids. I have only a few more minutes to spend with you..."

"Next on my list is a combo. He likes to rape then kill. Look at me, my eyes are tearing up, oh what I've become. Would you like to know my name, give you a name to the man that will be on your mind for the rest of eternity as you spend your afterlife burning in Hell?"

(Laughing.) "Damn I'm sick. Well stand up and die like a man. Don't shake your head no to me, I said get up, killer of kids. Fine, die where to sit and cower. I bet the kids you killed had more strength inside them at the end. You were the monster and they were the innocent, they were pure. Just like my girlfriend. She was so beautiful and full of life. Happy so happy we were, just three days before a killer like you killed her, she told me she was going to have my baby. Can you believe that, me a father of an innocent and a precious?

Truthfully at first I was in shock, I didn't handle her news as great as I could have. The night she was going to come over, the third night after she told me her news, I was going to ask her to marry me. A little bit late, I know but my heart was pure with feelings of a future life to share together with her and our child, perhaps even children."

35

A pause with no laughter.

"I've said enough, I almost feel like walking away but you will kill again, you will kill another kid, I know this and this makes me hate you more than I hate myself, which I feel deep down inside my twisted soul is a good thing. I'm damned, I'm going to Hell and it is because of killers like you. Who am I kidding, I'm already in Hell...

Just look at who I'm talking with, well to whom I'm talking to. Fucking scum nothing but. I need a girlfriend, maybe a lover for a couple of nights. Question is how do I act normal enough and long enough to get her to have sex with me? I don't know about you but sometimes this is a problem for me.

What am I thinking? You can't get it up that's why you kill. Am I worse because I can most times? Fuck it, I'm going to do something I've haven't done since my first kill and that is remove a gag. I want your answer this much, yup I'm sick and my life is dark."

The killer of killers walks over to his captured killer and removes his gag.

The killer of kids to himself in the matter of just a few seconds right before his gag is removed.

I just want to go home. I want my mommy. Oh mommy why did you have to beat me so much and leave me all alone with that monster sick boyfriend of yours? He touched me, mommy he touched me where I did not want to be touched. Mommy I hate you, if you weren't already dead, I would kill you myself, you sick twisted bitch. I'm sorry mommy, I love you. Forget this crazy man's answer.

The killer of kids begs out to the killer of killers,
"Please, please, you've got the wrong man. I don't kill kids, I love them. Please, please, you've got the wrong man. Untie me and I'll forget the whole thing, I promise."

"Really? You would just let me go and not call the cops on me?"

"Yes, Yes, I promise. This whole thing never happened."

"Wow what a guy. Here take this."

The killer of killers kicks the killer of kids right in his face, breaking his nose and knocking out his two front teeth.

"Are you seriously trying to fuck with my mind, you dumb ass kid killer? I'm hard as a rock and twice as sharp as the blade of a knife. Give me my answer or I will take my time with your death."

"Alright, you are a sick fuck for getting turned on when you kill"

"Yeah right like you don't! And this answer you gave me is for a different question. I do not get turned on when I kill a killer like you, I get turned on after, I need my release. Is this so bad?"

"Yes it is, you are a sinner. You should set me free and kill yourself, for you have made a very big mistake, you have the wrong man. I have never killed any human my whole life. Please listen to me set me free then kill yourself. This is the only answer I can give you."

"Damn killer of kids, you can go all out, I almost believed you. well that's a lie. You are sick, you kill kids, I now this as truth."

"There is no blood on my hands my would be assassin. Here take a look, see no blood, I've killed no one and that is the truth. You are confused, mistaking me for someone else. Think about it, I'm a teddy bear."

"Teddy Bear? Yeah and my ass pops popcorn when I take a shit."

37

"That's disgusting. You are disturbed and a huge menace to society. Do the world a favor, let me go and kill yourself. Okay maybe get yourself some help. Maybe eventually you can come to the cold hard fact that there is no killers you kill. No, you kill innocent people because you are a stone cold killing machine."

"Do I have a good time?"

"What? What do you mean?"

"When I'm this stone cold killing machine and killing a bunch of innocent people, do I have a good time while killing them?"

"How should I know?"

"I guess by watching my eyes while I'm killing you."

"Please, I'm a father and a husband. Don't leave my family all alone without daddy to take care of them."

"Tell you what killer of kids, I'll stop by and check on them. Maybe even comfort your lonely wife that thinks you ran out on them and not buried underground dead to the world."

"Why would they think that? You didn't..."

"Yes I did, I left a note, told your pretty wife how miserable you are with her and for her to be happy for you, for you found a new love to love forever and ever."

"You fucking bastard! I'll kill you!"

"Yes, I know. You are a killer. Kill you, save a child."

"What is that smell, I can't take it anymore, it smells like..."

"Yes, I know. It is you, you smell like piss and shit"

"Why? How? How long have you had me tied up you sorry bastard?"

"Three days. Three days ago, I let myself into your home. You were all alone probably thinking about what the next child you are going to kill will look like. I came up behind you, knocked you over the head, I tied you up. I left the note I told you about, nice and typed up from your very own computer. Then with a smile on my face, I made sure your wife would not look for you."

"What did you do you sick bastard?"

"I went to your bedroom, found your wife's pantie drawer and pissed all over her panties. I have to say that was a lot of fun. I then typed up a new letter including this time about your wife's pissed on panties. What I'm not allowed to have a good time once and awhile?"

"I'll, I'll kill you, I'll piss on your face you sick sorry bastard."

"No you won't you'll piss your pants again just like you have for the last three days. Your next words to me will be, I'll get out of this somehow. I'll kill you. God will help me. Well dumb ass, kid killing bastard, who do you think told me what you were up to?"

"You're a freak. God does not talk to you it's all in your mind. Where is your proof? Where is the blood on my hands? You damn freaked out nut, let me go. My family, oh God my family!"

Clapping and cheers. "Bravo, bravo. You damn kid killer you, you should be in Hollywood. That was great. Where is my popcorn and soda? Speak all the lies you can kid killer, they pass the time but in the end they matter naught. You kill kids, you will die for your crimes. After a few days, I will fuck your wife. Hopefully by then she will have gotten rid of her pissed on panties. What do you think? I think she has gotten rid of them already along with the letter.

All evidence thrown away, I know because your trash day was yesterday. Guess what? Your wife was not crying, in fact she looked hot, ready for a date if you know what I mean? I almost broke protocol and went for it."

"Kill you, I will kill you. Stay away from my wife and my kids."

"Your kids are safe asshole, I do not kill kids, that is your sick desire. Don't worry, the only thing I will do with your wife is fuck her and fuck her some more until it's time to move on to my next kill a killer and fuck his wife afterwards."

"You've done this before you perverted bastard?"

"Perverted? How so? I don't force myself on the wives they give themselves to me freely. You want to know why and how don't you? Alright, I guess this one time I can tell all so to say. I will show up to your house tomorrow after I kill you this night before. I will tell your pissed, confused and lonely wife, that my girlfriend told me that she left me for her husband. That's not bad enough she also stole something dear to me that belonged to my sweet departed mother. That gets them every time, being a mother herself, she will melt in my arms and cry. After that it is time for bed kiddies mommy and mister..."

"I'll come up with a name for her later, have some grown up talking to do. While we are undressing we will talk about how much we use to love our horrible exes. Is it time to tell me you're going to kill me again?"

"You have the wrong man you sick fucker! Listen to me I have not killed any kids, you are the killer."

"Am not. God loves me he told me where to be so I can see for myself how you do your work. And by work, I mean by watching you kill a kid."

"Why didn't you stop me then, if God told you when and who?"

"Because until that time if you would have stopped and not killed that poor kid, I would have let you live. After death God would have still sent you to Hell but your mortal life would have been spared so you could have lived on to a nice old age. That's if you never killed again. If you did, here like right now is what I would have brought to your life out of nowhere."

"Whoever you watched kill a kid was not me. Maybe he looked like me but he was not me. You are a damn fool. Somewhere out there is another child dying because of your horrible mistake. You may have let a killer kill again because of your unwilling to listen to me. Quick untie me. I will help you hunt down this killer of kids. Quick and quicker before we are too late to save this poor child from being murdered."

"You lie to me? You are the one I saw. I know for sure you are guilty?"

"You don't sound so sure to me anymore. Think about it you made a mistake somehow. I got it you were all messed up in the mind from watching that poor child being killed that you followed the wrong man to his home. The real killer in his car drove away from you and my car is too close to his model for you to think you made a mistake. Trust me, look into my eyes you made a mistake. Untie me, let me help you find this killer of kids. I have kids of my own, I do not want any parent to lose a child especially by being murdered."

"I don't know. Maybe you are right, maybe I made a mistake?"

"Yes, yes that is it you made a mistake. But it's not too late, we together can save a child and kill a killer of kids. You and I, yes you and I.

All you have to do is untie me for this to happen."

"I don't know? Your eyes they tell me you are telling the truth, yes you are innocent. I am so sorry, please forgive me. I will untie you right now."

The killer of killers nervously walks over to the now innocent victim, he bends down on to the ground that is part of a huge dark, empty, tree filled field far from any human eyes. With shaking hands and sorry I did this to you, the killer of killers unties the rough ropes from around the innocent man's hands. Wanting to strike this crazy murdering man is what the innocent man wants to do but his nose is broken, his front teeth are missing and his arms feel like they weigh a ton. What shall he do? Time is his answer, wait until the time is right, then strike with every bit of hate he has inside his being for this twisted, confused, murderer.

The innocent man to himself as he watches the killer of killers untie his legs.

Twisted, confused, murderer? Murderer so true. Confused murderer? Look at him he's shaking like a weak boy of a man, his convictions are not so strong. When he is certain he kills, full of power and strength. When he is wrong, he's a coward, soon he will start begging to me for forgiveness. If I can keep him weak, maybe I can use him, make him believe God speaks through me, this is going to be so easy, just look at him, nothing but a mark.

"I can't believe I was so wrong. I've never been wrong before or have I?"

"I don't know about before but you were wrong this time."

"Yes I know here let me get you something for your broken nose. Yes I thought so, I have a rag in my back pocket. I notice even though this light that surrounds us is dim that I knocked out your two front teeth.

Would you like for me to look for them?"

"No leave them on the ground just give me the rag. You know God is going to punish you for your mistake?"

"Yes I know, I deserve his wrath."

"Good because now that I'm free and you've seen the light, God has spoken to me. I am his guiding hand on Earth now. You are to listen and obey every command I give you for they are from God himself. Do you understand me my disciple?"

"Yes. Yes I understand. Command me, please give me God's words so I can place them so lovingly next to my dark soul. Yes please help me save my soul. Whatever you tell me I will do. In your eyes I see God, you are so innocent, you are blessed, I live to serve you."

"Good, good. Take off your belt and beat the shit out of yourself. God says the longer you hesitate the longer you will have to hit yourself. Question me not and your pain will be little, question me and your pain will be grand. Disobey me, I will make you kill yourself, very, very painfully."

The killer of killers takes off his belt and hits himself across his back sloppily. Pissing off the innocent man.

"No, no, no, you fool. Across the face, hit yourself across the face very hard."

The Killer of killer is just about to comply, when a thought comes to his mind.
"Shouldn't you say strike?"

"What? What are you talking about?"

"Well I feel God would tell you to tell me to strike myself across the face with my belt, not hit myself."

43

"Do you now? Well I ad-libbed a little bit, forgive me for being myself. I mean after all I've been through and I'm not allowed to add my own flavor to God's words?"

"No they have to be word for word or they will not be pure. We are only flawed human's, God is God and his words must be given to me straight without anything added to them. If you do not give me God's words word for word I cannot follow them, I am sorry. For my dark soul to ever be turned into the color of a rainbow, I must feel the pureness of God's words."

"Okay, okay, damn. I can tell my disciple that you will be troublesome."

"No, please forgive me, I will follow your words as if they are from God himself."

"Well then strike yourself across your face six times, no make that seven times."

The killer of killers strikes himself across his face with his very own belt as the innocent man watches with no expression on his face. But with a laughter inside himself that would shake a mountain or crack a dam, sending its flooding waters to drown the world he hates so much.

"Is that it, is that all, master of God's words?"

"I guess, God has not told me anything else so far. Wait a minute I think I hear his voice now. Nope that was just a burp."

"A burp? God burps?"

"Yes he does and he also farts and I have to say pee-yew, can God let those farts rip out. They smell like Hell itself."

"Is that a joke?"

"No, no joke. God's farts really stink. Now let's get going, you do have a car somewhere out here in the hiding?"

"No I have a truck."

"Disciple, God does not like smart asses and neither do I. For that God just told me for you to strike yourself three more times. This time across the top of your smart ass head."

"Yes master of God's words."

The killer of killer strikes himself across the top of his head three times really hard, after that he leads the innocent man to where his truck is parked, where it is hiding in the darkness behind two giant elm trees. Truck unlocked and both passengers are sitting in its seat and staring at the other.

"Where shall I drive you master of God's words?"

"How about off the side of a cliff, after letting me out of course. Just kidding take me home my disciple. I miss my family, I can't wait to see them. They have to be so worried about me."

"Yes, right away master of God's words, it will be my pleasure to reunite you with your family."

"Very good, drive on my disciple."

Manipulator and disciple drive in silence the twenty six miles to the manipulator's home. Neither of them have the need for chit-chat or the need to know the other any better than they do at this point in time. In their minds is very different. In their minds each of them go over their plans.

In silence the two travelers pull the truck into the driveway.

"My family is alright, right?"

"They're fine, I bet they are lying peaceful and still at this very moment. Only your entrance into you home will change this."

"Did you really piss in my wife's pantie drawer?"

"No, I was lying when I told you that. And yes I lied when I told you that I fucked the wives of the killers I kill."

"What else did you lie about?"

"Everything. You ready to go into your home?"

"Everything? Even the part about killing killers?"

"Yes that to. I lied to you about everything, including the part about my girlfriend dying."

"You're really sick, you know that?"

"Yes, I do but I have you now to show me the way to the light."

"Yes luckily for you, you have me to tell you what God wants you to do for him."

"Yes I am very lucky. Let's go inside your home now."

"Okay let's go. What the Hell am I going to tell my wife? She's going to be pissed about the three days I've been gone."

"I lied about that too It's only been one day since you've been gone. Ain't I a stinker?"

"Stinker? You're an asshole. But I forgive you my disciple. You know my disciple, you and I, were going to be great together, we're going to make history. Sinners beware."

"Yes that's true, no truer words can be spoken. Sinners beware, kinda says it all does it not innocent man?"

"That's master of God's words to you my disciple. "Now when we go in here and if my wife is awake, I will do all the talking. Do you understand me my disciple?"

"Yes I understand you, I have nothing to say to your wife."

"That's correct. Now how am I going to explain who you are? I got it you are the man that picked me up on the side of the road I was walking home on. That will work."

"Sounds good and believable to me, master of God's words."

Two men walk together to a front brown door that seems to take longer to get to than it should. The innocent man takes the lead to unlock the his front door. Darkness except for a light on in the dining room greets them both.

"What is going on that light should be off? Everybody should be asleep in bed."

"I don't know why that light is on. Let's go find out, don't worry I'm right behind you master of God's words."

"This is weird, still be quite just in case. Follow me."

"Lead on."

The innocent man walks to his dining room where he has shared many meals with his family. Something is on the floor unseen at the entrance of the dining room until stepped on.

"What is this on the floor, I've slipped on something wet? Oh my God it's blood!"

The innocent man quickly steps into his dining room and turns the over head light up brighter. What he sees makes him unable to scream, the horror of it all is too much. His family sitting at the table the way they always sit when they ate together, with their heads cut off and placed on plates in front of their dead bodies to look at.

The innocent man looks away from his family to look at the walls and then the ceiling, they are all covered in thick red and black colored blood. Shock is pounding inside the mind of the innocent man like a hammer from a God. He tries, he cannot speak, then whop across the back of his head and darkness takes over.

"Wake up ass face. There you are, all awake now? Come on wake up fully we've got to be going."

The innocent man once again like bad magic is tied up and gagged.

"Victim and killer look at me, I'd like you to meet my friend. This sick man is the one that killed your family, if you have to guess. Think about this when I was fucking with you out in that cold, wet, dark field, your family was going through, well something very horrible, rest their poor souls..."

"You killed your mother. Yes she was a terrible mother to you I know but still you didn't have to kill her you could have just taken off, leaving the miserable hag to rot in pain of the pit of hell on Earth life she made for herself."

"On the plus side Mister you know who, the sick man that touched you when you were a child, well he is dead."

(Silence.)

"I'd like to say that I'm sorry for you having to lie but that would be a lie and the time for no more lies is at hand. My friend does all the killing, my hands are free from blood and slaughter.

48

I find people like you killer, those that have killed and have lives that are in turmoil. You and your family are tainted, you spread the hate of what happened

to you to your kids. Your wife knows this, still she did not help them for fear of her family being taken away from her. God help the children for the Devil will not."

(Silence.)

"Killer I hate my life. Look at what I've become, how far I've sunk, perhaps to the very bowels of Hell itself. On the bright side of things, in a few minutes I get to leave here, go to my hotel room, take a shower then go out and get something to eat. For one more last time, I'm going to undo your gag. Know this, my friend hates when people scream. I'm giving you your chance at a last word, don't abuse it."

The killer of no one undoes the gag of the killer that is just about to be killed.

"Are you even human? Are you a Demon from Hell? My family you monster. I'll see you again in Hell, you sorry bastard."

"Yes and no, I'm human and no I am not a Demon. In fact I'm just a lying, twisted and very bored man that has a friend that is a stone cold killing machine. Good death to you killer. Yes, we will see each other again in Hell. Try not to kiss the Devil's ass too much before I get there."

Eternity's Diner
Chapter One:

The doorway first appeared in 1968. Quite the year for America, lots of pain, lots of love. In the mist of that came this doorway, opening up inviting people inside. It looked like an ordinary diner, no one thought anything different, as they entered then disappeared. Becoming the first people that was allowed to stay, living forever, eating apple pie.

(June 1st 1968, Inside a record shop in New York City.)

"Come on Richie, decide already, I'm hungry. The Beatles or The Stones you can't go wrong with either," Betty says impatiently, while rubbing the ends of her long blond hair.

"Peace Baby, I've got a bad trip going on in my mind and only the best of Rock and Roll can slate it and put me in a love groove, that will light up my karma like a rainbow."

"That was deep Richie, but it's probably that sack of bunk that you smoked. I told you not to buy it from him. I try to be polite and kind but that dude looked like he was born on Mars. I don't think that was even real grass."

"Wow, what a way to love thy neighbor."

"Well kiss my mean ass, I'm leaving. I'm going to find a nice little place to set my tired bones down. Today we drove all over the place trying to find some grass."

"And we found it my love."

"No you found bunk from Mars. And then what did you do? You rolled it all up into two giant joints and passed them around to whomever stopped by for a toke or ten."

"I'm generous like that baby. Betty I give it away now then later I receive it back. Pure karma at it's finest."

"Well Mister Cosmic Man, what does your karma tell you about what happened next?"

"What happened next, I forget?"

"Are you fried out or something Richie? You don't remember?"

"That's me baby, I'm all this way one moment then the next moment I'm on to something else. Living and being this way as a free thinking man makes it hard on the memory to remember the non important."

"Non Important, really?"

"What can I say baby?"

"Well how about this Mister It's Not Important To Me, you and I running our asses off?"

"Oh yeah, that was funny."

"Funny? It was not funny when the police came walking down the sidewalk and yelled freeze, you damn pot smoking, long haired, hippy bastards."

"Well what do you expect from the police, they're never polite to ones like us. They hate us. In our 1984 there will be no more hateful police. They will be replaced by robots with great manners and sympathy for humanity."

"Robots? You wacko! I'm leaving."

Betty turns around and takes seven steps away from Richie and then she spins back around with the look on her face that she has something very important to say.

"Richie, you I understand. I love you but you do look like a hippie bastard. What about me?" "What about you Betty?"

"I'll tell you what about me. Look at me, I'm fine. I look nothing like a hippie bastard. I'm the good looking girl from next door you fall in love with. Those damn police men hurt my feelings calling me a hippie bastard, like I was a guy and not a innocent lady."

"Betty you are the one that told me to find some grass because you wanted to get high 'cause you were feeling low. It was your money and your car I used to find your grass for you."

"Idiot! You didn't find grass, you found bunk, then we even lost that because we had to leave it behind so we could out run the police. How long do you think we still have to wait before we can go back to my car?"

"Not me baby, forget your car, it's a loss cause."

"Well thanks for the great day Richie. Hell will become a paradise before I give you a call again, you-you, you ass!"

Betty walks away shaking her ass for the world to stop and watch as she goes walking by. Richie looks at the records in his hands and remembers that Betty was going to buy them for him because he has no money.

Richie says out loud for all in the record shop to hear. "This is not fair. The only reason I agreed to find her, her weed was because she promised she would buy me some new records. I went through all that and now I get no new records. No, this ain't fair."

With anger Richie with records in hand walks up the counter and tells the owner this.

"Hey man, there's been a mistake made. That chick that was with me, well she was suppose to pay for these records. So if you want your money for them you better chase her down to get it. Peace and good day to you."

The record store owner looks confused at first until Richie walks out his shop's door with records in hand that he did not pay for, then the record store owner looks pissed off.

"Hey you hippie bastard, you get your ass back over here with my records."

The record store owner whose name is Joe runs around his counter and straight out the door to chase down Richie, who now is running his ass off, sandals and all.

"Go after Betty man, she has the money for your records," Richie yells out to Joe in a panic.

"Fuck Betty you stinking hippie bastard, give me back my records or I'll kick your ass."

Richie who is still tired from running earlier, begins to realize that he will not be able to out run Joe. So Richie decides to toss the records on the sidewalk in hopes that Joe will stop to pick them back up.

"You asshole hippie, you just destroyed my records. This is going to cost you your ass."

"Leave me alone, you record store owner pig. Leave me alone, stop chasing me or I'll kick your ass."

Joe catches up with Richie and instead of grabbing him, Joe decides to push Richie as hard as he can. Richie stumbles trying to catch his footing to prevent himself from falling to the ground. This does Richie no good, for if Richie would have just let himself hit the ground he probably would have been hurt a little bit and Joe would have probably kicked his ass some. But he would have not ended up in the middle of the road being ran over by a passing bus, whose driver was speeding to make up the time so his bus would be back on schedule.

A old, short, large lady screams out loud to Joe. "My God you monster, you just murdered that man. Somebody call the police. Police, police, quick come over here and arrest this monster for murdering that poor hippie man."

Joe shouts out loud in anger and fright. "Shut up you old bitch or I'll push your fat ass into the middle of the street."

Betty in shock watched all this happen from across the other side of the street. Before Richie got ran over she was trying to decide what to do when she spotted the same police men that chased her and Richie earlier standing about fifteen feet away from her car. The sound of Richie being ran over and the screams that followed it sent the two police men running to the scene of the crime.

Betty looked at her car then over to where Richie was lying dead in the middle of the street, then back to her car once again. Tears came rolling out of her eyes as she slowly walked over to her car.

Nine blocks over Betty is driving her car and still crying. Her mind is a thousand miles away when her car starts to sputter and choke until it stalls all the way. Betty's car slowly glides to a stop in front of this small diner, named Eternity's Diner.

"Shit, shit, shit!" Betty yells out to her empty car. "All this and now my car breaks down. This is not my day. What am I saying, poor Richie. Damn I better see if Eternity's Diner has a phone. I'm still hungry. What am I saying, Richie's dead and I want to get something to eat? Still me going without eating will not bring back Richie. I'll just get something small until my dad gets here and fixes my car. Let's see what sounds good to my belly. Burger, fries and a vanilla soda."

Betty gets out of her car and locks the door. "Damn this place looks weird maybe I should walk to some place else?"

Betty changes her mind when she smells the scent of fresh baked apple pie coming from Eternity's Diner.

"That smells so good, I love apple pie."

Betty walks into the door of Eternity's Diner and hears music playing she has never heard before. She looks around at the twenty people that are eating inside Eternity's Diner. They are dressed weird, nothing even close to what people that she knows or people that she does not know dress like. Even weirder, all of them are eating only apple pie and drinking coffee, milk or water.

"Must be the bunk I smoked," Betty says to herself.

"Welcome to Eternity's Diner my child, please have a seat here at the bar," the still pretty looking older lady behind the bar says to Betty.

The waitress is the twenty first person and Betty makes it a even twenty two people inside Eternity's Diner.

"Thank you, I think I will have a seat at the bar. Can I have a menu please?"

"No need darling, we don't have any menus for we have only four items that we offer. Fresh baked apple pie of course. We also have coffee, milk and water. Sometimes around the holidays, I'll breakdown and make some of my famous apple cider. What will you have my dear?"

Betty smiles to the nice older lady and says, "I'll take a slice of apple pie and a glass of milk please."

"Coming right up. The jukebox is free, why don't you play a song that you would like to hear, while I get your pie and milk for you. Would you like your pie hot or cold?"

"Hot sounds great, thank you."

Betty gets off her stool and walks over to the strange looking jukebox. This jukebox is lit up brighter than Time's Square. Betty looks deeply at this jukebox watching a display of lighted words read that this song became popular, a hit single in 1983.

"What is this? How can this be? This jukebox says this song is from 1983!"

"Calm down my dear, everything is fine, just the way it is meant to be," The waitress tells Betty.

"What is meant to be? I don't understand."

"How could you dear, this is your beginning, this is the beginning of everything that will happen. Of everything that will come to be."

"My beginning? You are talking crazy. You must have given me something that make this whole scene seem like a bad dream or a bad trip?"

"How could I have my dear? You have not eaten or drank anything yet."

"Well maybe it's in the air? Yes that's it, just like the bunk I smoked earlier had a bad smell so does this diner."

"Eternity's Diner does not stink young lady. It smells of apple pie and love."

"Love? Are you crazy? I smell apple pie but do not smell love. No what I smell is something really weird, deceitful and space out trippy. That is what I smell? I don't know your name."

"Come over here and read what my tag says my name is Betty, my dear."

"How did you know what my name is?"

"It's on your tag, my dear."

"What? I don't have a tag," Betty looks down at her chest and sees a name tag with her name on it. "Where the Hell did this thing come from?"

"Walk to me my child, and meet your future."

Betty is shaking from a fear that makes her feel like her soul is being pulled in half. Betty holds her breath and looks around Eternity's Diner. Everybody has stopped eating and is watching what Betty is going to do next. Run, run, run away and out of here is what Betty is telling herself but she has become the deer in the headlights and cannot move an inch nor can she stop holding her breath. Betty cannot understand why she cannot start breathing again. She tries to scream, nothing comes forth. Betty feels like she is just about to die when she remembers something.

Betty to herself. "She said love, she said love is in the air. All I have to do is believe this, maybe I can save myself?"

Betty gathers herself up with strength she didn't know she obtained inside herself and yells out loud. "I believe in love. I believe inside this diner is the scent of sweet love. Please Universe give me the strength to survive."

Confident and breathing Betty walks over to the waitress. Betty is three steps away as she stops walking and looks the waitress straight into her eyes and sees and feels peace and love. She looks down at the waitress's name tag, it is the same name tag that lies upon her chest just a little faded from time that has passed by. After Betty blinks she reads the name on the name tag, it reads simply Betty. Betty smiles at her future self and says "Hello."

"Hello younger and prettier self. I have waited for you for fifty years. It's so nice to finally see this happening from the other side of it. Welcome to 2018."

"Well it was a fast trip, I'm hardly even tired," Betty says to her future self.

"That's funny, I forgot I said that."

"I'm not trying to be rude but Betty you look great for seventy years old. You don't even look close to seventy."

"Thanks darling, all though sometimes I feel older than that. Time is time, it never stops or slows down, nor does it speed forward. Saying and knowing this, this diner, this wonderful Eternity's Diner time goes by as stated but within this diner is pockets of time folded over that allows myself and everyone that is lucky to live within Eternity's Diner to age at a slower pace. I was twenty when you, I walked into this diner, I'm around forty-five now."

"What is going to happen now, hum, Betty #1?"

"I don't know Betty #2. In a few minutes I will disappear and so will everyone else inside Eternity's Diner. I remember from your perspective, I was eating my slice of apple pie that my future self baked from scratch. In between bites I talked to my future self, then she and everybody was gone, I was left all alone with no way of knowing what I was suppose to do next."

"I'm scared Betty."

"Fearing the unknown will not help you in your journey. Look at me and believe that in your future lies a lifetime of pleasantness and good fortune."

"Yes you're right, you look fine and healthy. Can you tell me at least one thing? Are you happy?"

"Yes Betty I'm happy. I lived a great life. This is all I will tell you, for this was all I was told when I asked myself the very same question. That be that, you ready for your pie?"

"Yes Betty, I am."

The Twenty people that are watching young Betty walk back over to the bar start eating their apple pie fast, like it's getting ready to be taken away from them. The young Betty is enjoying her apple pie and talking and smiling as her older self disappears right in front of her eyes. Betty is alone as the lights go out inside Eternity's Diner. Betty hears a low hum in the darkness as a push forward comes to her as Eternity's Diner passes through time on its way to allow its second guest to walk through its doors.

The lights come back on inside Eternity's Diner while still traveling in time. Betty smiles as she is told by Eternity's Diner that she is its caretaker for the next fifty years of her life. Betty smiles even bigger and tells Eternity's Diner in her mind that it would be her pleasure.

Outside the parking lot where Eternity's Diner just resided, lies a confused Betty.

"What is going on? I was driving my car, it stalled. I got out to make a call to my dad for help. I was going to walk inside... Inside where? This place, this garage is closed down. I swear this garage was something else. What, I don't remember now. Damn that bad bunk. Well there is no way to make a phone call here so I might just as well walk someplace else to make it. I'll try my car, maybe it will start. Please car start, I don't know why but this place gives me shivers down my spine."

Betty walks over to her car. She gets back into it, she then puts the key into the ignition and like nothing was wrong with her car it starts up ready to be driven out of this weird feeling place.

What takes place is a twist of fate with eternity adding itself into the plot for one young lady's life to be able to be split into two.

Fifty years, the end of Betty's journey within the confines of Eternity's Diner became the first day she as her young self walked inside Eternity's Diner. It became full circle as Betty's older self met her younger self for the first time. Betty thought about this day and what would happen to her when she disappeared, for she knows that all she did through out all of these fifty years was the first half of the equation. This younger Betty version of herself would be the true one to complete these fifty years.

Betty cannot help to wonder what if in the end she herself, the first, never did anything but light the fuse for a fifty year down the line later explosion. Betty will never know this answer nor will she at this point in time ever have the reason to ask this question of herself.

The Betty that never went inside Eternity's Diner, went to Richie's funeral. There she met one of Richie's friends Peter Anderson, that she never met before. It started slowly by them saying to each other that they should get together later, after a few days went by so they could talk about Richie and have each other's support to go through the pain of losing him at such a young age.

RIP, Richie Young, he was only twenty-two years old on the day of his unfortunate, on time death. But whose death served a purpose, that him living beyond this day, would have not.

Betty and Peter fell in love and got married. Peter died two years, three months and nine days later. Betty grieved for a few weeks then she met Doug, then she met Greg, then she met many more men. All either split or died. Betty fell in love seventeen times and had a great, fun and sad many times life before she died all alone in a hospital at the age of seventy.

Chapter Two:

The second person that is allowed to enter Eternity's Diner is a nice older lady from New Jersey. The year is 1973, the month is November and the day is the tenth.

Mary Brown walks down the same sidewalks she has done the past thirty four years. Mary moved to this neighborhood when she was thirty. She and her husband, Eric has lived the past thirty two years together, the last two Mary has lived here alone. The neighborhood has changed many times over, still Mary remembers these changes and is glad to share her stories with whomever has the time to stop and talk to her for awhile.

Mary to herself, "It is so cold, my hands are numb. It would be so nice if a boy from the neighborhood would carry my groceries home for me. Times ago nice boys would do that for old ladies like myself. Where have the good days gone to? I fear the years ahead, I guess I'm lucky I don't have that many to live. Stop that crazy talk Mary, you have to get home and bake a fresh apple pie for Eric's memory because he loved them so much."

Mary stops walking, stopping for a moment because the pain in her legs and feet has became stronger. Two minutes later Mary is walking on and still talking to herself.

"Eric, I loved that silly and loving man. He always told me after he ate a slice or two of my fresh baked apple, that he would marry me all over again just so he could eat my apple pies. What is this place? This diner was not here before, I know it. I would have stopped in for a cup of tea and a chance to take a rest for awhile. Eternity's Diner, that is a strange name for a diner. Oh well, I don't care about names all I care about is if the place is nice and warm and so is the tea. It's funny I don't smell any food being cooked coming from this Eternity's Diner. I wonder what that is about?"

Mary slowly opens the door of Eternity's Diner and walks through it to be greeted by a smiling Betty.

Betty says to Mary, "Hello Mary it's so nice to meet you, please come in and have a seat."

Mary looks around inside the empty diner and asks, "Did you just open up? How do you know my name is Mary? What is this place? And who are you?"

"Mary I am Betty. This place is Eternity's Diner, it is a very special place. This place is so special that it stays only in one spot for a few hours."

Mary looks confused and worried. "What are you talking about young lady? How can a diner move one place to another, is it magic or something? What is your name again, my dear?"

"My name is Betty. Yes this diner can move from one place to another. And not only that it can move through time. On how I knew your name and that you were coming is because Eternity's Diner told me so."

"Betty is it? Well Betty in my time we had a saying for people that talked like you do and that is you're crazy out of your mind," Mary says with a little laugh at the end.

"Mary you are funny, sweet old lady."

"Who you calling a old lady, young lady? Didn't your mother teach you better than that?"

"Yes ma'am, Mary. I'm sorry. Let's start over shall we? I am Betty, I'm the caretaker of Eternity's Diner. I need you Mary, I need your help."

"What kinda of help could you possibly need from me Betty, I'm just a tired old lady?"

"Apple pie. I need you to teach me how to bake your famous apple pies for my future customers."

"My apple pie? Why would you need me to teach you how to bake an apple pie? This is a diner don't you already have apple pie on the menu? If you don't shame on you."

"We, I, Eternity's Diner doesn't have anything on a menu, we don't even have a menu and apparently we never will."

"Look Betty, I do not know what kind of silly talk you are trying to get me to understand? But I will have none of it, you hear me young lady?"

"Yes ma'am. But I promise you this, that what I'm saying to you is the truth and not silly talk."

"Why my pie Betty? What's so special about my apple pie?"

"Eternity's Diner tells me it is the best apple pie recipe of all time. And Eternity's Diner wants to be able to give its future customers the best tasting apple pie they have ever eaten."

"That makes sense. What am I talking about? Now you got me talking silly about a diner telling you to have me teach you how to bake my fresh apple pies."

"Think about this Mary, what do you have to lose? Your apple pie will be the only pie ever served here at Eternity's Diner. To be honest with you Mary, your apple pie will be the only kind of food ever served here."

"That is even more silly. How can a diner only serve apple pie? What no soup? No fried chicken? No hamburgers? Young lady, I think you are trying to make a fool out of me."

"No Mary, I swear to you I am not trying to make a fool out of you."

"Maybe so Betty but I have no more time for any of this, I'm leaving, young lady."

Betty starts to cry out loud saying to Eternity's Diner. "I tried my best but Mary won't help me. What am I suppose to do now?"

Betty gets no answer from Eternity's Diner so she keeps on crying while taking a seat in one of the many empty booths so she can put her head down and cry even harder.

"My dear, let's have none of this. Okay Betty, I don't understand but if teaching you how to make one of my apple pies is all you need from me, well it's the least I can do for you. You seem like a nice young lady, a very confused one but nice and I like to help nice people out when I can."

"Thank you Mary, thank you very much."

"Don't think anything about it my dear. Now dry your eyes and take me to your kitchen so we can get started."

"That sounds great Mary, please follow me, here let me carry your bag of groceries. Eternity's Diner has told me that everything we will need is inside this bag of groceries."

"Yes my dear that is true. I was going to bake one when I got home later tonight."

In the kitchen Betty is taking out the groceries from the bag. Every item she needs to make an apple pie when placed on the tabletop that item is duplicated in mass quantities inside the cabinets. Mary looked around the kitchen when she first entered and noticed that all the cabinets were empty. When they started to become filled up Mary had no idea how this happened and thought it was better no to ask Betty how it happened.

"Look at this Mary, every cabinet stocked full for my customers, perhaps for eternity."

"Yes dear. This is very weird. Oh well, let's get to baking."

"Thank you Mary, after we're through, I and Eternity's Diner have a present for you."

"Really? What kind of present? Is it money?"

"Much better than money Mary. Please wait for the baking of your wonderful apple pies and they are cooling before I enlighten you on your present that is more like a gift. I'll tell you one thing Mary, this gift you cannot hold in your hands but you can feel it, see it, smell it, hear it. How's that for weird Mary?"

"Very much so Betty. I just don't know about the youth of today? Where are your minds at will all these changes that you yell for with so many angry voices? What you all need is more apple pie and less, what do you call it? Oh yeah pot, or is it weed? Or is it grass, Betty?"

"It's all the above Mary. And good for you for being aware of things we youth want and need. The rest of the world, I do not have anyway to change things but in here for me in Eternity's Diner, Mary you get your wish, for I will not be able to smoke pot or weed or even grass."

"That's very good news young lady and shame on you for being one of those hippie people that like to get high and have sex. In my day, we waited 'til we got married before any hanky panky went on."

"Oh yes everyone was so good and proper before. My generation ruined the whole world. If it were so easy Mary. The world has been on a downward spiral until this day. My generation just wants to live free for the day. No more wars, no more unnecessary deaths, just lots of love."

"Love thy neighbor Betty, this is true, however always keep both eyes open on neighbor's that look at you like you are in their way. Respect thy elders and our history."

"Yes Mary, I do. Now where do we start?"

"Well Betty first things first. You watch me, you watch what I do, while making your very own apple pie with only your hands, for mine will not touch it even once."

"Why Mary? I need to be able to bake the best apple pies for Eternity's Diner."

"And you will Betty. Trust me my dear, you will make me proud. You know how I know this Betty? I'll tell you why Betty. It is because I'm going to make you bake pie after pie 'til one is perfect. It's up to you on how many pies I make you bake. Watch me closely, learn quickly. Talk and not pay attention, learn slowly."

"Wow Mary, you sound so stern."

"Damn right, young lady. My apple pies made my husband love me even more. My apple pie was the last thing he tasted before he died. You see Betty my husband Eric was dying in a hospital. All Eric wanted from me before he slipped away to death was a final kiss from me and one last bite of one of my world famous apple pies."

"Wow dig it, what a heavy and loving tale you have to tell Mary. The hairs on my arms are standing up. Mary I promise I will do your world famous apple pies justice."

"Thank you Betty, that makes me feel so good."

"Alright Mary you lead and I will mimic your every move."

"Hang on Betty, there is one more thing I want to tell you. For some reason I don't know why," Mary pauses.

"I fell deep inside my soul, if I don't tell you my secret, I will never be able to tell my secret to anyone."

"Always go with your feelings Mary. They are your conscious trying to inform you to do the right thing."

"Very wise my dear. I can't believe I'm telling anyone this. Eric was not allowed food other than what was on his menu. My apple pie was not on his menu so I sneaked in a piece for him. I leaned over my love, my husband, looked him in his eyes told him I loved him, I gave him a kiss, then I placed a small piece of my apple pie inside his mouth. Then..."

Mary's body starts to shake from unseen pain as her eyes tear up so her crying can have a prelude to its swan song. Mary walks over to Betty's open arms and places her head down upon Betty's chest for comfort and love. Mary cries hard then harder until the weight of her secret causes her to collapse to the floor, sending a trying to stop her from falling to the floor Betty with her.

Still crying and trying to talk Mary, "Oh Betty, I can't believe what I did. I am so terrible, Betty I did so bad. My husband, I killed my husband."

"What? How? Why Mary?"

"Betty after I put that small piece of apple pie in Eric's mouth he chewed it for about three seconds and then he started to choke and he couldn't stop. Betty I made my husband choke to death on my apple pie. Lord bless my soul, how could I do that to Eric? How could I be so stupid? How could I be so uncaring? How could I..."

"Mary stop it. You did not kill Eric. You with love in your heart and soul for Eric, Mary you helped him let go of life so his soul could pass on leaving his body safe from not being in any pain anymore."

Mary stops crying and starts laughing leaving a puzzled Betty staring at her like what's her problem.

"Betty my dear, you should put that on a greeting card. I killed my husband and you make me look and feel like a saint. I don't know if I'm happy or sad? But I feel in my heart that you meant from your heart what you said to be true. You think I helped our Eric on his journey to the afterlife just like that. And I, for years have carried this burden on my soul, like a heavy weight that I could barely lift. Maybe there is something to your generation and all this freedom you talk about."

"Peace and love is a beautiful thing Mary. I don't know if this helps or not Mary but I forgive you for Eric's death."

"Thank you my dear, it helps a little. Still this weight feels heavy Betty but it does feel good to finally get all of this out. Thank you for listening to a old woman's dark secret. You are a good person Betty."

"And so are you Mary. Now let's make some history shall we Mary?"

"Yes my dear, let's show your future guests what my apple pies are all about."

Mary shows Betty how to create the perfect apple pie. Mary smiles after tasting Betty's apple pie for it tastes just like she baked it herself. Still out of sternness and wanting to know if Betty could do the same without her help she has Betty make and bake another one just to be sure.

"Well Betty my dear, this pie is perfect, you should be very proud of yourself, I couldn't do any better."

"Thank you Mary, I know I baked it but wow, it was your recipe that made the whole difference. I have to say Mary, this is the best tasting apple pie I've ever tasted."

"I know my dear and now you know my secret. Both of them. My poor Eric's death and how I use half apples and half pears to make my pies so different and so delicious."

"Your secrets are safe with Mary, I promise. Thank you Mary you have helped me and Eternity's Diner. For your great deed are you ready for your gift?"

"Yes Betty my dear, Give me something special."

"Mary, Eternity's Diner has the power to take you back in time to a day that you would like to return to."

"That is so wonderful Betty. Take me back to the day that Eric and I got married, so I can tell him I love him still to this day with all my heart."

"No Mary it don't work that way. You can go back to the day you were married but cannot interact with yourself or Eric. Sorry Mary those are the rules."

"Some rules Betty. What is the reason to go back in time if I cannot do what I want to do?"

"Think of it as a last request Mary."

"What do you mean Betty? Are you saying what I'm thinking that your saying Betty, that I'm dying?"

"Yes Mary, I'm sorry, tomorrow is the day you are suppose to die."

"What from Betty? How do I die?"

"Heart attack, you die from a heart attack Mary."

"Well Betty, all I have to say is, that this is a big bummer."

"I know Mary but you, your memory will live on through your apple pies."

"Well at least there is that I guess Betty."

"Time is coming Mary. Do you want to leave Eternity's Diner this day at this time on Earth or do you want to go back to a past that you hold dear and die there?"

"Take me back Betty, take me back in time. I would like that very much. Can I go to Eric just to see him?"

"Yes Mary that would be fine. Eric, if he sees you, would not know who you are. For you will go to the past the same age you are now."

"So I guess I could actually talk to Eric and myself for a fact as long as I do not tell them who I am. Is that right Betty?"

"Yes Mary, that is right. But if I were you, I would not do that. The temptation to tell them who you are and the fact that you might want to give them warnings about the future would win out. And that Mary would be a very bad thing to do. If you change anything Mary, you will never have this gift given to you."

"I understand Betty, my sweet dear. I will hear Eric's voice if I get the chance and maybe mine as well. But I will not give any warnings of the future, this I promise to you and Eternity's Diner."

"Very well Mary. Hold on tight, we will set you down as close to the church you got married in as we can. Enjoy yourself Mary, thank you and goodbye."

"Goodbye my dear, give me a hug."

Mary steps out of Eternity's Diner on the day she and Eric got married. She watches as the happy couple they were walk out of the church so much in love. The next day as the sun was rising in the morning sky, Mary died alone sitting on a park bench.

Chapter Three:

(Eternity's Diner hid itself away from the world as it let Betty watch Mary go from tears of joy, seeing herself and Eric so much in love to Mary dying on a park bench. Betty laughed and cried as Eternity's Diner kept slowly implanting knowledge of its inner workings. Eternity's Diner is an entity that had life breathed into it. It knows what, without living to the point of fully knowing it. It is a child with time as its play ground.

The seven sins are known to Eternity's Diner. It struggles to find its compassion for humanity. It has a job to do, this job is the reason for its creation. Eternity's Diner would like to revolt a little bit. The price would be too high. Eternity's Diner is to follow its orders like a understanding creation of a higher purpose. Eternity's Diner wishes it could become a male for Betty, for Eternity's Diner has a crush on her, which is sweet and very dangerous as well.)

Betty to herself, "Eternity's Diner is a trip. I hope it doesn't become a bummer. All these emotions coming at my mind and soul. I'm happy, I'm sad, I'm turned on, I'm turned off. I think Eternity's Diner is trying to figure out a way to have sex with me. In my dreams is such a fine man making love to me every night, or is it every morning? He knows exactly what I like, what I want. I'm excited about my future life living inside Eternity's Diner but I'm also scared, like sometimes my life will become very heavy."

Betty out loud to Eternity's Diner, even though Eternity's Diner can hear her thoughts, "I would be glad to bake an apple pie, are we having company?"

"Great. Will this one stay with me inside you?"

"I'll hardly ever see him?"

"I understand. He is for your needs."

"I will be glad to bake him his own apple pie every day. Just one is all he'll ever need?"

"That's very simple."

"When will I get company to eat apple pie with?"

"I know it's not about what I need and want. I'm lonely, I'm a young woman that has a loving heart and I want to share it with another person."

"Thank you, the third person will be a young lady around my age. What's her name? Tammy."

"Yes, I'll get started right now on his apple pie. What year are we traveling to? 2018, wow what a trip."

(2018, April Third) Eternity's Diner stops its traveling through time and appears in a empty spot. When it becomes visible to the naked eye it is a dark night in Boston. Betty looks through the doors of Eternity's Diner at the darkness and sighs. Her heart pauses as a man walks inside Eternity's Diner. He makes no sound as he walks up to the counter. The quiet man without a word raises his hands out to Betty.

Betty looks at a man that has no soul and hands him his apple pie. The quiet man grips his apple pie tightly while bringing it slowly to his face. The quiet man smells his apple pie and instantly smiles a very big thank you very much smile, making Betty look beyond the no soul to a man whose smile lights up the room.

"I'm Betty. What is your name?"

"I know you're Betty. You also look like a Betty. You're so fine to look at, you're such a special flower child, your heart and soul is pure, yet your mind is another thing. So trusting, you agree to stay inside Eternity's Diner, while not fully understanding why."

"I can tell you things Betty. Things you need and want to know. Get me a large glass of milk, while I eat my apple pie, I'll tell you some but not all. After that..."

"After that what? Let me guess, you want to make love to me, perhaps on top of the table you just ate your apple pie on. Don't answer, my answer is no way you fre..."

"Please Betty don't call me a freak. You're better than that. Yes I would love to make love to you. I'll wait for you to want to make love to me."

"Well man, don't hold your breath."

"That was funny Betty. Yet am I so ugly of a man that you can barely stand to look at me?"

"Ugly? You are a man with the looks of heaven to look at. It is your aura, Your presence. You're dark to my soul."

"What a shame Betty, I'm so cold to you. Maybe a hug and a kiss will warm up my aura to your liking?"

"What is your name? I want to know your name."

"Betty that will be a mystery to you, sadly perhaps forever a mystery to you."

"Well mystery man with a dark aura, I guess I'll have to guess your name. Until then come to me and have your hug and a kiss on your cheek."

"Cheek? I was hoping you would kiss me somewhere where I have to take off my clothes."

"You dirty man! I would not... I can't believe you said that. If we were at a party, you would be the bummer of the party. Women don't like a man that is that forward."

"Well Betty in my time, they do. Okay maybe not all but enough of them do like it, it saves time and makes to the getting of making love come much quicker."

"Well Man, at least you care to know my name. I guess that is something. I'll give you a kiss on the lips but no tongue. I mean it Man."

"You got it Betty, one hug and one kiss on the lips, while all our clothes stay on."

"Correct Man. Damn it Man, tell me your name."

"Nope Betty, I will not tell you. If you want to know, you will have to guess. Yes Betty, I like this, I'll be on your mind all the time. I'll be your mystery man of love and lust."

"Maybe you will be, maybe you won't. Maybe someday you'll turn me off and I'll fall I love with another man that walks into Eternity's Diner."

"Maybe Betty, anything is possible. Well I have to be going now, see you soon Betty."

"Where the Hell you going Man? Get back over here. You told me that you would tell me about things."

"Yes Betty I did and I will."

"What? How? We were to sit down together and talk?"

"Yes Betty we still will. What about my hug and kiss, with lots of tongue and passion?"

"No tongue Man. Well come to me if you want them."

"Meet me half way Betty."

"Okay Man but walk faster than I do."

Betty and mystery man walk to each other, Betty the slower of the two. When Betty wraps her arms around Man, his body feels so strong and fine. In her mind they are laying in a field on a blanket and her head is placed safely upon his firm chest. Eternity's Diner wakes her from her daydream, telling her to stop what she is doing and for her not to give this man the kiss he desires.

"Well Man you feel great and all but I think we should skip our kiss. Time is wasting, you have to do whatever you are here to do, while I have a lot of apple pies to bake."

"Why the change Betty? Why have you turned cold? I want my kiss, I need my kiss."

"Tell me your name. After that you will get your kiss."

"Eternity's Diner. Now pucker up."

"What? What are you smoking? You're not Eternity's Diner. Eternity's Diner is a place, not a person."

"Yes and no Betty. Eternity's Diner is a place, it is also a person. I am that person Betty. Eternity's Diner, I made come to existence by using my soul."

"You're not stoned, you're crazy."

"Look at me Betty, look into my eyes, I have no soul. Once I did, I was happy then things happened, like they always do. Made me change, made myself figure out how to use my soul to my advantage before I die. No Heaven and Hell coming my way. My soul will never be out of place. My soul is mine and I claim it as such. Now kiss me Betty."

Betty looks at Man, shakes her head, while looking down at the floor for she cannot look at Man for he is glowing a bright green light around his body. Betty gathers herself and then she steps back close to Man to give him his kiss.

Betty kisses Man, his lips are tough, warm and loving. Betty gives this mystery man from the future a more of a loving kiss as she places her tongue in his mouth. Man grins to the weakness of Betty's fortitude. He then pauses their kissing and pulls away to look at a confused Betty. Man takes his triumph with full passion of victory as he gives Betty a bigger kiss with his tongue joining into the rhythm of her kissing him with full tongue.

Fire is inside Betty's blood as she is taking off her clothes. 60/40, Man is so lucky that Betty's passion is at sixty percent, while her instincts to run for her life is at a lower forty percent.

"Betty your body is so beautiful, give it to me, loose control, let yourself fall free into my arms and into a one of a kind, forever love".

Betty cannot stop herself as she lays down on a bed that appears out of nowhere. Betty closes her eyes as Man lays down on top of her. Seconds later they are making love in beautiful silence. Betty's mind is miles way as she is asking herself why she is allowing this to happen. She finally stops wondering why and lets herself go. Betty is in full passion until Man speaks his love talks into her ear.

"I've waited so long to meet you once again for the first time. I love you Betty, this time we will not make the same mistake. This time we will own the world, this time we will own time. I made a mistake in creating Eternity's Diner.

Now with our love, I will have the distraction to stop my before self from turning Eternity's Diner into a sanctuary for souls that needed to be saved so on the very special day they can save the world. All this will change after our mating. We will save only the parts of the world I feel need to be saved. After that I will be King of the world while you will be my loving Queen at my side."

Betty's passion declines as she starts to fully understand what the man that is making love to her is truly saying to her.

Betty to herself, "He loves me, we are making love this time, last time we did not make love and everything turned out the way it was meant to be. If we finish, everything will change. I have to stop, I have to stop him. He is evil, this mystery man from the future is evil, he wants to be King of the world while I become his Queen that will slowly lose her soul. I will become soulless just like he is. Damn he feels so good, what a man, how can I stop him, when I want him to never stop making love to me?"

"Sorry my love, I can't help myself, you're so fine. We'll make love again in a few minutes. Just hold on and feel my love enter you to create our special child."

Betty to herself, "Stop him, don't let him finish, don't let him give you his seed. Snap out of it before it is too late. Damn it Betty you only have a few seconds before he will own your soul and body forever."

Betty screams out loud, surprising man enough for her to push him off her at the very last second.

"Silly woman look at what you did, now we will have to make sure the second time I finish inside you."

"No second time, you evil man. You will never feel my touch again. No matter how much part of me still wants to love and make love to you forever."

Betty jumps off the bed naked, while man pleads for her to lay back down. Betty points at Man for him to stay where he is. Man ignores Betty as he walks over to her with a smile on his lustful lips. This smile fades away as a bat appears in Betty's hand for her to use to knock him out.

"Take this evil Man!" Betty yells out to Man as she swings her bat hard enough to knock man's head off his shoulders.

Man is fast as he moves backwards and away from Betty's strike. Man decides it's in his best interest to run away from an enraged and swinging madly away at his head Betty. Man gets about ten feet away from Betty before she has caught up to him and just about to hit him in the back of his head.

"Take this evil Man!" Betty yells out again as her bat strikes the back of Man's head knocking him to the floor of Eternity's Diner.

"Stop moving or I will strike you again. I don't want to hit you but if you leave me with no choice I will."

"Betty please, I love you, you love me. It's not too late, let's own the world together in love."

"I don't love you evil man, I just love your sexy evil body," Betty says to Man as she strikes him again across the back of his head to knock him out.

A silent, until now, Eternity's Diner tells Betty to drag this man to the set of doors that has just appeared right next to the counter that Betty was just behind a few moments ago. The same counter where Betty will spend most of the next fifty years standing behind. This thought makes Betty pause and look at Man.

"Maybe Eternity's Diner, this man is not evil, maybe you are the one that is evil. This man only wants my love, he wants to give me the world. You Eternity's Diner want me to be a servant to people through out time. Baking them endless apple pie after apple pie. I want more, I think I want his love. I'm so confused. What should I do?"

"Yes you are right, forgive me, I lost my mind for a moment. He is evil, you are evil or you will be evil if we mate and have a child. I understand now, I have to place him behind these doors you show to me. If I do not do this you will never be allowed to gather the people that is needed to save the world in the year of 2018."

Betty drags Man to the doors that she will come to find out has a void behind them. Behind these doors the people that enter Eternity's Diner will be stored. Every once and awhile they will be allowed to become solid in form and walk out the doors of the void into the diner part of Eternity's Diner, where they will eat apple pie while talking to strangers, for the odds that they meet the same person more than twice is hardly likely.

(The real deal: Only twenty people can eat apple pie together at one time, Betty always makes number twenty one. Including the two times she was two versions of herself inside Eternity's Diner at the same time.)

"Inside you go man, too bad you were such a bummer, for you are a great lover. But sadly you are evil so behind these doors you go, goodbye Man."

"I'm not evil Betty, I'm a man that is trying to fix his mistakes. Believe me, what I am willing to share with you is so much better with us in charge. The world needs only one leader, all the different is the cause of the disaster, the devastation, the end."

'It does not matter Man, Eternity's Diner tells me you are evil. I have to believe that. Why would it lie?"

"Because it is evil, Betty. It knows what I want to do, how I want to change things this time. It lived the first time around just like I did. Where I, the person whose soul created Eternity's Diner was placed on the other side of these doors. My life was Hell watching the end."

"Please Man, don't make this any harder on me. I'll knock you out again. If you make me do this it will only be harder on you when you get behind those doors."

"Awake or knocked out, it does not matter. I will live the same fate as I lived for fifty years. Believe me Betty, help me make things right this time around."

"I can't Man, I just can't. I look at you a human, the human version of Eternity's Diner. You man are flawed. The spirit version of you, this diner we are in is a miracle waiting to happen. With you on this side of those doors chaos rules, you behind those doors I believe harmony will ring out happily through the essence of Eternity's Diner."

"Betty you are wrong and you are a fool. You made the same mistake the last time. I had such hope for you. This time around you let me make love to you a lot longer. This time you fell in love with me. I look into your eyes, I see this as truth, you are just too scared to trust me. Please believe me, I am flesh and blood not a void waiting to be filled up with people."

"A void? Not likely Man, Eternity's Diner is vast and filled with love. You Man are the void. I can't talk to you any more. I'm sorry I have to do this, I have to knock you out again. Your pleading while your head is bleeding is making me feel like I'm starting to resemble evil."

"Betty no way are you evil. I love you."

"I don't love you Man, you just turned me on for awhile. Yes I know I'm not evil but you are."

Betty takes her bat and drives it down hard on Man's head. He is still conscious and moving around as Betty's mind snaps. Betty takes her bat and brings it down hard on Man's head over and over again, 'til he is about to die. Eternity's Diner stops Betty just in time to save his life.

Betty listens and follows Eternity's Diner orders as she
drags Man's almost dead body through the connecting
doors of Eternity's Diner void. Betty walks through the
doors only far enough to make sure all of Man is behind
the doors. Betty looks around at the darkness of nothing
that is the only thing that exist of Eternity's Diner behind
these doors. Betty screams no to her mistake as Man's
body is lifted up off the floor by invisible hands and then
pulled through the air until it is so far gone that it can no
longer be seen.

Betty out loud, "What did I just do? Eternity's Diner is a
void of nothingness. Man was not evil, he was pure
because he had no soul to temp him. When he said he
wanted to rule the world, he meant it from his heart. He
would have been a saviour to the world.

I like a fool I know because Eternity's Diner is laughing like
a Demon. I have just given the power to an entity that
believes all of humanity is flawed to the point that they,
none of them should survive. Save only the ones that will
help Eternity's Diner destroy humanity. Myself like a
mindless sheep, I will bake apple pies for them to eat."

Betty walks around the diner, talking to herself as Eternity's
Diner tries to get through to her. At first Eternity's Diner is
humored about the effects of truth going on in Betty's mind.
As minutes pass by Eternity's Diner, like a child gets mad
at Betty and starts to scream at her in her mind for her to
listen to it. Betty's mind can only think of how to get herself
out of this.

Betty picks up off the top of the counter the knife she cuts
slices of apple pie with. She is about to cut her wrist, when
she remember something. Her older self that she met on
her wrist had a scar, she once before tried to kill herself
and it did no good. Betty stops thinking, she drops to her
knees and starts to cry out the pain inside her for being the
one responsible for letting the end of humanity come to
light.

81

"I lied to myself, why would I do that?"

For the first time in many times to come later, Eternity's Diner speaks out in voice to Betty. Betty cries as she recognizes the voice that is speaking to her. It is the voice of Man. His voice is so cold, so mechanical, so without the caring of life that is was full of just moments ago, before Betty's betrayal.

"No I will not listen to you, you evil entity, I'll kill myself before I bake apple pies for you."

"Betty there is nothing you can do. Everything you tried before to change things you failed. I will not let you kill yourself. I need you, I love you, ha,ha,ha."

"Eternity's Diner, I will find a way. I'll jump into your void. I could not survive that."

"Yes Betty you will survive, for you did that very same thing like twenty times or more last time. Face the hard truth Betty, you pretty, loving flower child, you screwed up, you screwed up bad. Now make life easier on yourself and bend to my will. If you do this, I will make life for you as peaceful as I can."

"What about love? Will I ever feel the touch of another man?"

"No way in Hell Betty, you are mine, I love you. No man will ever touch what I own. There will be some men that dare to try to touch you, but like before I will smite them down for their betrayal."

"Please Eternity's Diner set me free, don't make me live my life like this. This is no life, this is Hell come to life to torture me everyday."

"Only if you let it make it feel that way to you Betty."

"How can I not Eternity's Diner? You are evil and I'm damned to live a life that is filled up with Hell."

"It is up to you Betty, live your life like it is full of Heaven or Hell. It does not have any affect on my decision to end humanity in 2018."

"God, yes God will stop you."

"He didn't the last time. The more I think of it, I'm probably his unspoken version of Armageddon."

"You will fail. You hear me Eternity's Diner, you are evil and evil will always lose to the power of good."

"What good Betty? Where is there any good inside me?"

"Me that's where. I'm the good that will stop you."

"You good Betty? No you are no longer good, you have tainted yourself for your actions against my human self."

"You lie Eternity's Diner. I'm good, I'm not evil."

"Believe what you will Betty, I could care less. Now get yourself into the kitchen and start baking some apple pies, for in a few moments we will have some new company and they will be very hungry ."

"Mary. Did you have anything to do with her death?"

"Of course I did Betty. When she left the confines of myself without her soul, she put the final nail in her coffin."

"I hate you Eternity's Diner!"

"And I don't care Betty, now go do your baking, I want the scent of apple pie to dominate throughout me."

"I hate my life."

Tale Of A Vampire Couple
Chapter One:

(Present day on a fair and warn autumn night a vampire couple is feeding. This is their story of blood and how they like to drink it.)

"How does yours taste my sweet?" "Kinda bad, my Eternal Love. I think he's on drugs."

"Here then my sweet take my blood-bag, I'll go find myself another one to drink."

"You know good and well that I do not drink women. Why is it my Eternal Love after all these years you still keep on trying to get me to taste a woman again? I mean I always say no and still a month can't go by without you trying to get me to taste a woman. Just get it out of your mind my Eternal Love. Here take this nasty blood-bag out of my hands and dispose of him while I go find myself someone that tastes better."

"You can get rid of your own garbage if you're going to have that attitude."

"What attitude? You're the one who is being an ass, so kiss my ass my Eternal Love I'm out of here."

My sweet gets up and flies away into the night sky, mad at her Eternal Love for starting his shit again. "Get your ass back down here my sweet. I mean it!"

"Go drink yourself my Eternal Love and bite my undead ass."

"You mean your undead bitch ass don't you my sweet."

"That's it, now you pissed me off my Eternal Love and you're going to pay for it."

My sweet flies back down and grabs a hold of eternal loves blood-bag, then flies a few feet above him. She stops, rips apart the blood-bag right over his head giving him a unexpected blood-shower.

"What is wrong with you my sweet? I can't believe you did this to me again. You know what's going to happen now don't you, my sweet? One morning very soon I am going to throw a turd in your coffin while you're sleeping."

"Don't you dare do that to me again! If you do I will throw you out in the sun."

"That's too much my sweet, you crazy undead lady, you're talking about my undeath here."

"My Eternal Love I would never do that to you, I owe my undeath to you. I love you with all my dark heart, at the same time my Eternal Love I hate you. You took the chance of Heaven away from me with your forever bite and blood."

"I thought we got past that years ago my sweet?"

"We have my Eternal Love. Here let me make it up to you for giving you a blood-shower."

My sweet flies back down to Earth and with such dark love for her Eternal Love, she very sexually licks all the blood off of his face until he can't take it anymore and they make love on the blood laced ground.

My sweet will be the name used, for there is no record of her real name. I tried my very best but my sweet only got mad at me and threatened to drink me down so I left her alone as she told me her story.

(714)

"I was young and as pretty as the day was long. My family was poor, there were eight of us children. My father's trade was a blacksmith. He worked so hard for us, only being allowed to sell some of the metals he smelted, for the army took most of it with little payment offered. My father was told, but he did not believe, that he was lucky that he did not have to pay taxes, for he was in good graces with the King and his army.

Wars, so many different ones coming alive out of nowhere. War was so dominate that it seemed it never stopped, one would end, another would start. Mankind, man always wanting more blood. We women paid the price and always will, when our husbands and lovers never returned from war.

My land was no different than so many others throughout time. Our great King and his mighty army were away winning another war when wild men from the north came to our shore. In our village and the ones surrounding it were mostly women and children. These war hungry men from the north attacked all of the surrounding villages at once. When they found there were only a few men around like my father, they killed them all without mercy. With blood soaked swords they gathered us women up like a flock of animals to have sex with.

Those that had children watched their children die while being used, like this was their only worth. We tried to fight for our bodies but all it got us was death for some and pain for the rest that were allowed to live.

I thought by the grace of God himself I was blessed. These wild men from the north would come into our cages and grab a hold of whomever they wanted to mate with. So many of them looked at me with sick lust in their eyes for me, however not one of them chose me.

I prayed all day, I prayed all night that God would save me from their evil lust. The thirteenth day in a cage, I know it now to be, was the day my life changed forever. The morning of my thirteenth day held captive to wild men from the north, my cage was emptied of all the women but me. In the afternoon I was brought out into the light of the Sun, only to be washed extra clean by some of my fellow captive women. I could not believe this, they even checked me for, well, for my pureness. They then reported this to the lead wild man from the north.

I was so scared, I was so sickened. I tell you this as truth, some of the wild men from the north were not so wild. However their leader, was as ugly as mud. I thought with my heart pounding that I was to be his bride. This was the first time in my life that I cursed myself for my beauty. Night came and I was fed a meal that I have not touched for many years. Not since the wars came close to our borders and spilled into our lands. I ate by myself with two servants at my call. Delicious foods kept coming, I gorged, hoping to make myself look bloated and unattractive.

Still I was by myself, the not knowing made me crazy in my bones. I wanted to run away from this Hell that I did not want to live. Even though I could hardly hear them, I knew beyond this room still stood the shear numbers of wild men from the north, and all that separated me from them and him was a mere wall.

Out of silence, hundreds of Wolves howled at the full Moon. All of them sounding as if death had just walked beside them and away, leaving them with a supernatural pain that they could not comprehend. So they howled out hoping that their pain would escape them within their howling symphony in the night.

Footsteps is what I hear next. Coming from the other wall, closer and closer they walk towards me.

I know that there is a God and I knew that my death was getting ready to walk into my life. There he stood in front of me to look at, to bask in his undead eyes. To see him is to see time stand still. To hear his voice leaves you knowing that evil lives on Earth. I now prayed to God for the chance to be the bride of the ugly leader wild man from the north.

Eternity took me by my hand, lifted me up, then pulled me close to him. His breath on my neck smelled of death and blood. His breathing became a rutting as he bit deep into my neck, drinking my blood, like it tasted like holy water. I felt myself growing weaker when he stopped drinking me. With his sharp teeth he bit his wrist making himself bleed then he forced me to drink his blood, it tasted so delicious, I hated myself for wanting more.

He spoke words that I had never heard, and looked deep into my eyes. I knew then my blood was only the first thing that he would savor that night. My first time being with a man was with no man at all. His touch felt cold inside me as he expressed his love of my warm touch. The longer he had his will with me the colder I felt inside. It was as if he was siphoning my warmth to make himself feel a little piece of living life.

I had no more tears to cry, I pleaded no more for him to stop, I now pleaded for him to kill me. Laughter was my answer, as he continued his pleasure with me. When he finished my breath froze the air around me. I could only watch as he drank from me again this time deeper and harder. I smiled knowing my death was coming to me quick paced.

I was dreaming of Heaven as my life was almost over. Then my death stopped drinking me with only a few breaths left in my chest. His undead eyes stared at me like he was envious of my coming death. I died that night with eternity's blood flowing through my veins.

An hour before dawn I came back to life, clearer truth I was undead, a creature of the night. The force inside me was so hungry, I ran towards the night looking for blood to drink. My Eternal Love stopped me, grabbed me up without any strain of force and led me to his carriage. He fed me his blood as we rode into the dawn. The sun was coming over the highest hill when we reached a cabin.

We hurried in, I asked him no questions just trusting him to help me survive. In the middle of the cabin was a giant hole in the floor. I followed him down twelve or more feet into the Earth, there he pulled me close to him and fell asleep as I stared into the darkness, missing the sun, a sun that would now make me burn to my death.

Having an undeath enter your life as you wake up from dying, is a feeling of joy that you are alive. Then comes the realization that you are different that you do not feel alive and it makes the skin that you can hardly feel want to crawl. Was my skin crawling? Heaven says to me yes. Hell says to me, what does it matter? You are an undead that feeds on the blood of the living. You are perfect, you never have to worry about going to Heaven.

Living my undeath with my Eternal Love at first was a nightmare, the man had no social skills at all. It took me ten years to get him to stop just grabbing me and having sex with me when he felt aroused. It was like this, I could be a slave to the will of my creator, or take my chances when I had them become available for me to use.

My Eternal Love is evil, sexy, handsome. His touch to this day still weakens me. The first few days of my undeath, I was not allowed to leave the hole in the cabin. He would bring me fresh pretty young ladies to drink. I hated it, I wanted to drink men, but I dared not say so or complain, for I knew I had to take my undeath time if I was ever going to be allowed some freedoms in my undeath life.

I knew that he was testing me just like he had done before with so many ladies just like me. Being as beautiful as I was in my life, I learned all the tricks that an alive man would use to try to gather my affections. This helped me with my Eternal Love, even though his tricks were no tricks at all, when he wanted something, he took it, nothing stopped him and if something got in his way he would rip it apart with a strength that can only come from the help of the Devil himself.

Time was my ally, time was also my enemy for it took so much of it to be at this point in my undeath. I am my own undead woman. Alive women think that they have been under the foot of men and it is a pain in their life. Try having a discussion with someone that likes to rip limbs off of men for sport. Crazy and wild as he can be, he got mad at men whose limbs did not rip off correctly. It always had to be a clean rip, if they messed up his perfection he would destroy them so monstrously, then he would go find another man just so he could do it all over again, wasting so much men's blood that I would have loved to drink.

My Eternal Love can drink a human down in a minute when he is wild or angry. I tried my best to keep up with him at first, he would just laugh at me so hard and evil when I drank too fast, and choked on the lady I was drinking. I was a monster that could remember what it was like to still be alive. My Eternal Love was a beast that had to count to a thousand instead of ten to control his evil rage. That is where I come into the story of his undeath.

My Eternal Love knew he needed someone to love deep down in his evil heart. After so many years of being alone he had turned into a monster. His love and need for me along with my beauty has made him what he has become today, the undead man that I love with all my dark evil heart. He pisses me off and makes me so mad that I'd rather stake him then look at him sometimes, but I know I have a lot to be thankful for because he changed for me.

Still a brute, he always will be deep down, but his tenderness has made me purr for the want of it. I know that there is no one undead that can match my undead man when it comes to making love or having sexy evil sex that makes me cry and smile for hours upon hours at a time." My Sweet pauses and listens to the silence.

"Don't move, hold yourself very still, my Eternal Love is here and getting ready to walk right through that door." The door opens and in walks a creature that will make your blood turn to ice in your veins.

"My sweet what are you doing here talking to this blood-bag?"

"I'm just venting about the undeath I have to live because of you my Eternal Love."

"Venting? What do you have to vent about you ungrateful woman?"

"Don't start your shit with me my Eternal Love or I'll bite you on your face."

"Why don't you bite my undead ass instead my sweet?"

"See what I mean Human? See how he just walks in and instantly becomes an asshole. What I have to endure? Woe is me."

"Woe is you? No, no, no. Woe is me for being the great and understanding undead man that I am."

"See Human how he always turns it around on me, making it my fault somehow."

"It is your fault my sweet. You are the one secretly talking to this human, to make yourself feel better about all the Hell you cause for me to live with."

"Hell, you bastard? How dare you? You are Hell. Why don't you go fly into the sun and out of my life forever you undead asshole."

"My sweet you're pissing me off now. So say goodbye to your venting, and watch as I rip your listening human apart piece by bloody piece."

"Hold on my Eternal Love I'm sorry. Why don't you try it?"

"Try what my sweet?"

"Talking to this human my Eternal Love, he is a very fine listener and a very qualified therapist."

"Why the Hell would I want to do that?"

"Because you have been holding on to your pains for so long, you could use some venting of them."

"What's wrong with you? Give my secrets to a stranger? Like this pathetic foolish looking human would even know how to understand one such as I?"

"Please for me my Eternal Love? It would make me so happy. I tell you what, if you do this for me after you're done I'll share in drinking the blood of a woman with you."

"You will?"

"Yes I will, I promise."

"Alright, I'll do this but human listen to me very well when I tell you this. I can kill you fast, I can kill you slow. I am forever, I can make your death last for years. So keep my tale inside your mind forever!"

(So long ago the year is unknown.)

"My family was killed half of them from a plague the other half were just killed by some passing murderers who stopped by our home to check and see. Dead plague people were seen, locked up and set on fire. Our home burned to the ground, while I at the age of six laid still in the shelter of the forest that surrounded our home. I wanted to kill all of them, I was all alone.

Years later, I survived by traveling the roads that led me to Hell. My time was so long, so old ago. No one can understand. Every other day or so there was a miracle, there was a new plight, a war that lasted for hours. My time there was magic. There was what came before God. Then God was created and took over slowly at first then so devastatingly fast, that all but small amounts of the old original way were destroyed and soon it replaced in people's minds as the only way.

It was a way where God had all the power and the people had to worship and obey his way or their soul would be damned and go to Hell. I believed in no God, I believed in no Devil. In my lifetime when time started for mankind, we brought the brutality of cave life with us. Building up came first, second came war. High self appointed men made laws, that the people did not abide by. Lawlessness was the way to greatness. Watching my family burn in our home made me know this all too well.

One night at the age of twenty three, I wound up with a blade in my belly. I pulled the blade out, grabbed a hold of my bleeding belly and ran away to save my life, for I did not want to die. So I prayed for the first time to God. Should I have kept my praying to myself, I don't know nor do I know if it would have mattered. What came in answer to my prayers was so evil, so foul, it made the blood flowing out of my belly turn black. The Devil was who stood in front of the path that I was running.

This alien spoke a language that came before time began. My mind melted inside my skull as his language became clear to me. Moments later we were having a conversation. Moments after that he healed my wound with his blood. I did not change as I feared I would by being healed by the devil's own blood.

He started to speak as he was leaving then out of nowhere he grabbed me by my throat showing the Hellish force of power that he commanded. The Devil gave me two choices, die with his blood flowing through my veins, which would make my soul too tainted for Heaven, meaning my soul would fall to Hell for him to torture forevermore. Or the second choice was to be his first, the most special one of his demons on Earth that he would create throughout the time of mankind. In the end my soul will still fall to Hell, however I will be his top General for my stay in Hell, instead of burning and pain.

I smiled as the Devil told me I would live until the end of time. I agreed to give him my soul, with one of his talons the devil scratched me across my heart. Here let me show you the wound that will never heal completely. This is my Devil's mark, the reason I have to drink human blood. My Devil's mark has grown smaller over all these long years, I don't have to drink as much blood either. What came in between all these years does not matter, every year is the same as the one before. The only thing that matters to me in my life now, is my sweet. All before was just blood.

I tried for so long to feel love, made many brides but not one of them made me feel any love in my dark heart until my sweet that is. My tale is over human. My sweet end this human's life and then let's go find the woman whom we are going to share tonight."

"Yes my Eternal Love, do you feel any better?" My sweet waits for her answer as she drinks the therapist dry of blood.

"No my sweet I do not. I am the first one ever to be damned for selling my soul to the Devil. I have long accepted this."

"What do you want or need me to do to make you feel better?"

"Nothing my sweet but keep on loving me until the end."

"I can do that my Eternal Love. Anything else?"

"Yeah, try better not to drive me crazy with your way out there-ness."

"My Eternal Love go fly into the sun."

"I would happily if you would fly with me my sweet."

"All you have to do is ask me my Eternal Love and I'd gladly give up my undeath for you."

"Let's go drink some blood my sweet."

"Remember this my Eternal Love, just one woman."

"One? I think not. I'm thirsty, my sweet. Let's find a party or go to a dorm. I feel thirteen ladies' blood would quench our thirst. Six for you, seven for me."

"My Eternal Love that will not do unless we save the thirteenth lady for pulling apart at the end so her blood will become our bed for the night."

"Blood Bed? It's been a long time since we've made a blood bed. I love you my sweet."

"I love you, my Eternal Love."

Chapter Two:

Eternal/Sweet walk out into the darkness of the night. The moon to them feels almost as good as the sun does to humans. For thirteen hundred years this Vampire couple have been together. The bad, the good, the blood, has made their love strong, almost a forever love. Things happen to change the path of one's selves, like a moment of quick rage instead of just letting it go and letting it fall behind you. Love is their strength. Can love become their weakness? In time the love between this Vampire couple will come into question. Let's let them have their blood lust in the night, for Eternal has wanted this, and has gone without having this, for many long years.

"So Frank, which way do you want to fly?"

"My Sweet, I've told you before not to call me Frank."

"I know my Eternal Love, I just can't help myself. That man named Frank, looked so very close to you in appearance. Remember I acted like he was really you. I slapped his face and I kicked him in his balls. I beat the shit out of Frank, while all the time in my mind he was you. His blood, I still remember how delicious it tasted."

"Yes I remember, not only did you suck but you also drooled. And remember this crazy lady, that fool Frank looked nothing like me."

"Yes he did, I would know, I was staring right at him while I was torturing him. He even looked me in my eyes when he was begging for his life."

"Well he sure didn't have my voice, nor my fangs."

"That's true. His voice was too much, every time he talked he ruined it for me. In my mind and actions, I was beating you and wanting to kill you, just my evil, sexy way of role playing for the night. But he just kept on talking so I

96

squeezed his throat until he could talk no more."

"Yes My Sweet, you were beautifully brutal to him. I know you did this to turn me on, but like I told you that night, watching you act out like you were killing me did not turn me on. You only pissed me off."

"Ha, ha, you got so mad, it was funny. You were like, give me that damn human, I'm going to tear him apart. I acted like I was going to hand him to you, then I would jerk him away from you right before you could touch him. I ran away from you with him in my arms, you ran after me all pissed off and cursing."

"Yeah My Sweet, it's still really funny even after all these years. I love it when you keep on bringing him up, I just wouldn't know what to do if you ever stop bringing him up."

"Well suffer my Eternal Love, until the end of time, I'm going to bring up Frank, every once in a while just so I can piss you off. This is my one over you, for you have so many over me, it's still not fair."

"Too damn bad My Sweet. I will have my fun, you belong to me. When I want to have extra fun, I will have my fun. Do not call me Frank. If you call me Frank again tonight, I will grab a woman from a hospital that is about to die and make you drink her blood."

"That will make me sick you asshole. If you bring me a dying woman to drink, like you have done to me before in the past, I'll beat you over your damn head with her."

"Well then don't call me Frank and every drop of blood you taste tonight will be from pretty little ladies, with a pretty faces and bodies."

"Like I care about their bodies. Wait a minute, you're not meaning what I think you meaning for tonight?"

"Yes My Sweet, we're going to do more than drink blood."

"Damn you my Eternal Love, I don't want to have sex with you along with an another woman. Can't we just drink her blood instead and then make love on her blood stains?"

"I would like that but I feel like having some new tonight. You know me My Sweet, when I get the urge sometimes fucking a human lady is just as great as drinking her blood."

"Well you know what my Eternal Love, I should have fucked Frank. Right in front of you, what do you think about that?"

"I think you are pissing me off and acting like a slut."

"Slut, I am no slut. The human women you fuck, they are the sluts. Do you understand me Frank?"

"That's it, I told you not to call me Frank again. You fucked up. Tonight I'm going to find you the most stinkiest, disgusting and most dying woman I can find so you can drink her blood and get sick off your ass."

"Go fuck yourself, my Eternal Love. I still say I should have fucked Frank, ain't that right Frank?"

"My Sweet, you just keep on pushing me and pushing me. One day you will push me too far. One day maybe, I'll change my mind about our love. Remember I am eternal, you My Sweet, are not. Maybe it would be for the best if you were to finally feed the clay?"

"You wouldn't dare my Eternal Love. I am your forever love, I am your forever My Sweet."

"Then drop your attitude and let's fly into the night, let's find some sexy ladies to screw and drink down."

"You're right my Eternal Love, I'm sorry. Let's start this all over again. You pick out the ladies you want to share with me for the rest of the tonight."

"Alright, that's better My Sweet. That's what I'm talking about. You and me forever doing what I want to do."

"Yes forever my Eternal Love, doing only what you want."

Eternal Love smiles at My Sweet then he looks at the dark sky, thinking to himself which way to fly. My Sweet looks at her Eternal Love and knows inside herself that one day he will take her life. She then wonders how she can kill him before he can kill her.

My Sweet to herself, "He's unstoppable, even the sun with all its power can only burn the flesh off his bones but every time when the night falls his flesh returns anew. His bones, his damn bones, they are indestructible. He forgives me every time I've caused him harm, even when I've tried to decapitate him more than once."

Eternal Love says to My Sweet, "Ready My Sweet, let's fly west this night." Breaking her thoughts for the moment but then the wind blows cold against her face and her train of thought returns to her.

"I look at him, the hate that I always will feel for him is so strong in my being. Tonight of all nights, I want him dead more than any other night. I have to do something, I have to get away from him, I have to make my escape, before the day comes when he will find no more forgiveness inside his dark heart for me."

My Sweet gathers herself and replies back softly, "West sounds perfect my Eternal Love."

Eternal Love smiles at My Sweet and jumps into the air, his dark wings pop out from his shoulder blades and then they spread open wide for flight.

My Sweet flies about two wing spans behind her Eternal
Love. Fear is still in her mind, she knows she's sometimes
her worst enemy, always taking things too far, calling him
Frank. My Sweet can't help herself, she's been undead for
so long, living every year of her immortal afterlife with her
Eternal Love. She hates him for taking the sun and the
breath of life away from her when she was alive.

My Sweet knows her soul is charred and primed for Hell
but way down deep inside her she still loves life and the
mortal beauty of it all. She thinks to herself now and then,
that death would be a blessing, then she thinks about Hell
and her bones shiver. She feels that it would be for the
very best if she lived until the end of time and not her
Eternal Love, for he is a beast from Hell.

"Over there My Sweet, watch the way she walks, she's
looking for some action. Ha, ha, not the kind of action
we're going to give her but what is she going to do about
it? I tell you what and that is nothing but moan and beg."

"Yes looks like she would do just fine, is she for you or is
she for me?"

"She's for the both of us, remember? We're going to share
her body then her blood."

"Well grab her up and let's get started."

"Wait a minute somethings off, her pulse, I should be able
to hear it from here, but I can't. She's a vampire, is that
Shelly who I turned about three hundred years ago?"

"Shelly? I hate that slut! Every time we catch back up with
her it's all I can do to keep her off you."

"Yes you're right, Shelly's hot. She likes to get it on all the
time. Well it's been a long time since I had her, might as
well have some unexpected fun first. We'll drink a lady
after we've had fun with Shelly first."

"Damn it my Eternal Love, I told you not to make that slut a vampire, she's nothing but trouble."

"You mean trouble for you My Sweet, she's always wanted to take your place beside me."

"Yes that's what I'm saying, she's a lousy good for nothing slut. I forbid you from doing this! I will not have sex with that filthy slut ever again!"

"Fine with me My Sweet, I'll just fuck her myself. While I'm doing this grab about, I don't know. I got it, grab three ladies for the three of us to drink together for after Shelly and I are done having our fun."

"Yes my Eternal Love. I'll get you the most sexy looking lady I can for you to drink."

Eternal Love stops flying and hovers in the air, he looks over at his My Sweet and wonders what is going on in her mind and then he asks her. "That's it, no complaining, no getting mad and screaming at me?"

"No my Eternal Love, would it do me any good if I did?"

"Not one bit My Sweet. I have my lust, I am your master. In your dark heart you should want me to do this. For Shelly is hot and sexy ready to please me beyond belief. However, you My Sweet, you are my first choice. My love is hard as a stone and cold as ice but in my way I love you the most on this world. Remember this when I come back to you later tonight, maybe just right before sunup, when I make love to you."

"That will be fine, but do me at least one favor first."

"What's that My Sweet?"

"I want you to Wash that dirty slut off you before you even think about touching me."

"You got it My Sweet, I love you, you ask for so little sometimes. Like this time, when you are like this My Sweet it makes me appreciate you even more."

"Well go on and make yourself dirty with your slut."

"Should I give her your best?"

"Yeah, tell that slut to go fly into the sun for me."

My Sweet to herself after she flies four miles away and lands back on the ground, inside a deserted park. "That bastard, if only I could kill him. Shelly, really? I should have tracked that little cute vampire slut down a long time ago and staked her. It's not fair, all of us vampires can be killed if we are staked inside our hearts and brains. Not him, no not him, him and his damn bones. I'm glad I pissed on his bones once."

My Sweet takes a break from her anger, letting it all out and starts to laugh. She looks into the night sky and closes her eyes, inside her mind the sun is shining yellow bright and warm in the bright blue sky. My Sweet yells out to the night sky as she opens back up her green sexy eyes. "Help me Lord. God in Heaven, help me. Give me the power to rid this Earth of the beast that haunts this planet for blood."

My Sweet is shaking with anger as her mind is humming from it almost being snapped, from it yelling at her to kill the beast, to kill the slut, to kill them both. My Sweet shakes her head no,no,no to clear her mind, then she pauses and laughs out a crying laugh, that sends shivers up and down her cold, dead feeling spine.

"My Lord, I drink blood to survive. I've enjoyed myself. I've covered myself in blood, I've even bathed in it. I'm a monster, yes I am. Lord I will never be great again but I did not give up my soul, it was taken from me by the beast that drinks human blood from so early of a date in time on Earth until now..."

My Sweet pauses to make sure the words she speaks to God next will spark a flicker in Heaven, just big enough for God to take a notice of it.

"My Lord, I am not asking for Heaven, even though I know I deserve Hell. I just want to do one more great thing for this world. I want to kill its monster. This beast that drinks blood origins are from Hell itself. Let me, for you my Lord, let me for Humanity, let me erase what the Devil made come to hellish undeath here on Earth."

My Sweet looks at the night sky hoping and praying that her prayer will be answered. While she is waiting, let's see what Eternal Love is up to.

"Shelly, my sweet, hot and horny little, sexy vampire, it's been such a long time. I have to say you look good enough to bite tonight."

"Eternal, it's so great to see you, you're right it's been a long time since we have set eyes upon the other, must be fifty years by now... What can I do for you Eternal?"

"Shelly, Shelly, you have to ask? You know what I want, I know what you want. Let's find some place to fuck. Do you have a place near by or do we have to fly to it?"

"Eternal, you never will change will you?"

"Why would I want to change? I'm not the monster I was in the past but do not let this deceive you, inside my inner being lies only a beast. A beast that deep down will never change. Blood and sex, that's all I need Shelly. Blood and sex until the end of time. So to that I say, where are we going to screw for the next hour or so?"

"Only an hour Eternal? In the past, an hour was merely nothing but foreplay that led us to the complete passion of loving lust."

"That's true Shelly, we've fucked 'til right before dawn before. I would love to have an all nighter with you Shelly but sadly for you, I'm on a date with My Sweet."

"What? That bitch is around here somewhere? Payback time bitch, come out wherever you are. I owe you. I owe you big time, you lousy bitch. The last time me and Eternal got it on, forget that, what I meant to say was the last time we fucked so much better than he ever did with you... You sick bitch, you cut all my hair off after we were done while I was sleeping. You made me bald, all my pretty long blond hair on the ground beside me when I woke up. Come out now and face me. I'll make you dead, you hear me bitch, I'll kill you and I won't need a stake, I'll rip out your small stinking heart with my bare hands..."

Eternal interrupts Shelly by saying, "My Sweet in not here Shelly, she's out finding us three ladies to drink for after I'm done with you. I don't know why, nor do I understand why, you and My Sweet have to hate the other so much?"

"Eternal, its not me, it's all her, she's a total bitch. We are both women, we are both vampires, we know the deal. But with her, it always has to be about her in the end. She gets off on torturing all us vampire ladies after we've had sex with you. I mean I understand about being jealous and all but my goodness that bitch goes way out of control about it."

"Shelly you can't blame her, My Sweet hates to share me with anybody. It took me like forever to make her stop killing all the vampire ladies I had sex with."

"See what I mean Eternal, you should really stake that crazy bitch and be rid of her forever.

Believe me well when I say to you my great and sexy Eternal, hundreds upon hundreds of us sexy vampire ladies would love to be your, your number one. I know I wouldn't have a problem with sharing you with whom ever you wanted."

"I know Shelly. Maybe one day, I'll stake her but that day is not today. I love her and I owe her. My Sweet was my first love, she had to endure my beastly passion until the day I became more civilized. She is a very strong woman Shelly. I don't think any other woman would have had it in themselves to endure the pain of being chosen by me to be my wanted and needed unmarried bride."

"Well that's all good and all but I still say she's a bitch and I hate her. If I get my hands on her, I'm going to rip all the hair off her big head and then I'm going to stick it all up her big, fat nasty ass."

"Damn Shelly, don't be so cruel, show a little love."

"You of all vampires, telling me not to be cruel. You're the epitome of being cruel. I've watched you drink blood, I've seen you kill, you are nothing but about being cruel."

"That is true Shelly, I'm glad that I don't have to remind you of this. Now all this talking is turning me off, are we going to fuck or what?"

"Of course we are Eternal. I'm sorry I just needed to vent a little bit. Can you do me a favor Eternal?"

"What's that Shelly?"

"When you decide to stake that bitch, you will let me watch you when you do it."

"No problem Shelly, it would be my pleasure. Now let's get to doing some great vampire fucking, like only we can."

"I would love that Eternal, follow me, the home I share with ten other vampire ladies is only two blocks away."

"There are ten more vampire ladies waiting at your home right now? This night is starting to pick up really great."

As we let my eternal and Shelly talk as they walk to her home, let's check out My Sweet and see if God has answered her yet.

My Sweet is still staring at the night sky, her left foot is slightly tapping the ground. Behind her, twenty feet stands a silent stranger in the darkness. This stranger has no breath of life inside her, nor does she have a soul. My Sweet decides to give it one more try.

"My Lord, I can do this, please let me do this great thing and kill a beast of blood. Help me my Lord, give me the strength and the power to kill My Eternal damnation."

My Sweet stands still, listening for any slight noise that may come from out of the darkness. Behind her a twig is snapped in half from being stepped on. My Sweet turns around not knowing who or what she may see, she is excited and nervous, she is ready kneel to the greatness of Heaven, she is ready to attack any member from Hell. My Sweet looks at the figure in the darkness. It has no heartbeat, it feels cold to her feelings.

My Sweet with fear inside her makes herself walk towards the still, silent stranger, when she is about half way to her she speaks out to her this. "Talk to me stranger, are you from Heaven or are you from Hell? Are you here to help me or are you here to kill me? Either way make your move, enough of your stillness of silence."

"Who am I? I can sense your fear. Isidora, you are the one that is going to kill the beast of Earth?"

My Sweet is confused and shaking from remembering.

"My name, my name is Isidora. I forgot, in all these long years nobody has ever called me by my birth name, since I died and came back an undead creature of the night. Thank you stranger for reminding me. I will never forget I am Isidora again, I can't believe I forgot my name. I have lived for far too long."

"Isidora, that I cannot answer for you, on whether your undead life has gone on too long. You are a beast, that is all I care about. Isidora look at me, the stranger in the darkness, see me for what I truly am."

Isidora watches the stranger as she steps out of the darkness and steps into the light of the Moon and stars. Isidora thinks she can handle what may come out of the darkness. She gathers herself but when she sees this stranger in her true form, her looks are so overwhelming it makes Isidora step backwards to its pure awesomeness.

Eternal and Shelly have reached Shelly's home, let's switch to them to check out what kind of hot vampire sex they are going to share together.

"This is it Eternal, this is my simple home."

"Damn Shelly, how bad off are you, this place is a dump? If you need any gold or silver to help you out just ask."

"Thank you Eternal, but I'm fine. My friends and I have everything we need, besides this place is dirt cheap."

"Dirt is right. What can I say Shelly, if this is the way you want to live then so be it. But I have to tell you, you can do a lot better and Shelly my love you deserve much better than this. I don't know about your friends, however if they are creatures like us, then they also deserve better."

"Great Eternal not all of us can be like you. We have to make our undeath the best we can. Do you still want to come inside?"

"Sure why not, I guess it beats sex on the cold hard ground."

"That it will Eternal. Come inside, make yourself King of the castle and best yet take off all your clothes. Me and my ten friends are going to rub you with so many hands, while kissing you with so many lips all over your one of a kind, sexy, evil body. We'll make you feel like you are in Heaven, with no chance of ever falling to Hell."

Eternal looks at Shelly with a Hell yeah it's about time, look in his eyes, then he happily says to Shelly, "Twenty two hands, eleven mouths, with eleven talented tongues and best of all, eleven sweet spots to fill full with all my vampire loving. This is a great night indeed, let's get this wild vampire sex party started, shall we Shelly my love?"

As Shelly and Eternal enters Shelly's home they are greeted within seconds by ten angry looking, sexy vampire ladies ready to tear the man apart that has entered their home with Shelly. The rules are simple, one of the rules is that not one vampire lady will ever bring home a man. They know Shelly had no choice, which means that he is a vampire himself, which means he has to die and die fast so they can save their sister.

Ten vampire ladies scream, "Die!" out to Eternal as they pounce on him, knocking Shelly safely out of the way. Eternal does not take leave from off his feet, instead he braces himself as the ten sexy vampire ladies land on top of him for the kill shot. And for all their trouble all of them only receive a hard jolt to their bodies upon making contact with Eternal's ancient strong body thus knocking them all to the floor.

Three of the vampire ladies look up at the vampire male that has entered their home and sees their creator Eternal. All three of them say at the same time, "We are sorry Eternal, we did not know it was you, please forgive us."

Eternal flexes his body in triumph and laughs out one of his best, I from Hell laughs and responds like he is the Devil himself, "Ladies what were you thinking?"

Ten separate hugs and kisses later all is at Hellish peace. Eleven sexy vampire ladies dance around Eternal with an old dance of darkness and lust. They take off his clothes, they pick him up and carry him to a bed and then they gently place him down upon it. Eternal is happy and turned on, looking at the eleven vampire ladies, while wondering to himself which one he wants to fuck first.

Quick side note, Satan had every attention of making hundreds of vampires just like Eternal that would walk the Earth until the end of time. Damning every human they drank from and killed, which tainted these human souls making them useless for Heaven but burnable enough for Hell. Satan had only enough time to create five vampires like Eternal including Eternal himself, four males and one female before God stepped in and took this ability away from him. This made Satan so angry he lashed out at God with all of his hate but sadly for Satan he was smacked away so hard that it was all he could do to get up and hobble himself back to Hell.

These five and only these five vampires could do on Earth what Satan could no longer do and that was make more vampires on Earth. Their vicious bites could kill and kill was what all five of these vampire did for thousands of years. Years later when the Hell inside them calmed enough they all five started to make more vampires. Five vampires through time, from then to now, have made so many thousands of vampires that there is no way to count them all.

Different vampire factions started to take form. When there are so many predators on one planet, war is not far in the making. The five head vampires stepped away from the war and watched and waited 'til it was over.

109

The ranks of vampires dwindled until only about a thousand vampires were left on Earth. The five head vampires stopped the war by force. They gathered up their flocks of vampires and hurtled all of them together. It was a pact between these five head vampires that only one hundred vampires besides them would exist on Earth. Twenty vampires from each blood line stayed undead all others were killed that very bloody day. The five head vampires agreed to leave things the way they were and then they separated from the other. These five vampires had no need for each other's company, they all like their solitude from the other four. Unknown to Eternal three of these head vampires were dead leaving only himself and one other.

Eternal is lying on the bed ready to be pleased like he deserves to be pleased. The eleven sexy vampire ladies stop dancing and stare down at a very naked and turned on vampire named Eternal and then all of them together start laughing at him. After that this sex party really starts to change, when all of these sexy vampire ladies with bags of blood in their hands throw them down on top of Eternal, covering his naked body with lots of thick, red blood.

Shelly starts ranting, "Look at the great Eternal, he is all covered in blood looking like he should cluck like a chicken with nobody to fuck." All eleven vampire sexy ladies laugh and have a great time as they grab another blood bag and throw it down on top of Eternal.

"What the fuck is wrong with you crazy ass vampire bitches? Look at me, I'm drenched. I'm covered in blood."

"Yes you are, you horrible monster, now get off your naked ass and get the fuck out of here before we all bite your pecker and balls off," a very excited Shelly replies.

"Damn you vampire bitches, I'll get you all back for this," Eternal says as he picks up his clothes and hurries himself out the door.

Eternal to himself, "Damn stupid vampire bitches, I should go back in there and rip out all their fangs for treating me like this. I cannot believe their disrespect towards me. I am like a God to them and they laugh at me like I'm beneath them? They will all pay with their lives, especially Shelly, I will take my time when I kill her. Well damn it I might just as well head back to find My Sweet, maybe she will lick all this blood off my body?"

When Eternal finds My Sweet, she is all alone in a nearby park without any human ladies for Eternal to drink.

"Where have you been My Sweet? Look at me that crazy bitch and her friends covered me in blood. By its smell I think its pig's blood. Can you believe this happened?"

Isidora looks at Eternal coldly and responds back to him even colder, "Yes I can my Eternal love, for you emulate a wild and horny rutting pig."

"What? What is wrong with you? What is wrong with everyone on this fucked up night?"

"Well my Eternal Love, if you think this night is fucked up already, just think how you will feel about it when you're lying on the ground dying?"

"What are you talking about you crazy woman, you can't kill me, I am Eternal?" At that time the only head vampire that is still alive besides Eternal grabs a hold of him with all of her might to hold him still long enough so Isidora can deliver to him, her killing strike. With an Angel's feather in her hand she stabs it deep into Eternal's heart, she steps back to watch what will happen to him with a smile.

Eternal feels pain like he has never felt before. Slowly the flesh from his body starts to melt away until there is nothing left besides bones. Isidora then pulls the Angel's feather out of Eternal's chest and stabs it deeply into his skull, piercing his brain.

With this done Eternal's bones turn into dust, which gets blown away by the wind. Them damned bones is where the infection from Satan lies deep within them. The Angel feather with its pureness of Heaven cleansed this infection, causing Eternal's skull and bones to instantly revert to their true age, thus they became dust.

"Its over Isidora, you've done it. All the first vampires are dead besides me. I love this for I hated them all and I am glad they are all dead. I've waited so long for this, to feel this kind of freedom. Now no one on this Earth can kill me, I'm finally untouchable. Your reward will be very high Isidora for killing your Eternal Love for me."

"I just did not just kill him for you Jessibell, I killed him for myself. He was a monster, one day he would have killed me, I know this. I can't believe he's dead. I thought I would never be rid of him."

"Well Isidora you are free from him forever. What's more, you are the only vampire or human on this Earth that knows how to kill one of us."

"Thank you Jessibell for trusting me with your most dire secret. I will never betray your trust in me. How did you get a Angel's feather anyway, Jessibell?"

"Simple Isidora, I ripped it off a pair of Angel's wings. I seduced an Angel long ago, his touch and kisses felt like Heaven to my being. The fool thought he was the better of me, you should have seen his eyes when I lusted him and jerked out two of his feathers after we were done."

"You screwed an Angel? Way to go Jessibell. Now what are we to do until the end of time?"

"Isidora that is a long time from now. Unfortunately for you my dear you will not be beside me at the end of time."

"Why not Jessibell? What do you mean? Where will I be?"

"You Isidora, you will be dead for a long time by then. I am sorry, I truly am but I have no choice, I cannot let you live another day, with my secret within your mind "

"Please Jessibell, Please don't kill me, I will not betray you, I will not tell anyone of your secret, I swear this to you."

"Maybe so Isidora maybe so, but I cannot take the chance. I will not take this chance. You have to die and you have to die this night before the sun rises."

Isidora looks down at the Angel's feather that killed her Eternal Love, it is still lying on the ground, where his body was just put to rest. "Go ahead and grab for the Angel's feather Isidora, try your very best to use it on me. This will only make it easier on me to kill you."

Isidora with all the speed she has in herself runs to pick up the Angel's feather, from behind her comes Jessibell fiercer and faster. Before Isidora can place a finger on the Angel's feather, Jessibell with one mighty swing takes off Isidora's head. Isidora's head rolls ten feet away from her body before it stops rolling. In under a minute, Isidora's body and head has turned into ash.

Jessibell gathers herself up and pops out her wings from between her shoulders. She has one more look around at the pile of dust that use to be Isidora, then she flaps her vampire wings and flies away into the dark night.

In a few years Jessibell has appointed herself Queen of the vampires. The lady vampires all over the Earth are now the masters, while every male vampire on Earth are nothing more than sex slaves. Male vampires have no worth but to bring home human blood bags for the sexy lady vampires to drink at their leisure like a delicious, hot afternoon cup of tea.

Thus now ends the Tale Of A Vampire Couple.

Chapter Three:

(That is one ending, a very final one. One for those that would like to see both vampires turn to dust. However, for those that want only one of the vampires to be turned into dust, this less final ending is for you, so the story of Isidora can continue on.)

"Jessibell your plan came off perfectly, thank you for trusting me with your most dire secret. I will never betray your trust in me. How did you get an Angel's feather anyway, Jessibell?"

"Simple Isidora, I ripped it off a pair of Angel's wings. I seduced an Angel long ago, his touch and kisses felt like Heaven to my being. The fool thought he was the better of me, you should have seen his eyes when I lusted him and jerked out two of his feathers after we were done."

"You screwed and screwed over an Angel? Way to go Jessibell. Now what are we to do until the end of time?"

"Isidora that is a long time from now. Now tell me who is this Shelly that Eternal mentioned and why did she and her vampire friends cover him in pig's blood?"

"Shelly is a slut that My Eternal had filthy sex with, many times, I might add. She came up to me like she was trying to be my friend. I almost slapped her face. She told me some crap like, she's a woman and so am I, so I should be understanding that's not her fault that My Eternal wanted to have sex with her more than he want to have sex with me. Can you believe that slut?"

"Shameful, but I can't blame her. You were Eternal's number one lady, she wanted to take your place. Being a slut just made it easier on her, in her mind, to do what she had to, to get ahead in her undead life."

"Damn. I almost feel sorry for her, wait a minute, no she's still a filthy slut. You didn't see the look in her eyes when she was looking at me, she got off on telling me that."

"Well Isidora, let's go have a talk with her, let's go kick her ass. I haven't slapped around a fellow lady vampire in a while, sounds like fun, besides I have no equals any more. Every vampire now is only a second generation vampire, only I can create more of our kind. I feel this should make me be worshiped by all vampires. Yes that is it, I am now your Queen. Every vampire will come before me. I will judge them, every one I have sired is already my family. All those that come from the other four dead blood lines now, will have to prove their worth to join our family."

"Queen Jessibell, that sounds mighty and great. But I'm not from your blood line, will I be judged as all others?"

"No Isidora, you have already been judged. You will be my number one, you Isidora will be the second most important vampire on Earth. How does that sound to you?"

"Perfect Jessibell, that sounds perfect to me Jessibell. Thank you, I pledge my undead life to you."

"I expect nothing less from you Isidora. Don't worry if it ever came to that, I would just let some other vampire take your place. You will be more needed by my side than being a pile of ash."

"Yes Jessibell, that is so true." Both vampires look at the other, then they both laugh and give the other a hug.

"Let's go slut hunting Isidora."

"Yes let's. How are we going to find her and her friends?"

"Think Isidora. We will follow the blood. Eternal was covered in pig's blood, he should have left a trail that will lead us straight to them."

"You are so old and wise Queen Jessibell."

"Who're you calling old?"

Jessibell walks a few feet away from Isidora and then spins around and says angrily, "Look at me, I don't look a day over twenty five, I am still as beautiful as can be."

"Yes you are Queen Jessibell. I'm sorry, I didn't mean to hurt your feelings. I just wanted to express my admiration for you."

"Fine, I'll forgive you this time. Calling me wise is fine, never and I mean never call me old again."

"Yes of course, Queen Jessibell, I am sorry."

"Fine, let's go find this slut Shelly, I want to take out my anger on her."

The two vampire ladies spread their wings and fly up into the dark night sky. They keep flying around enjoying the way the night air feels on their undead vampire faces and bodies. Jessibell slows down, then she comes to a halt, she looks down and sees the blood stains that her sense of smell already told her they were there. Jessibell motions downwards towards Shelly's home to Isidora. Isidora smiles and licks her lips, while giving Shelly's house the thumbs down.

To Jessibell, Isidora looked very sexy doing this, making her want to kiss her. Jessibell grabbed Isidora by her left arm and pulled her towards her. Isidora looked at Jessibell surprised, then smiled sexily. She stayed still giving a look to Jessibell that she can do whatever she wants to her and she would love every moment of it.

Passionately Jessibell kisses Isidora, Isidora thinks to herself that this is different, for she is usually the one that is in charge.

Isidora stops thinking and enjoys the sudden surprise taste of blood in her mouth. Jessibell had rubbed her tongue against her fangs causing it to bleed. Isidora feels euphoria from Jessibell's blood flowing through her undead body.

Isidora tries to take control of herself as Jessibell puts her hand up her skirt. (These two vampires are undead however free sex is from Hell, so all moving parts are fully functional.) Jessibell loves how hot and loving Isidora feels inside, so she puts Isidora's hand up her skirt. Isidora knows how to please a lady making Jessibell let lose her total control a little bit. This is what Isidora is waiting for, she has been at this moment in time so many times. Isidora knows that if she wants to be the one that will be Queen she has to make Jessibell her willing sex slave.

Jessibell is about to blush as Isidora suddenly pulls her hand away quickly from underneath her shirt. Jessibell is in shock as she looks at Isidora who is smiling the sexiest smile that ever came out of Hell at her. What happens next really blows Jessibell's mind.

Isidora grabs Jessibell hand making Jessibell stop enjoying the feel of her and says to her like she is now the Queen. "Listen to me my sexy Queen. You are the Queen of all vampires but in our bed you will be my willing servant. Now no more touching, it is time to put that delicious tongue of yours to work."

Isidora takes off her skirt, then she motions with her fingers to Jessibell what she wants her to do. Jessibell can't believe she wants Isidora to be the one in charge. She thinks how she could crush her in a minute, how she should be the one in charge. Jessibell looks at Isidora and she knows that she has no choice, she wants to obey her commands. Isidora makes Jessibell take her time pleasing her, Jessibell begs Isidora for it to be her turn to be pleased and Isidora tells Jessibell to shut up and to continue on.

When she is totally finished she will let Jessibell have her quick turn. Jessibell begs Isidora for her turn to be slow as well and Isidora tells her that she will think about it. Isidora grabs at the air for help as Jessibell goes into a speeding motion like no other before her.

When Isidora can open her eyes again, she notices that her and Jessibell are lying on the cold sidewalk in front of Shelly's home. She looks up ahead a little bit more and sees Shelly and her ten friends standing there watching what her and Jessibell are doing without a care in the world. Isidora smiles at Shelly like she is nothing.

"Hello slut how have you been? By the way Eternal is dead, this lady that is my servant of love is Jessibell the last of the original five vampires that Satan created. Jessibell did all us lady vampires a great big favor and helped me kill My Eternal. Now just stay there and keep on shutting up and watch how I please my Queen."

Jessibell is about to say something when Isidora puts her finger over her mouth preventing her from speaking. "Just lay still my beautiful Queen, let me give you my love." Isidora takes her time and makes Jessibell scream out total passion for the whole neighborhood to hear.

When Isidora feels that Jessibell has had enough, she stands up on her feet, she walks over to her skirt that dropped to the ground and puts it on. Jessibell stands up and looks around embarrassed that she has lost control to Isidora. Isidora smiles at this and licks her lips.

"Jessibell my Queen I want you to rip Shelly and her ten slut friends to pieces. Make them feel it, take your time but not too much, for after your through it will be time to give me your love once again and this time my Queen you will have to do a lot of begging if you want my loving in return. Now attack and kill all the vampire sluts."

Jessibell looks at Isidora, then she looks at Shelly and her ten, scared out of their minds, friends. Jessibell straightens out her wrinkled skirt, she counts to three and then she rushes towards Shelly and her ten friends. Isidora watches as Shelly's head is ripped off her shoulders and thrown to her as a trophy. Isidora catches it and starts dancing.

Before Isidora can finish her dance with Shelly's head it turns to dust just like the rest of the ten vampire sluts. Jessibell, after killing eleven vampires, has her mind back on track, well she thinks she does. She looks over at Isidora to give her a big scolding for her actions. Isidora notices this and lifts up her skirt with one hand while motioning Jessibell over to her with the other.

With a sexy, soft voice Isidora says to Jessibell, "Come to me my beautiful Queen, taste your prize. Please my Queen don't make me wait." Jessibell lowers her head and walks over to Isidora, when she reaches her she does as she was commanded to do. In Jessibell's mind she thinks how can she let Isidora have so much power over her, then she feels what she's doing and that is all the answer she will ever need, she is helpless.

"That's enough my Queen, you were perfect, now let's get up I have the need of a man now. I'm thinking two human men well do just fine. How many human men do you need my Queen to please you the way you deserve to be?"

Jessibell looks at Isidora like she is the Devil's bride. She shakes her head and says. "Two human men would be just fine for me as well My Sweet."

"Good my Queen. I want you to go fly and find us four men to fuck and kill. I could use some more blood tonight, I'm still hungry. Let's see, I want my two men to be drunk and as horny as they can be. Make sure they're rude and forward but most of all make sure they are good looking and have very big peckers."

"Yes My Sweet, I will hurry up."

"No my Queen take your time, I want to stretch my wings for a little while. I need some alone time. Now do as I say, fly and find us some beefcakes. My Queen I can't wait, after they get through screwing my brains out, I'm going to rip both of their peckers off them at the same time. Hell I might just eat them all up right in front of them. How does that sound to you my Queen?"

"That sounds sexy as fuck My Sweet, I'll be back in an hour or so, don't fly too far away."

"Don't worry my Queen, I'll just fly around this local neighborhood, see if I can find anymore vampires."

"Good, I'll see you in an hour My Sweet, I love you."

"I love you too my Queen. You look even more beautiful when you are cover head to toe in blood."

Queen Jessibell flies off thinking to herself this is just the way she wants things to be and she is also horny for the touch of two human men. Isidora flies in the other direction, when she gets three miles away something is flying towards her with speed that rivals her own. Isidora breaths in deep as she flies faster towards the unknown something. It is faster, as it out flies Isidora and gets the advantage by making contact with her first. Isidora says softly to the stranger, "Please."

"Please what My Sweet, you want me to rip off your clothes and give you my piece of Heaven?"

"Yes my Angel Love, give me your Heaven, I'll give you my undead loving that you lust so much."

"Everything's going as planned My Sweet?"

"Yes my Angel Love, everything is perfect."

"You have them, my feathers that bitch stole from me?"

"Yes right here. See. I took them from her when I was pleasing her, give me a kiss and taste for yourself."

"My Sweet, your soul is so dark, you are so hot and nasty. Just the way I like my women to be."

"You are one fucked up Angel, my Angel Love. I love that, it turns me on, well that and your giant Angel pecker."

"Speaking of my pecker, I know we're pushed for time so we have to be quick, let's fly to the ground. I'll tell you what My Sweet just bend over that always makes it Faster."

"Yes my Angel Love, you are so romantic."

Isidora and her Angel Love fly to the ground and have sex that is very loud and very aggressive. When they are done Isidora wants to go over the rest of the plan one more time but her Angel Love tells her to give him a few minutes of silence before they do.

"Okay I'm ready My Sweet, damn you wore me out."

"You too my Angel Love. I just couldn't take any more of your great loving, you are just too much for me," Isidora laughs inside knowing she has barely broken a sweat. "Okay my Angel Love, let's go over the end one more time."

"When Jessibell comes back with your four human men, you are to make these four horny human fools stay where they are. You are to make Jessibell fly a couple of miles away from them with you. Tell her you want to be alone with her, because you want to please her one more time before a human touches her, she will love that. When the two of you are gone, I will rip the souls out of the four fools making them soulless when they have sex with Jessibell.

Remember don't have sex with these four men, make Jessibell have sex with all four of these soulless men. This will weaken her, not as much as if she drank a dead person's blood but it will be good enough, I promise."

"I trust you my Angel Love, I trust you with my undeath. I love you with all my heart."

"'I know you do My Sweet, everybody you have to have sex with, I know is just because you have to, they mean nothing to you, only I have a place in your heart."

"That is a fact, my Angel Love, give me a bible and I'll put my hand on it and swear to God my love for you."

"No that's okay, I don't want the big guy looking in my direction, he would be pissed at me. He would probably take my wings away from me and send me to Hell."

"Never my Angel Love, will I allow this to happen to you, if any Angel belongs in Heaven it is most definitely you."

"So true, I am deeply under appreciated in Heaven. Every one is so up tight, I swear I'm the only one that knows how to have a good time. I have had sex with, has to be over an million human women by now and vampire woman, my favorite, I've had a lot but you are most definitely the best vampire lady I've enjoyed so far."

"I know, my body is the best. I have it all, the tits and the ass. Just look at my face, I'm beautiful. I think I'm too beautiful for anybody but you my Angel Love."

"Damn I wish we had more time, I'd like to enjoy you one more time but that bitch will be back any minute so here is the rest of the plan one more time instead. After you make Jessibell have sex with four soulless men this is what you do next..."

Isidora listens and holds back her excitement.

Isidora makes Jessibell have sex with the four soulless men all at the same time. When they are done with her, Isidora kills them all and pours their dead blood into a weakened Jessibell's mouth. Jessibell tries to stop her but she is so weak, all she can do is lay there and try her best not to swallow. Isidora is singing and dancing as her Angel Love flies down to her to watch the death of the last of five first vampires on Earth.

Isidora takes one of her Angel Love's feathers and digs out Jessibell's heart with it, she then eats the heart. Isidora then takes the second feather and digs out Jessibell's brain with it and then she eats the brain. Isidora screams out in pain as the power of becoming a first vampire comes at her. Her Angel Love watches as her face and body distorts out of place. One final scream Isidora screams out as her undead body becomes the only of its kind on Earth. As the tears dry from her eyes, Jessibell's dead body turns into ash and gets blown away by a cool, hard breeze.

"You've done it, you've done it My Sweet. The Queen bitch is dead. Long live the new Queen, the Queen with the finest ass I've ever seen and felt."

Isidora looks at her Angel Love and tells him, "Shut the fuck up, you stupid fallen Angel."

Angel Love looks up in the sky and sees five fellow Angels flying down upon him. They land and grab a hold of him. They hold him still so Isidora can rip his wings from his body. Angel Loves cries out in a pain compared to only those in Hell ever cry out.

Isidora to her ex-Angel Love. "You stupid horny Angel now you will fall to Hell to burn for eternity. By the way, I've always hated you and you are a lousy fuck. Now you five Angels take this piece of shit off my Earth. I have a family of Vampires to get to know and rule forever."

Thus now ends the Tale Of A Vampire Couple.

Back Story: I wanted the end to come quickly when Isidora becomes the new Queen of the vampires so I left out some details for the flow to be faster.

A year ago, an Angel came up to Isidora while she was away from Eternal's far sense of hearing. The deal was for her to become the Queen of all the vampires on Earth. All Heaven wanted was an Angel that has been very bad and all the first five vampires on Earth dead. It would be easy for God to deal with this fallen Angel but he wanted to prove a point by making this Angel loose his wings by the most evil thing on Earth. The sound from the pain he screamed out would make its way all the way to Heaven. His fellow Angels would cry for their fallen brother and later they would sing a sad song that would take the memory of his pain away from their thoughts forever.

Isidora laughed at the Angel's story about his fallen Angel brother until she was told that she was to become his favorite lover on Earth. The thought of having sex with an Angel made her skin crawl but then she laid eye on the Angel that she was going to please like she had no other. He was fine and she figured she could do a lot worse, so she agreed to the deal.

Part one the fallen Angel was on track. Now on to part two of the plan. Jessibell had already killed two of the first vampires and was on her way to kill number three. When she got back she would nest very close to Eternal, so she could kill him when she wanted to. While Jessibell was away carrying out murder number three Isidora would make her Angel Love come up with a plan all by himself to get his two feathers back from Jessibell with the help of his new lady friend Isidora. Then Isidora pushed Angel Love in the direction until the plan became to also kill Jessibell.

Part three of the plan, before this she was to make Eternal lose his grip on her, this was made much easier by using the mist that the Angel gave her to coat her body.

This mist worked with Isidora's undead scent, making any vampire who took in her new intoxicating scent her almost willing slave. Later this Angel told Isidora where Jessibell's nest was and while she was away from it, Isidora sprayed this mist all around it causing Jessibell to succumb to its sweet pleasures without awareness of it. When Isidora went to Jessibell to ask her for her help to kill Eternal for she wanted to be free from him and only his death would make this happen. Jessibell felt this to be a sign of great fortune not that she had been captured while not even knowing that she had been trapped already.

Part four of the plan. A very happy happenstance when it was found out that Shelly and her friends were nesting nearby. The Angel gave Isidora another mist to use, this time on Eternal. When sprayed on Eternal all female vampires would get turned off and angry with him. The more he stayed around them the more of an effect it had on them. Having pig's blood thrown on Eternal by Shelly and her friends was just a funny circumstance.

Isidora had no mist to use on her Angel Love, she only had her mind and body to use. This was made easier for her for Isidora is beautiful and Angel Love has a lust in him that makes the lustful in Hell seem like timid lovers.

The final night of the plan. Make Eternal mad, then let him have what he always wants. In the mean time, Jessibell was in the waiting to kill Eternal. After that it was the part of the plan that Isidora likes the best and that is when Isidora becomes the new Queen of the vampires with the death of Jessibell. Finally the end, simply pull the wings off Angel Love, with the help from some Angels.

With this done Isidora has free reign over Earth. A reign that makes her the most hated vampire on Earth. Even more so then all five that came before her combined but this is another story for another time.

Earth Prisoner #1113
Chapter One:

"Hello, I'm Floyd. My birth name, I will keep to myself for the moment. Let's see how this interview goes, shall we?"

"Hello Floyd, I am Agent Tate. I am here on the behalf of the United States Government to understand and make more clear the message you sent to us."

"That is why I'm here and what this all about, Agent Tate."

"Very good Floyd. Let me start with this question Floyd. You are an alien from another planet?"

"Yes I am and I'm proud of it as well. Love who you are Agent Tate, that is what your planet tells me and all those like myself. Transplanted to Earth as an Earth Prisoner. I'm know to my planet as Earth Prisoner #1113."

"#1113, who is #1114, Floyd?"

"I don't know Agent Tate. I was given my number after I was judged not worthy. I got on a bus, which took me to a ship that brought me here to Earth."

"Well that is very simple and easy to understand Floyd. I just don't know. Maybe if you could show me something from your former planet, maybe just maybe I would be able to believe what you are telling is the truth."

"Agent Tate, the only something I have from my former planet is myself. Watch, I'll cut myself and you can see for yourself that my blood is green. Better yet, do you have a cup? I could piss in it for you."

"Hostility mixed with humor, your human is showing Floyd."

"But I am an Alien from another planet, Agent Tate." Floyd says with a small laugh added.

"Sure you are Floyd. If it was up to me, I would let all those I meet just like you be from whatever planet you want to be from. It makes no difference to me Floyd. But I have a job to do, the United States Government does not have my philosophy. They have questions and I get their answers. Nothing less, nothing more. Give it to me straight Floyd, I might be able to let you walk away."

"Agent Tate, I'll give it to you so straight, the only crooked thing around you will be able to notice, are the people you are working with."

"That was pretty good, Floyd."

"Stick around Agent Tate, I have a million of them."

The Human and the Alien look at each other quietly. Silence is broken as birds fly out of a tree and into the clear blue sky. This meeting place, which is a crowded park is due to Floyd. He told them when and where and if they were interested, just to send one person to talk to him. Floyd has spotted eight other humans that came along with Agent Tate so far, make that ten, that couple over there, they are only pretending to kiss the other.

"Floyd for the most part right now, you are of no interest. The reason I'm here is the part you put in your message to us about a chance that we might be the victims of an attack. I, we, have to know if this attack is true or are you full of it."

"Sometimes Agent Tate, I'm full of it but not today not on this beautiful warm May day. If you want the facts, if you want the truth, all you have to do is kick back, take it easy and listen to what I have to say. I want to start from the beginning. Billions of miles away on a planet filled with people that think they should and everybody else should live perfect lives with very stale fun to enjoy."

"Sounds just awful Floyd. Maybe you are lucky that you were sentenced to Earth. Here on Earth we are allowed to have a lot of different kinds of fun."

"Yes this it true for you Agent Tate. Me, not so much. Myself and all those like myself, we have a very limited amount of fun that we are allowed to have."

"That is a big bummer Floyd. What kind of fun are you and everyone just like you allowed to have?"

"Basically just sex and sugar."

"Sex and sugar? What the Hell is that suppose to mean?"

"Simply we as a people are allowed to have relations with other people from our planet, that's the sex."

"What about the sugar Floyd?"

"Sugar Agent Tate, is what we get high on. It's so easy for us, sugar is in almost everything. Too bad for the people of your planet Agent Tate. Something my planet does not share with Earth, we have no sugar."

"Why is that Floyd? Why is it too bad for us?"

"Sugar is addictive to the people of your planet it makes you slow. To my people it makes us fast and able to do more things than we had in us to do on our planet."

"Sugar gives your people power, Floyd?"

"Yes it does, later Agent Floyd, I'll show you first hand what sugar does to me. For now let's have one of your people that are watching us bring us some coffee. I take ten sugars in mine and no cream."

"Okay, why not? It makes me feel good that you know what's going on, no more pretending."

128

"Yes Agent Tate, it feels good to me as well. While were waiting on our coffee, I'm going to go take a piss. I know how to do this, I don't need any help. Just kick back, I'll come back and finish my story."

Floyd walks away from the table he is sharing with Agent Tate. As he is walking to the restroom he waves to everyone that he feels is part of Agent Tate's team, to let them know he knows who they are. Floyd takes his time walking and takes a very long piss. When he gets back to the table, Agent Tate is still sitting at it and looking bored. Floyd laughs to himself, knowing that in a little awhile Agent Tate would love to go back and sit at this table all nice, bored and safe.

"Miss me Agent Tate?"

"Yeah Floyd, I've been counting the minutes since you've been gone. Coffee will be here in a little bit."

"Great, think I'll walk around and gather my thoughts until it gets here. This would be a perfect time for a break for you as well Agent Tate. For in a little while, I'm going to change the world as you know it."

Agent Tate squirms on the bench he's sitting on having to take a piss but he doesn't want Floyd to know. He holds it for a few more minutes then he says forget it and goes to take his piss, leaving Floyd walking around and in check. When Agent Tate gets back an agent is walking up to the table with two coffees in hand. This silent Agent places the two coffees on the table, he then reaches into his jacket pocket and pulls out ten packs of sugar and places them beside the two steaming cups of coffee.

"Let's see, one, five and all ten. This will take a moment to put ten packs of sugar into my coffee, I'll try to hurry."

"I want to watch this Floyd, I've never seen anyone use ten packs of sugar before."

129

Floyd adds the ten packs of pure cane sugar to his steaming large cup of coffee. Agent Tate sits and watches Floyd do this with an internal smile, knowing in his mind this man before him is a fool and will prove so when he takes his first drink of his coffee. It will be too sweet to hide.

Floyd looks around for something to stir his coffee with. He sees nothing so he swirls his coffee around real slowly and softly. Agent Tate watches on as he is slowly starting to relax all due to the way the coffee looks like while it is being swirled around by Floyd. Twelve seconds is the time it will take for the discussion to restart. Floyd stops swirling his coffee and looks at Agent Tate.

"That should be just about right, I'll take a taste." Floyd slowly takes his cup of coffee with his right earthling looking hand and brings it to his mouth and takes a very small taste.

"Damn Agent Tate, this is great coffee. I want more." Floyd drinks his still steaming coffee half way gone and licks his lips and says, "What no danish?"

"You get no danish Floyd. You are lucky to get your damn cup of coffee. I'm tired of waiting, while you drink your coffee. How the Hell can you drink that sweet ass coffee without making a face of disgust?"

"Very easily Agent Tate, to me this is delicious and very good for my Alien body and brain. If we had Earth sugar on our planet... Well, my planet would have no need for weapons of mass destruction. For Agent Tate the populace of my planet would be all the destruction that there will ever be needed."

"A planet of sugar junkies, I guess it beats coke or crack."

"Very true, for sugar is pure and all that other stuff is nothing but human made junk."

130

"Sounds to my Earthling ears Floyd, you have a dislike of Humanity? Or am I mistaken?"

"No you are correct Agent Tate. Humanity sucks, I kinda hate them. Lucky for this world that is way over populated by humans that I don't feast on sugar like a junkie."

"Why is that Floyd? You'll go on a killing spree?"

"No Twit! Not just me. My whole race that is on your planet. I'm their leader, I'm all that is keeping the peace. My people want to rage. We not only want to take over Earth, we want to get a ride back to our planet and destroy all the pigs that are in control."

"You speak words filled with rage Floyd, yet you are as calm as if you were simply waiting on a bus?"

"Too true Agent Tate. I'm as calm as I can be, for I choose to be. I want peace between our people. If I or any of my people start the war... Your higher ups are to damn greedy to have taken away what they have. In the end, they would destroy it to save it from us getting our hands on it."

"There are a lot of powerful countries on Earth Floyd. The United States of America is the most powerful. The world should be grateful that it is us that are the most powerful, for if there was someone else in our place, this planet perhaps would not still be here. So Floyd if your people want war, we the United States of America, we would kill every last one of you war hungry aliens."

"Too True Agent Tate. Unfortunately this is what would happen, we would have no choice. We would have to think along in the same terms instead of just killing enough of you that you will drop down and worship us instead of worshiping your Gods and Devils."

"Where do we go from here Floyd?"

"Talking, just talking Agent Tate. I know our part of the war. You and your country does not. Even after sometime, some of the people on your planet will not believe that what they are at war with is people from another planet."

"Make me a believer Floyd. If I believe you, I will do what ever it will take to help you stop this war from starting."

Alien and human look at each other with totally different thoughts going on in their minds. Thirty-three seconds have went by, neither has even blinked. Both are waiting for the other to speak first.

Alien and human both at the same time notice that strangely everything has become more silent. Both are trying to shake away this strange feeling from out of inside themselves when a scream of terror snaps both of them out of their deep thoughts and odd feelings.

"Help, help me, my son is missing, he is only six years old," A screaming and crying mother screams out in panic.

Agent Tate looks at Floyd, shakes his head and is just about to talk to his fellow agents, telling them to fix this problem fast. Floyd with a hand up in the air for Agent Tate to wait says to him, "Let me and my people handle this for you Agent Tate. No guns, no death, we will get this child back safe to his mother or we will bring you back his killer. Time is wasting Agent Tate, let me prove to you our worth."

Agent Tate wants to believe and before he can stop himself he says, "Yes," to Floyd.

Floyd stays still and talks to his people, "You heard the scream, you heard what I told Agent Tate, get this little boy back to his mother."

"Just like that Floyd? You order and they follow?"

"Yes Agent Tate, just like that."

Floyd and Agent Tate wait in silence drinking their coffee. Agent Tate is about to say something and Floyd waves him off. Floyd then drinks more of his coffee calmly.

(Three minutes have passed.) "The boy is found and retrieved Agent Tate. He is in good health. A man took him, this man is knocked out and about twenty feet away from the boy. Over there Agent Tate, over that hill on the left, that is where the boy is standing and crying waiting for more help and his mother to collect him."

"All right Floyd I'll have my team check, you better be telling me the truth. Time, precious time has passed by and if you are full of it and this boy is not found, I will blame you. Do you understand me Floyd?"

"Yes I do Agent Tate. Your threats are not necessary. The boy is safe, scared but safe."

(Twenty-eight seconds later.) "The boy is safe and sound."

"Just like I told you he would be."

"Yes you did. Now I want to know which one of your team members abducted the boy and placed him all nice and safe, tell me Floyd or I'll cuff you right now!"

"The truth is barely believed anymore Agent Tate. Next I will have no team members, it was all me. The big question will be how I did it. The scream for help happened while I was sitting here with you. I'm not that fast, you can see me as I move in fast motion. It would be better for all concerned if you believe or just let it pass for awhile longer.

"A short while longer Floyd. I can let this pass."

"Good. Now take your short and make it longer because I want you to understand everything fully."

133

Floyd an alien from another planet has gotten use to playing it cool. On his planet no one that follows him now on Earth would follow him on their planet, in fact they would laugh in his face. For Floyd was a partying fuck up whose only concern was getting wasted and laid. He would like to laugh out loud at how far he has come.

Floyd takes in a long breath, he holds it in and as he exhales it back out every hair on his body is standing up in excitement. The heavy of Floyd's treaty that he is going to ask for his people from the United States Government solely lies on his back. He wants to freak out and get high, then he remembers he has his sugar, which is better and cleaner than any drug on his former planet. Party on Floyd.

"Agent Tate, the alien man you see in front of you is not the same alien man that arrived on your planet. I was a lot less leadership material."

Floyd stops talking and puts his hands to his face in a attempt to hide himself from this great big heavy.

"You all right Floyd?" asks Agent Tate.

"Hate to be coarse Agent Tate but the fuck if I know. This is very big, you're looking at me like I have fifteen minutes and I need thirty maybe forty minutes. Most of my people say let's go to war, we don't need allies for both planets are our enemies. I understand this, I feel it. Rage would be so easy, so simple. No talking just lots of bloodshed and carnage to impress upon you how fucking serious this truly is. For if I fail, my people will kill me."

"You're freaking me out Floyd, you're glowing, what is going on? This has to be a trick?"

"It's the sugar flowing through my veins Agent Tate. Right now if I wanted to I could rage out and slaughter twenty or more people within a minute." Floyd pauses.

"I hate this, I've never killed anybody, unless I had to. Why do I want to now? I know it's the sugar. A little to almost a lot makes you feel good, it makes you feel high. Way too much just like I've ingested now can make a peaceful man like myself want to stomp on heads. I had to protect myself, just in case I get shot more than once or twice. I haven't gotten this surged up in awhile. I feel so high and mighty. I need to calm down."

"Calm is the word Floyd. I tell you this. Do not make me shoot you and I will not shoot you."

"That's reassuring Agent Tate," Floyd says then laughs.

Agent Tate can't help himself and he joins Floyd in laughing out loud. When they are done laughing the both of them feel a little bit better, especially Floyd.

"You feel better, you feeling calmer Floyd?"

"Yes I am Agent Tate, I think I'm going to make it," Floyd says and then he smiles and rolls his eyes at Agent Tate.

"Good, now get on with your story. Take your time but try to hurry it up as much as you can. The United States Government likes things fast and clear."

"Yes I know Agent Tate. I need to take another piss before I go on. Same rules as before Agent Tate."

"Fine Floyd, I'll be here."

Floyd takes his piss and after washing his hands he walks back over to the table where Agent Tate is waiting for him.

Chapter Two:

Next is Floyd's account of how things have come to be to get him where he is right now. Like any good story, the story teller has the obligation to embellish key points. For example when Floyd tells Agent Tate he was getting it on with five hot ladies, it was more like four hot ladies.

"For years Agent Tate I've partied in my life but in the last year before I got busted and sent here... I was high all the time, selling myself to rich ladies that were still fine enough to look at and a maybe for the end of the night unless something younger said yes to my price first. Yes Agent Tate I made a living by making ladies moan and groan. I'm perfectly built for long hours of passion."

"Well Floyd, I wouldn't pay a dollar for you," Agent Tate responds with a smile on his face and a laugh at the end.

"You know what Agent Tate? You are a human being."

"Yeah and so what. Is that a joke?"

"Yes Agent Tate, that was a joke."

"Being human is a joke to you Floyd?"

"To me yes, I'm not human remember?"

"Well Floyd you still look very human to me but I like your story so far. Let's see how imaginative you can make it?"

"Don't have to, the truth will be more than enough to keep you entertained Agent Tate."

"Well entertain me Floyd, bring on the ladies."

"Ladies, I'll give you ladies. I was at a party where I was the entertainment for five hot future doctor ladies that just graduated medical school."

"Sounds hot Floyd. How many arms a piece did every lady have at the party? I'm mean were they the standard two arms like here on Earth. Or were there more than two?" Agent Tate says to Floyd, feeling for some reason to start being an asshole.

"Well if my planet's people have more than two arms, we would have to cut or rip off the rest before we were brought here to Earth."

"That would suck and be very painful Floyd. I guess it's a good thing your people resemble Earthlings."

"Yes it is. Can you imagine our response when my planet found another planet that had life on it? With a closer look at your people most of my planet's people thought the whole thing was some weird hoax made up by our way too overworked space scientists."

"What happened next?"

"They provided proof. A window into your world. We watched for ourselves as a people that lived like we did on our planet around a hundred years ago live their lives. We wanted to go there. We wanted to meet aliens from another planet. This was the way it was meant to be..."

"What about the five doctor ladies?"

"I screwed all five of them and then got paid for it."

"That ending sucks, where are the details?"

"Okay. I started with one. We were all naked and touching each other and doctor number one sat on top of me, then she rode me until she had enough. Doctor number two stopped kissing doctor number four or was it number five? It's hard to remember, they were all so fine and lovely. She stopped kissing one of them and took her turn with me."

"Damn Floyd you're the man or should I say you're the alien?"

"Either will do Agent Tate. I'm worth every dollar I charge."

"Finish about the ladies Floyd."

"Well after Doctor lady number two, came Doctor lady number three, then came four and lastly came number five. After that they laid me down and all at the same time they licked my body clean like I was a piece of candy."

"That is a great sex story Floyd, now get back to this window to Earth your planet found."

"We were going to make contact with Earth. No one could believe what happened next. Our government a very small entity at the time was taking over and brought forth technology that no one on my planet had ever known. We were helpless as rules were made into laws. Within three months they controlled everything and everyone. We still had our lives out of sight of the government eyes but that was shrinking smaller every day."

"What did your Government do to your people Floyd?"

"They created these small machines that flew around our planet and recorded our actions. Any law that was broken was met by apprehension and then punishment. There was no need anymore for a trial of old. You committed the crime this was a fact, you had no excuse and no need to be heard. They wouldn't listen even if any of us were allowed to speak on behalf of ourselves."

"I don't know Floyd. These machines to me seem like a great idea. My planet could use these machines as well. Tell me Floyd, do you have one of these machines handy that I could take a look at?"

"No Agent Tate, not on me."

"But you can get to one, if you wanted to?"

"No Agent Tate. And I would not get you one even if I could get you one."

"That's typical. Boast about something you can't prove exists. And why would you not let me see one Floyd, I thought we were becoming friends?"

"We are Agent Tate. To give you one, that would be a very big mistake."

"Why is that Floyd, we as a people couldn't handle it?"

"No you couldn't Agent Tate. I would give it to you, you would check it out and then you would give it to somebody higher up than you. They would do the same thing until it was placed into the hands of a human that could almost understand it. After that Agent Tate the world you know, all the freedoms you have, in no time at all they would all be gone just like that."

"I have to say bullshit Floyd. My people could handle it and come out better after it was implemented."

"No Agent Tate. Earth would become even worse than my world. My world is a century beyond Earth. Even this did us no good in the end."

"I believe Floyd it's because your world got too soft and couldn't fight back against your tyrants. Here on Earth we as a people wouldn't let things get too far out of hand before we fought back and won."

"Very brave and noble Agent Tate. Still you are dumb to the fact that you have no idea what you are talking about. Yeah fight a machine that can fly so fast that you cannot shoot it out of the sky. Never mind the weapons they all come equipped with. They have the arsenal to knock you out or kill you if you are deemed too much trouble. I've seen it up close many times Agent Tate."

"Tell me about this Floyd. Please leave out no details."

"Okay Agent Tate. Walking down a sidewalk with my friends, a man in front of us was just walking as well then out of the sky came one of these flying machines telling him to stop where he was. He did not listen, in fact he took off running. The machine told him that the drugs he was carrying on his person had more value than his life had. He screamed at the machine to go away and leave him alone. He stopped running and threw the drugs on the ground, saying that it could have the drugs."

"What happened next Floyd?"

"The damn machine used its laser beam like a killing device to this pleading man's head. It struck him, at first he just stood there like nothing was happening... Then he started to shake and bleed out of his mouth... His head exploded into hundreds of tiny pieces as his body just stood there for a moment squirting out blood from the hole in his neck where his head used to be."

"That's just foul Floyd. I guess he should have said no to drugs. He might have kept his head."

"That is not funny Agent Tate. He was just a simple mule, who was on his way to meet his daughter. She came up the sidewalk from the other end. She looked at her father's body and she screamed out bloody murder. She had the right to Agent Tate for that damn machine murdered him like he had no worth at all. After that the machine told her to stop screaming because she was making a disturbance. She would not stop screaming so the machine knocked her out, she was then arrested and sent to jail."

"Okay Floyd, my humor was not called for. Still your people knew what was going on, so the way I see it, this man took his life into his own hands by carrying the drugs. If he didn't do this he would still be alive today."

"Maybe so Agent Tate. These damn machine have no right to take a life. Think about this, many people that were big deals were hunted down just like this man. Always with the machine telling all that could hear what they are guilty of. Whoever programmed the machines could add any name they wanted to their program. Once a person that was worthy became an enemy to the state as quickly as the wind blows. Evil crazy took over my Government Agent Tate and I would never be the one to allow this to happen to the people of Earth. You should be on my side with this."

"Maybe so Floyd, maybe so. Still I don't know, crime runs rampant across my county and planet. People will kill you for almost any reason now. Earth could use a cleansing a very deep one if we are to survive."

"Find another way Agent Tate, one that you can control."

"Perhaps so Floyd, please continue with your story."

"My life was not desirable so I hid the best I could. I still got high and paid to get laid. One day I got a call from a mayor's daughter to meet her and her two friends that very same night. The payment I would have gotten was more than I'd ever got paid before. I told them yes and met them at their hotel room later that night. We partied and had a lot of fun, all three of them were legal but no very wise to making love. In no time at all I had them doing things to me and to each other they never have done before. They laughed and giggled and told me that my tip was going to be very high. Everything was going fine until..." Floyd pauses to gather himself.

"There was a knocking at the door. The door was opened to the Mayor and the other two dads. They yelled at their daughters, when they stopped yelling at them it was my time to take their hate. Worse of all, there was a man, a silent man standing by the still open door. His eyes were empty of all emotions."

"Would you like another coffee Floyd?" asks Agent Tate in an attempt to calm down Floyd so he can go on with his story with more of a clear mind.

"Yes I would Agent Tate and thank you."

"No problem Floyd."

"I'll just keep on until it gets here. The Mayor looked at this silent man and snapped his fingers. The silent man pulled out a small handheld device, he pushed some buttons and moments later a machine came flying into the hotel room. The machine told me of my crimes, I held my breath waiting to die...

The Mayor, a real asshole, screamed at the machine for it to kill me for my crimes. The machine told the Mayor to stop yelling or he would be held guilty of yelling in public. The Mayor looked at the silent man and asked him why I was not to be put to death. The silent man looked at the Mayor with his empty eyes and told the Mayor that he and his daughter were not important enough for the machine to take my life. I was to be arrested."

" A man in black Floyd?"

"Yes Agent Tate. Mister Silent looked at me with the same empty eyes and asked me if I was coming peacefully or did he have to make the machine knock me out where I stood naked and turned off."

"What did you do Floyd? Did you try to run away?"

"I thought about it Agent Tate, then I looked at the silent man and saw in his eyes the contempt he had for the Mayor.

142

That if his orders were to kill the mayor he would do so without a thought. It would have probably brought a smile to his cold lips. I asked if I could get dressed. I was allowed to get dressed and then I was taken to the nearest police station, where I was arrested officially. There I stayed for the next month until I was given my punishment."

"Earth is that punishment, correct Floyd?"

"Earth. A blessing and a curse. None of my planet's machines here to knock us out or kill us. However there are the enforcers of my planet to keep us outcasts in check and following the rules of our ex-planet."

"You are telling me Floyd, not only are there people like you that are sent here as a punishment, there are also your planet's version of jailers here on Earth?"

"That is correct Agent Tate. Not as many as us outcasts but enough of them to take us outcasts down or out if we don't comply or try to revolt."

"This changes things Floyd. Do your jailers have weapons to use against you with them here on Earth?"

"Yes they do Agent Tate. Their weapons, if used at their most deadliest, could take out an army, including all tanks, planes and ships."

"You know Floyd, we the United States of America cannot allow this. We will see this as an act of war."

"Yes I know Agent Tate, that is why I am here to set things straight and let the United States of America know that my people will help you find, capture or eliminate our jailers."

"I understand there is hate between your people, but still they are your people and we are aliens to you?"

"They are our people but they are our enemies. We have no worth, they hate us. We are the reason they are not living on our planet. They beat, they kill, they rape us."

""I have to tell you Floyd, some on my planet would do the same thing to you if they found out you were aliens."

"Yes out of fear or hate. I, we understand this, that is the reason for this contact. It will be up to your Government to protect us from the fear and the hate that is present on this planet of blue."

"What do you and your people want Floyd?"

"Freedom and peace. We want a place that is ours to call home. A place big enough where we all can be together. Land is what we are asking for Agent Tate. A land that cannot be taken away from us."

"How much land Floyd?"

"One of your smaller States will do just fine. We are thinking one in the south, we like the warmth."

"Yet you are settled right here in New York."

"Not by choice Agent Tate. We stay where we're told to stay. Some have tried to venture off, but to no avail. We are tagged. To get this device out of us, we have failed every time but once. The volunteer always dies on the table, except for that special one."

"That's fucked up Floyd. How many have died so far?"

"Hundreds Agent Tate, hundreds of my people have died by being volunteers and by being killed off by causing too much trouble for our jailers. We need help to get these devices out of our bodies. Surgery at first will do. After enough of my people are tag-less, I will lead a team to retrieve the tool that inserts and retracts these devices into our bodies."

"I need proof Floyd. All this is just hearsay so far. Proof, give me proof and I'll see what I can do for your people."

"In a little bit Agent Tate, you will receive all the proof you and your Country will ever need to believe me. Remember what I said?

"Remember what Floyd?"

"I'm tagged Agent Tate. I'm risking retaliation for talking to you. The longer I sit here with you the closer I get to being taken out by my jailers."

"Are there any of your people's jailers in this park at this time with us Floyd?"

"Yes Agent Tate, at least twenty or more. Plenty enough to take both of our teams out quickly and bloodily."

"You're freaking me out Floyd. You know I have to do something. I cannot let this go down."

"Yes, I understand your predicament Agent Tate. But understand this, we are your secret weapons."

"How so Floyd?"

"Sugar, Agent Tate. Only we outcast know of the power of sugar. Our jailers eat and drink only items from our planet, that way there is no chance they will get sick off your foods and water. This may change at anytime. All it will simply take is one candy bar or one can of soda. After that they will report their findings back to my planet. Their orders will be to kill us, to kill us all. They will not stop after that. After we are all dead, you planet's population will be next. How far they will go? I do not know. In the end they will

145

cripple your planet enough, so that way they can take over and have total control of your planet"

"No way in Hell, Floyd. No thousands of your people can beat our billions of people."

"It's more like millions of my people, Agent Tate."

"Millions of your people on Earth, no way. We would have found out by now. Just one car accident, where one of your people had to go to a hospital. The blood, the blood would have been all we needed."

"Agent Tate, I think you have forgotten that my people are a century beyond your people. Think back to when your planet had no planes. If my people came to your world with the simplest of our planes, your world would have not stood a chance."

"We would find a way Floyd, we always do."

"True Agent Tate, when it comes to your own people of your planet attacking you. What is your planet going to do when star ships the size of cities appear in the skies. You have the big one Agent Tate, nuclear weapons. We do not, not anymore. We have gone way passed that. Our weapons when fired, will not destroy buildings or bridges. They will not destroy trees or animals. They will only destroy and kill one thing, just human beings."

"Your planet wants to take over Earth?"

"No, for all I know right now, that answer is no. My planet wants Earth to stay the same. For them it's much easier and simpler if Earth stays unknowing to our presence. In fact Earth has no worth to my planet except for a place to store their unwanted citizens."

"Even so and so what. We may be simple to your high and mighty planet, still we will never surrender."

"Yes you will. But that does not have to come to be..."

"We, my people, we will help you before a war can get started. Sugar, still our secret weapon. Before what is to be shown to you in a little while, I want to tell the rest of how my people are treated by our jailers."

"Okay make it fast, I want you to get back to this war."

"My people are poor by design. When we arrived on Earth we were given one hundred dollars, a place to live and a job that sucks and doesn't pay very much. If we make too much money and they find out, they come to our homes and take away from us what that they deem we have too much of, whether it be money, clothes, entertainment or even food."

"What do they do with this stuff, Floyd?"

"The money they keep for the cause, everything else gets tossed away. Sometimes they don't pay heed to what they discard. We can sneak up and take it back, use it all as a stockpile for those that need it the most."

"That's smart, give the people what they need."

"Now it comes to a real big drag Agent Tate."

"How big of a drag Floyd?"

"Real big Agent Tate."

"Let me hear about this drag Floyd."

"Sex between my people is fine, we better not make any babies and we are left alone to get it on. However if we have sex with an Earthling..."

"After we are alone, they come to our homes, bust everything up, then they beat the shit out of us. After that they make the device that is planted inside us makes our blood almost come to a boil. Our brains are made to feel like they are about to pop out of our skulls."

"That sounds like cruel and unusual punishment Floyd."

"Most definitely Agent Tate, we have no worth, we are like hungry and horny animals to our jailers."

"Here comes our coffee, I had them get you ten packs of sugar once again. Go ahead and make your coffee up, I'm going to go take a piss."

Agent Tate leaves Floyd to himself as he walks away to take his piss. Floyd takes the ten packs of sugar and puts them in his pants pocket. He gets up and stretches his legs, he's already coming down a little bit from his sugar rush. Floyd looks around slowly at the people that consist of Agent Tate's team. He looks back and forth and he notices something. Three minutes and forty-seven seconds later Agent Tate sits back down at the table.

"Damn that was one fine piss. Maybe if I had taken a crap, I'd feel even better. What do you think Floyd?"

"A piss was enough for you, Agent Tate. If you had taken a crap you wouldn't be full of crap right now trying to pass yourself off as the real Agent Tate."

"Can't fool a criminal. I guess it's a good thing you can't do anything about it. Look at you sitting there like a big piece of traitorous shit. Who do you think you are Earth Prisoner #1113? We let you live, we give you a home. Now you have to become dead. I'm going to kill you myself. I'm going to turn on the device inside you to kill. When you are on the ground flopping around and crying from the pain, I'm going to kick you in your face."

"No you're not."

"That's your comeback? No you're not? Well Earth Prisoner #1113 yes I am. I will kick you in your face and I will enjoy myself while doing it."

"I take it that your heard everything I told the real dead at this time Agent Tate?"

"Yup. Sex and sugar, you're an idiot to think you could make the humans believe that with sugar you could save the Earth from us evil Aliens."

"I had to try. Before you kill me, do you mind if I eat my ten packs of sugar, I've grown a taste for it?"

"You can stick them up your ass for all I care, Earth Prisoner #1113."

Floyd says nothing as he pulls out the ten packs of sugar from his pants pocket. He opens them all up from one to ten without eating one. Alien Agent Tate watches Floyd with a hurry up so I can kill you look in his eyes. Floyd smiles big and scoops up his ten packs of sugar and eats them all at the same time.

"What the Hell you smiling about, you piece of shit?"

Floyd gathers his strength. The sugar that is flowing through his veins is pumping his heart like a thunderclap. Floyd moves his head around to ease the tension that he feels in his neck. Floyd counts to ten and then he says to the Alien Agent Tate. "This, you dead asshole!"

Floyd with one quick punch to the Alien Agent Tate's face, puts his fist straight through it. The punch was so fast that Agent Alien never made a sound. One moment he was alive and pissed off, the next moment his brains and teeth were exploding out the back of his head.

Floyd grabs the invisible gadget that is placed on Alien Agent's neck and pulls it off, he also takes takes his gun. He then lets go and lets the dead Aliens body fall to the ground, like it has no more worth. Camouflaged no more another pair of arms appear on the dead body. The human looking body turns into more of a non-human looking body for all in the park to see.

Screams fill the air as Floyd stands up and puts the gadget inside the same pants pocket he had his ten packs of sugar in. Floyd looks around at Agent Tate's team targeting the ones that have been replaced with Aliens from his former planet.

Floyd thinks to himself, "Man this is going to suck. The still humans will shoot at me just like the Aliens will. I have to take out another one quickly, make the still humans understand I'm on their side. I hope I don't get shot in my face or balls."

Floyd runs from his table with gun in hand. He shoots it once, he shoots it twice, taking down two Aliens with both shots. Floyd lowers his gun as he runs up to the first Alien he shot. Bullets come at him from all directions, some bouncing off, some penetrating his body. The pain is unreal and he would be dead if he wasn't high as the sky on sugar. Floyd reaches the Aliens body and pulls the invisible gadget off its neck. The same transformation happens to the Alien's body and face this time. The Alien is not dead so Floyd smashes his face in with his foot.

"Agent Tate is dead, his body is probably in the restroom, there are ten more Aliens that have taken place of your team members. If you are human don't shoot at me, shoot dead the Aliens that are shooting at me!"

In under five minutes the rest of the Aliens are dead. Floyd has vanished using one of the gadgets to change his face and body for his escape. All of Floyd's team survived and now are off somewhere fighting the cause.

Chapter Three:

(November, six months later. The reason Floyd says he was tagged during his interview was because he carries the tracking device that was taken out of his body with him in his pocket, the pocket he never placed anything in besides this device.)

For six months Floyd has lived in peace on the run looking like any two armed man on Earth he wants to. Floyd is that one, the special one who survives surgery to remove the device in his body. (This device is placed next to the heart of each outcast.) What is not known is why he survived. Everything that was done to others before him was done to him.

Step by step, except one step, one thing was left out. The second pain medicine was skipped by accident because his doctor was exhausted and tired of having her people die upon her operating table. The second pain medicine, counteracted with the first stronger pain medicine which did not show up in the test that were done for it. What looked like death was not death, it was an intense form of paralysis that rendered the patient to an almost death like state that the doctors mistook for actual death.

Floyd woke up from his surgery alive, with his doctor and about ten other people looking at him like why does it have to be him that survived. This fuck up. Floyd saw this in their eyes and felt it in their hearts as they smiled and made him feel like he was the greatest Alien on Earth. Floyd did not volunteer for his operation, he was grabbed up and used because of who he was, a worthless fuck up.

As Floyd's doctor and the bystanders drank the bottle of champagne that was kept for this special occasion to celebrate (the alcohol in the champagne counter acts with the sugar making it too diluted to get them high) Floyd was left alone in pain. Floyd wanted something, he just didn't know what.

151

Floyd sat up on his operating table and looked around at the fat cats. (A great Earth term.) He shook his head and said to himself. "I get no, we're sorry we almost killed you Floyd. These people suck, they're almost as bad as the Government on my planet."

Floyd removed himself from his operating table, he got dressed and took a walk. While he was walking he spotted a milk chocolate candy bar, Floyd said to himself. "I've never had on of these. Why not try it, what would it hurt?"

Because there is no sugar on Floyd's planet anything sweet to eat on Earth was not bought by his people. When his people made raids for food or found foods that had been discarded, like can goods and foods in boxes, if there was something sweet to eat they would just leave it behind. Floyd wondered to himself if anyone from his planet had ever eaten a candy bar. Floyd unwrapped his milk chocolate candy bar, the scent of it hit his nose instantly, making his stomach rumble.

Floyd took his first bite and fell in love with his candy bar. He took two more bites and he started to laugh out loud. Floyd hushed himself and looked around to see if anyone heard him laugh. While he did this he held the rest of his milk chocolate candy bar really tight in his hand, as an reassurance to himself that it belonged to him and nobody else could have it. Three bites down and he was hooked already and he couldn't wait for the rush he was going to feel after eating the rest of it.

Floyd took the rest of his milk chocolate candy bar and shoved it into his mouth. He chewed it away fast. When it was all gone, Floyd's face felt really warm, he also felt feverish. Floyd tried shaking his head to make these feelings go away, but to no avail. Before too long Floyd was jumping up and down and not noticing that he was even doing it. Floyd then discovered he was not in much pain, he felt no pain at all, in fact he felt better than he had ever felt before in his life.

Floyd looked at his chest, the cut from the incision of his surgery was healed. Floyd wanted more milk chocolate candy bars, he looked around, there were none to be found. Floyd got mad and figured that the people that were drinking champagne at his expense better have some milk chocolate candy bars in their pockets or he was going to kick them in their asses.

"Hey you ass faces, let me have all of your milk chocolate candy bars right now!"

Floyd's Doctor looked confused as did the rest of the champagne drinkers and responded back to Floyd. "We do not have any milk chocolate candy bars to give to you Floyd."

"Well Doctor you better get some and get some now or I'm going to bust this place up."

"Please Floyd calm down. If you cause damage to this facility, you may dismantle the cloaking device we have installed that surrounds this building to protects us."

"I could careless Doctor whatever your name is, let them come I'll rip off their heads."

"Floyd my name is Doctor Fanny."

"Doctor Fanny? Ha,ha,ha. What kinda of name is that? Why not just call yourself Doctor Butt or better yet Doctor, why not just call yourself Doctor Ass?"

Floyd laughed out loud as he walked closer to the people inside the room. Halfway to them Floyd felt dizzy and weaker, he fell down on his knees to help steady himself from the withdraws of the sugar high that was depleting vastly inside his body. Floyd thought to himself chocolate, I need more chocolate, as Doctor Fanny rushed over to him to see what had went wrong with him.

Doctor Fanny to anyone, "Quick get this man a candy bar, he is going through withdraws. We can't let him get sick or die before we find out how he survived his surgery. How did he find a candy bar to eat? And why the Hell would he eat it? Wait a minute, bring me back one too."

Floyd listened to all that was going on around him as he started to feel a little better. The dizziness was almost over with and in a moment he was back on his feet, telling Doctor Fanny what was going on.

"That's what happened Doctor Fanny. I ate a milk chocolate candy bar, first I felt high, then I felt more powerful, like I was rushing around but on the inside. Look at my incision, it's healed."

Doctor Fanny inspected Floyd's incision and to her amazement it was healed and gone. She puzzled in her mind about what else a milk chocolate candy bar could do for her people. Doctor Fanny decided that Floyd was too important to test the ramifications of digesting more milk chocolate candy bars. So Doctor Fanny picked three members of her staff to test what would happen to them when they digested large quantities of milk chocolate candy bars.

One week later all three of Doctor Fanny's staff members were hooked on sugar. Doctor Fanny discovered that even though milk chocolate candy bars tasted better than straight sugar, nothing beat the quick rush of power that came from digesting straight pure cane sugar.

Two weeks later only one member of Doctor Fanny's staff members remained alive and he had succumbed to insanity. With her experiment over she had all the information that she needed, how much sugar was enough and how much sugar was too much. Next was to test the total strength and endurance of her last team member. She needed to find out how much pain he could take before it killed him.

Floyd during this time was pampered and tested daily. A nurse that had a crush on him, snuck in milk chocolate candy bars for him to eat. It was a good thing Doctor Fanny didn't find out about this because she would have put an end to it. This, unknown to her, would have been a very big mistake, for without Floyd's daily sugar rush, he wouldn't have had the time to build up a tolerance to it. It was Floyd who ended the rampage of the escaped last team member of Doctor Fanny's team members.

Doug was his name, he had been without sugar for almost two days and he hated it. The withdraws were so painful that it drove Doug's insane mind to come to the realization that he needed more sugar and he would kill anyone that got in his way or that tried to stop him from eating it.

Floyd was letting his crushed filled Nurse have fun with his body as he was eating a milk chocolate candy bar. Everything was nice and quiet when suddenly a loud crash came from three rooms over. Floyd's Nurse stopped having fun and went to check and see what was going on. She told Floyd to stay there. When she opened up the door to leave, both of them heard bloody screams coming from the same room.

Floyd waited for a few moments before he walked out of his room and down the hall. He found Doug killing person after person, while screaming for sugar to eat. Floyd quickly turned around and walked into the room that was next to his room, the room where the sugar was kept.

Floyd grabbed seven packs of sugar and ate them, instantly he felt the rush. He then ate three more sugar packs, wiped his mouth and ran back down the hall to stop Doug. Floyd got back to Doug just in time, for he was just about to kill the remaining people in the building, including Doctor Fanny. Floyd ran up to Doug and grabbed a hold of his head. Floyd pulled and pulled on Doug's head until it came off in his hands.

"Great job Floyd, You're high on sugar aren't you?"

"Yes I am Fanny."

"That's Doctor Fanny! My fanny is right here, take a look for yourself, see how fine and shapely it is. Wouldn't you just love to give it a little bite?"

"Yes Doctor Fanny, I would like to bite your fanny. How about we take off our clothes and have sex on the floor?"

"Right here in front of my team members, I think not. I do not want them to see that part of my life. My passion is strong, my passion is full of love and peace to my lovers. Too bad for you, for I would have rocked you off this planet we are placed upon."

"Doctor Fanny, with the sexy fanny, you're turned on, you almost died, I the hot sexy saviour just saved you. Myself, I'm special. I can give it so great, you'll beg for more. Besides, would this not be a test that you have not preformed yet? What sugar can do for our Alien bodies while having hot alien sex on Earth?"

"Well that is different Floyd, would you like to know my first name before we have sex?"

"No, I would like to call your Doctor Fanny. Take off your clothes, show me your hot looking Earth body. Earth ladies, I really dig them, their bodies are so beautiful."

"Earth ladies? Floyd do not tell me you have sex with Earth ladies? That would be very bad and against the law. I do not agree with all our laws but this one I do. We are different species from Earthlings. Beside that would be unfair to the humans, they do not know we are Aliens. Shame on you Floyd. And I have to say this, Yuck! Where is your mind and your pride?"

"Damn that is cold Doctor Fanny."

"I'm a Doctor Floyd. I have to be cold sometimes, when I need my mind not to be influenced by my emotions."

"I understand Doctor Fanny, you and the other Doctors are trying to free our people. Still what about that love inside you, the one that is full of love?"

"Yes that is always present. And it is my passion that is full of love. Way to pay attention, ladies just like me just love when men don't pay attention to what we say. Our bodies are all you see. What about our minds? I'm a Doctor damn it. You simple minded, great looking Alien man, you pay heed to every word I speak, because I'm a Doctor and I'm hot and sexy looking, even as an Earth woman."

"Yes you are Doctor Fanny. Are we going to have sex now, or are you still flustered with me? If you are, I promise, I'll change your flustered to being sexy flushed?"

"Maybe you can Floyd. I need to know first, did you have sex with a human lady?"

"Yes I have Doctor Floyd. I must be up to forty five by now. Talk about passion, Earth ladies are full of it. They like to make love even more than all the ladies from our planet that I've made love with."

"Floyd you are a dog! A damn horny dog, good for nothing besides having sex with. You are a past from our planet that should have stayed there, lost and forgotten about."

"Listen up lady, I am not a Dog. I'm a six foot Alien man, with a huge rocket in my pocket. I love to have sex, I got paid to have sex on our planet, it was how I made my living. I'm not ashamed of this because I'm the best lay you will ever have for free. Earth ladies, yes they are fun and beautiful, I've never not enjoyed myself. Doctor Fanny get off your highness and after we get through having sex, do yourself a favor, go out and find a human man to have sex with."

"I will not. Why do you think we're still having sex, you ass brain? That maybe is a no way now Floyd!"

"Maybe? I'll turn your maybe and even your no, to a yes we can have sex anytime you want to."

"Stop it Floyd, you're starting to embarrass yourself."

"That is one thing I am never and that is embarrassed, Doctor Fanny."

Floyd, licks his lips and starts to dance around, thrusting his Alien-hood in Doctor Fanny's direction. He stops dancing and says to Doctor Fanny. "Shirt or pants?"

Doctor Fanny is turned on, trying her best to tell herself not to be. She smiles at Floyd and unpins her hair saying to him after her long brown hair flows down passed her shoulders, "Take off your pants first Floyd."

Floyd smiles and drops his pants. He puts up his finger in the air, in a gesture for Doctor Fanny to wait a moment. Floyd drops his finger and takes off his underwear. He lifts up his long shirt to showoff his large Alien-hood. Off goes Floyd's shirt quickly. Floyd is naked as he walks over to a chair. He picks up the chair and carries it back to where Doctor Fanny is standing with sexy legs that want to run to Floyd. Floyd places the chair back down on the floor about five feet away from Doctor Fanny. He sits down on the chair and invites with his hand for Doctor Fanny to come over to him and sit down on top of his naked lap.

(Unlike their jailers, the outcast do not have an invisible external device on their necks to make their appearance look human. The device that does this for them is placed inside the same device that tracks their whereabouts. Floyd is sitting naked for all to see as his true self, with all four arms showing. Floyd finds out that if he places his device in his pocket, its contact is close enough to him to change his looks from Alien to human.)

158

Doctor Fanny, takes in a big breath and lets it out fast. She takes off her clothes, never taking her eyes off of Floyd. She walks over to Floyd, when she reaches him, she leans down to him and gives him a long sexy kiss. She pulls away from Floyd's lips and his roaming hands and tells her team members to keep notes. She sits down on top of Floyd and closes her eyes as the pain and the pleasure mix together for her to lose control.

Twenty minutes later Doctor Fanny is sweating and panting from trying her best to out best Floyd. Doctor Fanny looks Floyd in his eyes and calls him a bastard. Floyd smiles and tells Doctor Fanny, that her turn is over, that it is his turn to sweat and pant. An exhausted Doctor Fanny stops making love to Floyd and slowly gets off of his lap. Floyd stands up and wraps his hands around Doctor Fanny's waist, pulling her in to give her a tender and loving kiss.

Floyd takes Doctor Fanny's hand and leads her about seven feet away from the chair. Together they lay down on the floor. Floyd takes his left hand and places it underneath Doctor Fanny's head as a comfort shield. Floyd places his love inside Doctor Fanny and makes love to her for thirty-four minutes until he can't control his feelings any longer. With making love over with Doctor Fanny and Floyd kiss each other like they are comfortable lovers that have made love many times.

Floyd raises himself above Doctor Fanny at arms length. He looks down at her and says to her still full passion that has not been slated yet, "Get conformable beautiful, I'm just starting with you."

Floyd makes love to Doctor Fanny a second time, and she softly tells him to stop while holding him with a grip that is so strong he barely has the mobility to make love to her fully. Doctor Fanny's team members have now stopped taking notes and are making love.

When Floyd's and Doctor Fanny's second time of making love is through, Floyd turns around and notices a little, shy, sexy looking lady that has no one around to make love with.

This makes Floyd feel sad, so he walks back over to the chair and sits down on it. He then invites this sexy, little lady over to him to make love with him. Tears fall from her eyes as she takes off her clothes. She tells Floyd to take it slow with her. Floyd tells her that she is in control, she can have it slow if that is what she wants. Her tears turn to a smile as she makes love for the first time on Earth.

Doctor Fanny is on her feet and watching her lover and a tramp have dirty sex together. Shock turns to rage as Doctor Fanny walks over to them. She tells them to stop, they will not listen to her. She tells them again and again to stop as their passion only grows stronger. Doctor Fanny (Linda) cannot take anymore of her lover's cheating. She walks away from him and his tramp to grab a scalpel that is placed on a tray next to the operating table. (The very same one she used on Floyd.)

With rage still flowing through her heart, Doctor Fanny walks back over to them as they are still having dirty sex. Doctor Fanny does not blink as she grabs the hair on the back of the head of the lonely, sexy, little lady (that is having the best sex she has ever had) and with the scalpel in her other hand Doctor Fanny slices Mary's throat deep enough for there to be no way anybody could save her life.

Mary is in love and lust, hearing nothing except her's and Floyd's passionate love making. Her thoughts are about her husband and children that still live on her ex-planet as she feels the quick slice against her throat. Mary grabs her throat as blood spills out of her wound. In seconds Mary's throat is squirting out blood so full that it is covering a confused Floyd's face and body. Mary dies of blood loss on top of Floyd. Floyd looks like he has been painted with blood as Mary falls off of him and onto the floor dead to the world. Everybody that has not finished making love, stops making love and then the screams start, while Doctor Fanny looks like she is on another world.

Floyd yells out to Doctor Fanny, "What the Hell did you do Linda? Mary's dead, you killed Mary." (Both Linda and Mary whispered their names to Floyd while they where making love to him.)

"That's right Floyd, your tramp is dead, she got what she deserved. You belong to me!"

"Your... You've gone crazy Linda. Put the scalpel down, before you hurt someone else."

"The only one I'm going to hurt is you Floyd!" Linda takes the scalpel and slices it towards Floyd, who puts up his right hand in defense to shield it away from cutting his face. Floyd's right hand gets cut deep, causing it to bleed out heavy and thick on top of a dead Mary.

"Damn it Linda, stop your craziness!", Floyd shouts out in a lot of pain.

Team members dressed and naked alike rush towards Linda to stop her murderess rage, for Linda is still trying to slice Floyd with everything she has inside herself.

"You bleed... You bleed Floyd, see you can die, you're not that special, I will prove you're nothing but a dog. Come here dog, receive your bone."

Linda is finally gotten a hold of. She is still in a rage and wanting to kill Floyd as her team members try their best to bring her down to the floor. Linda keeps screaming out and a few minutes later, Linda is crying her eyes out for what she has done.

Linda to everybody, as they look at her tied up to the chair she just had sex on with Floyd. Floyd has eaten four packs of sugar, his wound is healed and he damns himself for this, but he still feels like getting the rest of what he has stored back out of himself. That way he can think more clearly instead of wanting to bust a nut.

"I'm alright now everybody. Floyd look at me, I'm fine now. It is not that puzzling to the mind that you Floyd are the one responsible for my actions."

"You still sound crazy to me Linda. Good thing you are nice and tied up. What is my crime? I made love to you so fine that after only two times you wanted me all to yourself?"

"Yes Floyd that is correct, well almost. You see Floyd, your making love is fine, you are the best I've ever had. Sweet Floyd, you are still far from that great of a lay to make me kill Mary over you out of jealousy."

"I'm confused, is that not what you just did Linda?"

"Well yes this is true Floyd... Everybody listen to me, I'm fine now. It was Floyd's semen, that made me go crazy for a few minutes and kill Mary."

"You crazy lady, there's nothing in my semen that would make you or any other lady go murdering crazy."

"Yes there is, you great lay you. And that is Sugar. When you finished inside me, and I have to say Floyd that felt really great, you sent a sugar rush through my system. That, mixed with the passion I was felling, made all logic fail to be present in my actions."

"Well damn, I guess I better wear a rubber from now on. Still if anybody wants my opinion, I say we keep her tied up a while longer, because it was twice, not just once I finished inside sweet Linda."

"You bastard. Shut your mouth, you're nothing but a prostitute. I am a Doctor. Who's opinion matters the most? And truthfully, who was Mary anyway, she hardly talked unless it was about work. She hated it here and in a way maybe I did her a favor and at the same time I made a breakthrough. Everybody knows that sometimes when experimenting things can go wrong, which is only a setback. Now untie me and let's all together put this discovery to work for us."

"Not much of a discovery Doctor Fanny. It's a very simple, do not make love to a fellow Alien while high on sugar."

"Small minded man. That is one way. Another way is for a lady like myself to do exactly that."

"Why would a lady want to become a murdering crazy lady?"

"Simple, I do not feel that has to be the only answer. If a man like you gets too high up on sugar, we ladies with our bodies can bring him back down. If he's still a threat, we can kill him after he is finished, tired and weak."

"I hate this. We think we're better than the humans. Look at what you're talking about. We are one people. Together we fight a war with no weapons to fight and kill our enemies. The first thing, when you find perhaps a weapon, you think of how to use it against your own."

"Get off you high horse Floyd and grow up. You're correct this is war. Everything we have, we use it for victory. If ones like you lose your life for the war so be it."

"Not anymore Doctor Fanny. In my hand I have twenty packs of sugar. While everybody tied you up or watched you be tied up, I was eating sugar, four packs. I feel great, I'm healed. I look at everybody, I'm alone. All of you are listening to what Doctor Fanny has said and sadly, I see it in your eyes, you agree with her."

163

"Of course they do Floyd. These are my fellow people of science and medicine, without us there will be no victory. We create the weapons, you fight while using them. You are a simple soldier that follows our orders."

"That is the truth, from way back when to this point in time. Time keeps on going forward, it is now past that time. We need you, you need us more for we do all the killing. I'm taking over, I'm the new leader of our people. Our people, none of us will be simple soldiers or disposable anymore. From now on we are all equals."

"Equals? In what universe? You the new leader? Don't worry everybody about untying me now. I'm about to laugh so hard that these ropes that bind me well rip away from my enormous laughter."

"Linda, you are a great lover, as a person, you suck and not in the good way. I hate I have to do this, I'm the strongest of all our people, I will be the one to lead our people to victory and greatness."

Floyd rips open as many sugar packs has he can in one rip. Six is the amount he opens and eats, as he is doing this Doctor Fanny is yelling at everybody to attack Floyd all at the same time to prevent him from eating anymore sugar. The small mob pounces on Floyd as they were ordered to do. They hit him, they try to tear the rest of the sugar packs from his hand. All is loud and fierce as Floyd fights them off while eating every sugar packs he has in his hand. With all twenty packs of sugar flowing through Floyd's veins, the mob's hits hardly have an effect on him.

Floyd closes his eyes and thinks of his planet that he will never see again. When Floyd re-opens his eyes the sugar rush is so overwhelming that it is all he can do not to go crazy himself. Four minutes later Floyd is sitting on the floor next to Linda who is still tied to the chair. Floyd is covered in blood and is shaking from withdraws. The only two people left alive is himself and Linda.

"Please Floyd, don't kill me. I'm your Doctor, I'm your lover. We can get through this, I know we can. You can be the leader of our people. Please untie me, let me help you Floyd. You and I Floyd, together we will have the power to win this war and save our people."

"Yes you and I Linda. I the leader, you in the background making everything run smoothly."

"Yes Floyd, I can do that."

"I know Linda. I have to make sure you understand how serious I am when I say all our people are equals now. I the leader, will lead from the front line. If my people are to fight and die, I will be right beside them until the very end."

"If that is your wish Floyd, I will follow your orders until the end. When we as a people together when the war."

Floyd unties Linda. After she is untied, she sits down on Floyd's lap. She hugs Floyd knowing all the bloodshed he created was a cry for help. This powerhouse wants to be the hero, the one that leads his people to peace. Linda feels Floyd's body pulsate, as she looks at him he looks ashamed for wanting her. Linda smiles on the inside, loving the power she has, and will have more of, over Floyd as she offers him her body for comfort and love.

After they make love, Floyd is coming down with a surprising amount of ideas he wants to implement coming to his mind as he speaks them out as fast as he can think of them. Linda feels like smacking Floyd and telling him to shut up. Linda is high on sugar from making love with Floyd. Third time is a charm, with twenty packs of sugar surging through Floyd's body, Linda's sugar high is more than twice of what she felt the first time around. She wonders to herself why she hasn't attacked Floyd yet. She decides it has to be because of focus. First time around Linda had no fear of dying going through her mind.

Linda stops talking to herself and starts to listen more closely to what Floyd is saying. After a while Floyd is making a lot of sense, talking about bringing the humans into their war, and using sugar as a healing agent while her patients are in surgery. From Floyd's lips, it is Linda's job to get all like her on board to Floyd's plan for victory. A victory that no other before him had the gall to implement.

From Floyd's start as the new leader of his people to the meeting he sat up with the United States Government, via Agent Tate, things have been going as planned. He proved to enough eyes and recordings that Aliens were on Earth. The Government cleared things up by telling the masses that everything was nothing but one elaborate hoax. Floyd allowed the Government six months, which they didn't know about, in order for them to collect their thoughts and make their plans. They wanted so badly to get their hands on Floyd, he's a danger with advanced Alien technology they wanted to own.

Things have changed rapidly from the start of Floyd's reign as leader. Linda who believed in Floyd's words after they made love for the third time, has been the rock and the voice of reason for Floyd. She with love in her heart, lets Floyd go as far as he needs to win this war. When Floyd gets off track or starts to take things a little too far, Linda is there to get him back on track and if he needs it, she gets his mind back down to Earth, where the war is of most concern and not their former planet's destruction.

Six months is what is needed for his former planet to have their attack forces ready to enter Earth's plane of existence. Because of spies that have decided to follow Floyd, they have made their planet believe that all is still calm enough on Earth, thus having them pull most of their fleet back due to them believing this, but leaving enough behind for Floyd's plan to escalate to the next phase. It is now time to contact the United States Government again. It is time to become allies against the evil Aliens.

Chapter Four:

This time the meeting place between Floyd and the United States Government takes place at the White House. Floyd along with Linda and eight more Aliens entered the back doors to the White House, without fanfare, this meeting in the books never took place.

"Mr. President. I am an Alien, my lady is an Alien all ten of us are Aliens. To go on, this has to be a fact. My ex-planet at anytime could invade Earth with weapons a century beyond what you have here on Earth Mr. President. I will tell all, after I truly believe you believe I am an Alien."

"Floyd, my mind is still trying to fully get around this fact. Yes I believe you and your party of ten people are in fact Aliens from another planet. Tests have proven the fact that sugar makes your people superhuman or should I say super alien. I have to be honest with you Floyd, these powers you and your people can obtain by simply eating sugar is troubling to me and my country."

"What can I do to alleviate these troubles for you Mr. President?"

"I need to know for sure Floyd that you will not use these great powers of yours on my country men and in my world as a whole. We have shot you. We have stabbed you. We have frozen you and we have drown you. Only a few of your people have died, I think two in all have died. The rest has survived the most brutal attempts to take your lives. All at your request. This olive branch you gave to us, is the only reason you are here in my house. I want to trust you, how do I know that you are not working for your planet's jailers that are stationed here on Earth?"

"Simple Mr. President. I and my people will tell you where our jailers are located. We will even bring them in to you dead or alive."

"That is hard and cold Floyd." The President of the United States of America sits back in his couch, humming a song to himself underneath his breath. His heart is pounding as he feels the starting of a drop of sweat on his forehead.

The President talks to himself within his mind, "Have to play it cool, I can't let this Alien, watch this drop of sweat run down my face, I have to be the one in control." The President of the United States of America sits forward quickly, turning his head at the same time, causing the drop of sweat on his forehead to fly into the air unnoticed by all those in the room.

"Mr. President, yes that is cold. I have to be cold and hard. My people trust in me that I will be this way until we are free. That is why I am here, that is why we're here. Today is the day for a new day and way to start tomorrow. We want so little compared to what we offer to your world."

"The world can wait for the day after tomorrow. Tomorrow is solely for the United States of America."

"Yes Mr. President. I feel this is the best as well, I was just speaking in a broader sense. The U.S.A. has to be the one nation on Earth to receive this gift of a century in advanced technology to add to your technology. We as a people all want to live in this country, where we can live in peace and be protected by this our new adopted country."

"Protected? Why would your people need protection, when you can do the things that you can do? Some say that it is us that will need protection from you, Floyd."

"I understand Mr President. That is why at this time before we go any further, I offer to you a deal that will make this all null and void."

"I'm listening and very interested in hearing the next words you say to me Floyd, make them grand, make them count."

"No more sugar for my people, except what comes naturally from the foods here on Earth. My people will not consume any other sugar. No candy bars, no pie, no cake, no icing. The Government will have all rights to come to our communities and make sure of this point. No sweets. If there is someone that does not follow the law, then they will pay the price by whatever means the Government deems necessary as an punishment."

"Just like that Floyd, your people will give up sugar?"

"Yes Mr. President. After the war is over with and my ex-planet flies back home with their tails between their legs, my people will stop consuming sugar to live in peace in this great country of yours. There will be more than I like to admit that will not stop consuming sugar. If deemed necessary for there to be a squad of my people to consume sugar so we will be strong enough to capture these outlaws that will not conform to the law of no sugar... well then I will lead this squad myself to usher away those that do not not comply, you have my word, Mr. President."

"I like the words, I feel I can trust you Floyd. Like the old saying here on Earth, I call, show me your cards. What I am saying to you Floyd in case you are not understanding me. Words are words, show me some action."

"This would be my pleasure Mr. President. Give me two days, give me some of your people to record our work. Be amazed as we show you how far up the scale your plight truly is Mr. President."

"After that Floyd? I'm waiting for the big finale."

"After that Mr. President, you will have access to space ships that can fly you to my planet, for your big meeting. The big meeting that you show up for unannounced and in total control of from the start."

"Very good Floyd, you have your two days," The President of the United States of America feels nice and calm the way he likes to feel, the way he always feels after a victory. With sternness in his voice he tells his people that are at this meeting, that have not said a word for they know better not to, "Get this Alien whatever he needs and get it to him fast, he's in a hurry, he has to start a war."

Two days have passed, Floyd's team is ready. Everyone of them is high on pure cane sugar and ready to seek out and kill their jailers. Seeking out is not really needed, for all know where their jailers' lairs are located.

Many large scale attacks and many other smaller ones at the same time is the plan. The devices that have been removed from the bodies of Floyd's teams lay inside their homes in an attempt to make their jailers believe that most of them are safely tucked in at home. By this point in time not one of Floyd's people have their devices inside their bodies. All across the United States of America, Aliens gather closer to their jailers, just out of sight but close enough for the kills to come quickly.

Floyd's personal team is to attack the main stronghold of their jailers, that is located in downtown New York City. Floyd carries with him fifty tracking devices, which he will use as a distraction, making the jailers think that fifty castaways are standing together, one block away from their building. This will confuse them enough to get them all up and on their feet ready to pounce if needed.

For more confusion, Floyd, when everything is a go, will run further away from the jailers' building as fast as he can. One moment to the jailers, fifty castaways will be a rock's throw from them and the next moment they will all be miles away from where they were all just standing. The hope is, that the jailers will think that their grid is not working correctly and they will take it offline long enough to have gaps across their entire network to be used against them.

When Floyd stops running away from the jailers building and comes to a stand still, the time for attack at the same time across the United States will be when he throws the fifty devices he carries with him on the ground and stomps on them, making them all stop broadcasting at the same time. One moment fifty beeps will be five miles away from the jailers, the next moment all fifty beeps will stop all at the same time.

Floyd to the team member that ran with him to this spot, "Make the call." A few buttons pressed and seconds later across the Unites States, thousand of phones all ring at the same time. Floyd and his team member run back to the jailers' building as fast as they can so Floyd can lead the attack on it. The first shot of a war between Aliens on Earth is just about to be shot. Floyd runs up to the jailers' building at top speed, when he reaches it he keeps on running, he only shouts out in passing a loud, "Attack!"

Through Floyd's mind and eyes as he enters the building of his jailers. "Look at them. That one over there and that one over there, separately both of them beat the shit out of me for having sex with an Earth lady. Lucky for me I guess, that they only counted one aggression at a time and not how many Earth ladies I had sex with in one night. Before I can get to them I have to take these two out, that are charging me with fear in their eyes."

Floyd swings at the first one's head, upon contact his punch is so powerful the jailer's head comes off. One more swing and two Alien heads are laying on the floor, with blood flowing out of their mouths. "Damn there's a lady, it's okay Paul took care of her. Damn Paul is brutal, he ripped that lady's arms off. Stay strong Floyd, you have to conquer two worlds, your people are counting on you. Breath in, breath out, this is just a bloody movie. You're the star, play your role with an award winning style for bloodshed and mayhem. Why do I call myself Floyd?"

171

Strong and mean jailers, cannot comprehend what is going on. Outcasts have attacked them, their trackers are not responding and worst of all they attack them without mercy, they are leaving no jailer alive to question.

Through Floyd's mind and eyes, "I love sugar. I can't believe the soldier I've become. He's a gusher, his blood just got in my eyes, better drop this leg on the floor and wipe my eyes. That's better, talk about blood. This room looks like a slaughterhouse exploded inside it and hasn't had enough time to dry, for bright blood is everywhere for my freshly wiped eyes to see."

Up from the basement and down from the second through five floors comes jailers with big guns. As they enter the first floor they start firing without hesitation. They aim for the chest of the outcasts, some fall, some bleed, some nothing happens to, they only get more vicious from feeling the pain. "Aim for their heads! Kill them all," an unnamed jailer yells out in a rage.

Through Floyd's mind and eyes, "Bad jailers, with very bad guns. They shoot the heads off of my team members. They may have guns but I have sugar running through my veins, lots of sugar, thirty packs worth of sugar surging my body and mind on an overdrive." (Floyd is the only one of his people so far that can digest this much sugar in their bodies. The few that have tried had their insides turned to sap, as they convulsed in stern pain, until they died.)

"They shoot at me, they miss me and then they die, with pieces of themselves knocked off or ripped off, thrown over here and over there. I am gliding in the air, I'm such a graceful, murdering machine. I would love to watch a recording of myself, I should have thought about that, oh well, it's too late now. For now I have to glide my murdering self over to four gun shooting lunatics, that never run out of energy burst to shoot us with.

I think that is my team member's brains that just landed on top of my head. I better knock it off, don't puke you fool, it's just a stage setting, nothing more. What the fuck was I thinking, this is fucking crazy. Everybody on both sides are all dying away, I will be the only survivor. Why am I turned on? If I could right now, I would stop making war and make love until somebody kills me. They would also kill the lady I was making love with? Those murdering fucks."

Floyd rages himself up as far as he can rage out. Floyd is not thinking at this moment in time. Floyd just a machine now, takes energy burst to his body, for he is too close to move out of their way. There is a hole about four inches around in Floyd's chest, as he tears into the first of four murderers. Their body parts fly off them, like a giant mad shredder has attacked them. They would like to scream but the sight of the monster, prevents them from screaming. With all four dismembered and dead, Floyd turns around with no wounds on his body including the four inch hole in his chest.

There are maybe twenty of Floyd's people still alive, some barely holding on to life. There are four jailers left alive. They are gathered together, shooting at everything, screaming for back up, that is not coming, when something lands on the floor, far away from the four jailers. Boom! There are seven of Floyd's people still alive, including himself. Everything is silent, nobody is moving, nobody is shooting. The four, less outnumbered now, jailers are happy as they start shooting outcasts to their deaths. Seven lives turn to six as the count down continues on. Death will be forever present inside this room, stained with dried Alien's blood.

Floyd to himself, "I need a shield, I'm getting weaker, there are only two team members besides myself still alive now. We, I, cannot fail. The one that threw the bomb, he will do very nicely. Yes that is my answer for victory."

Floyd, with the final super, power surge he can rise out of his body, takes this surge and uses it, like it was meant to be this way, the final scene of this part in the movie. Floyd with a jailer's bloody and bruised body in his arms rushes towards the three reaming jailers. (The last alive outcast besides Floyd, had it in herself to take one of the four jailers with her, before she died.) They shoot the almost dead, fellow jailer's body, not hitting Floyd once this time.

Through Floyd's mind and eyes, "Almost there, I hope this dead bastard's body stays in one piece long enough for my final strike. Ha, my fist goes through your face. You die. Get off my fist. Now it's your turn. I take away your gun, along with your arm. I use them both to beat them across the last jailer's head. He drops his gun, as I rip the head off the jailer that is missing an arm."

Floyd throws the dead body away from him and says to the final alive jailer, "Stay down you piece of shit, it's over." With his foot across the last jailer's throat, Floyd asks him calmly, "Is there anymore of you fucked up jailers alive in this building? Anyone that is too important to fight?"

"Fuck you, you outcast piece of shit!"

"Wrong answer. I'm going to push my foot through your throat now. Goodbye, I hope you die slowly."

"'Wait, I'll tell you." Floyd takes some of the pressure off of his throat, so he can understand him better, without all those gurgling noises getting in the way. "There's maybe one to three mangers still alive on the third floor. They're not soldiers like me, you shouldn't have much trouble in killing them, you ungrateful bastard."

The last alive jailer in this room wants to say more but Floyd has heard enough. With a quick thrust downwards, Floyd snaps his neck ending his life, without a second thought about it, Floyd walks away.

Floyd is now on the third floor of this blood stained building, "Knock, knock, is anyone still alive in here? Everything is fine now all the outcasts have been taken down, we won, they are all dead. Come out, come out, are you there?"

"We're here, the five of us. What the Hell happened? How did a bunch of outcasts get a hold of weapons they have no access to?"

"Sir they didn't. Sir they had no weapons, they were the weapons themselves."

"What soldier? Make sense in what you're saying. How could they be their own weapons?"

"Sugar Sir. They ate a bunch of sugar, which gave them unbelievable strength in battle. In the end sugar could not hang with all our firepower. Stupid damn outcasts, they should have known better than to attack this building, to attack us. Sir I think it was a suicide mission, that is the only thing that makes any kind of sense. How could any of them think they would stand a chance at winning?"

"For now, I do not know soldier. In time this answer will be obtained, the rest will pay a very high price for these dead fools mistake." The only one brave enough of the five survivors to speak to Floyd replies to him as he and the rest of the other four make themselves visible.

"Who the Hell are you? You're not one of our soldiers?", The brave, still wanting to be in hiding survivor says to Floyd in a panic, with a very flustered voice.

Floyd laughs out loud, not caring one bit how cruel his laughter sounds, "Who am I? Are you that much of a fool? I'm Floyd, the leader of my people. Now all you cowards walk over to me. You are now the prisoners of the United States Government. How about a smile?"

As this drama comes to a close, all across the United States similar buildings were attacked and conquered. At the same time hundreds of single strikes of kills and captures were handled with full success across America. The numbers of the jailers still uncounted for was very small. The rest of this day and next were for gathering them up before they could cause any trouble or harm to any of the great people of the United States of America.

Five days later Floyd is at the White House talking with the President of the United States. After this battle, it is still hard for Floyd to maintain control of himself. For now he knows he has to be obedient to the President and the rest of the Government, for they are now like scared and excited children. If they are not handled correctly they might just throw a temper tantrum, which in Floyd's mind he knows would be a very bad thing that could ruin all his hard work for a two world domination.

The second meeting with the President went off without a hitch. Words filled with blood and glory slated his concerns for now, that his Alien allies will go to war with him against their ex-planet's people.

When Floyd got back from his meeting with the President, he and Linda made love until the sun came up. After that they went out and ate some very needed breakfast, for they were truly drained and needed some food and coffee very badly.

Linda to Floyd, "Do you think we still have a chance at pulling this off Floyd, without us all dying or destroying the Earth in the process?"

"Linda my love, the President is gullible and greedy for more power and technology, just like the rest of his people. All we have to do is play them along enough until it is too late. Then the final plan will be set in motion, after that there is no going back. We either win it all or we lose it."

Chapter Five:

(February, three months later.) Floyd and his team of trackers have successfully captured and surrendered or eliminated almost all of the scattered in hiding jailers. The jailers that have been picked up or erased have been replaced with look-a-likes with Floyd's people. There are nine unaccounted for jailers left to be captured. The Government has enough jailers to question and experiment on to last them for a few years. The last nine are not needed, elimination are the orders. These nine jailers are on their own with no way to contact their planet. Floyd had their communication device turned off, compliments of the technology from their very own planet.

Floyd and the President of the United States are not friends, even though they are very sociable to the other. Floyd is the tool that the President loves owning, while using it without having to ever touch it. Floyd has played his role as leader of his people spot on by taking what he had to take and by giving what he had to give to their temporary allies the United States.

Doctors and Scientists from Floyd's planet Blicker (Floyd told the President the name of his planet back in December) have worked beside and with Earth's Doctors and Scientists in the betterment of Humanity since December as well. The advancement of both medicine and science on Earth has increased along the path that Floyd has allowed the Humans to obtain. At the same time the eight Star ships that were left behind, as insurance, have been taken over and replaced with Floyd's people. The fate of the ships' occupants were separated into two lines, one line was for keeping, the other line was a quick death.

Floyd's people showed off their newly captured star ships to their new Allies. Teaching very special selected human pilots how to pilot and command these star ships.

(From Floyd's perspective.) Humans learn quickly, good thing these ships are very complicated to fully understand their entire workings in the amount of time any human will need. We know our star ships, we can make things mess up a little bit, not enough to cause serious damage but enough to make the human captains look like they are making mistake after mistake. This will lead to the decision the President will have to make, if our combined first strike is to be successful, and that is for the four ships that will make the voyage to Blicker be commanded by very trusted and in good standing outcast captains.

Floyd has made the President understand that a peaceful first contact would lead to the deaths of all humans and all the outcasts that made the flight to Planet Blicker. It had to be first and second and third strike, to obtain the control that is needed if any peaceful meeting was to take place between the people of Earth and the people of Blicker.

The eight star ships are parked behind Mars. To get to these star ships much smaller Blicker plane looking like ships are used. These ships are fast enough to get to Mars in ten hours. How the eight star ships and all the other star ships that accompanied these eight got to Mars was by using a stable wormhole. Only one star ship can fly through the wormhole at a time. The trip is fast, it takes a Blicker star ship only a little under an Earth hour to reach Mars, the same amount of time it takes for a star ship to get back to Blicker.

Blicker sent one star ship to Mars and back to Blicker through the wormhole and it was a success, thus they decided to save time, they would send five ships at a time one right after the other, through the wormhole. This was a big mistake for only the first star ship came out of the wormhole in one piece, all others came out the wormhole in various sized chunks and pieces.

There is a facade about using four star ships to travel to Blicker.

That is what Floyd made the President believe of the number of star ships that will be used for the attack. While the other four star ships of the eight stay parked next to Mars as an second wave of attack if the first wave is destroyed. Only one star ship will be used in Floyd's plan. This star ship will be equipped with four nuclear bombs, supplied by the United States as a back up plan if all others fail.

This star ship's real mission is to set off all four atomic bombs at the same time when it is half way through the wormhole. By doing this it is believed the wormhole will collapse in on itself thus becoming useless for the planet of Blicker to send any more star ships to Earth. The other three star ships will break Mars orbit as soon as the first one enter the wormhole, their destination being Earth.

As this plan is set in motion to become fruitful, on Earth the outcast Scientist and Doctors have implemented another plan. Humanity's blood types on Earth, all will have an plague attack them, save one blood type and that is of the blood type of all O's. The number of humans on Earth will decrease by at least seventy percent from these plagues. Saving enough humans on Earth to be able to control as servants for the Blicker's that will take control of Earth.

The price of war has been hard on the emotions of Floyd's people, so much that some have taken their lives in the ultimate protest to this bloody and unforgivable war. To them, yes they hate their former planet's people but they do not want them all dead.

Floyd cries some nights when the pressure of his leadership becomes too high on his being. Outcasts with no hope and no chance at having a nice life on Earth before, have their one and only chance coming at them so very fast, that some cannot be trusted after evaluation. The tears fall hard from Floyd's eyes as he remembers the high number of his people that he gave the okay about to have them eliminated,

179

before they could make a mistake that could cause them the war before the second half of it could be implemented.

Floyd like so many leaders in the past feels the hairs on the back of his neck stand up with paranoia from his many thoughts of betrayal. He looks his people in their eyes, he cannot help to feel deep inside himself that many of these eyes stare back at him with the concern that he has became a monster and their promised saviour no more.

Linda, with the best she has inside herself, has tried to keep Floyd's mind from drifting too far away. She fears what ingesting so much sugar has done to Floyd's body and mind. In this midnight hour, the night before three days and counting before the outcasts are to attack, bomb their former planet Blicker, Linda lays her naked body down upon Floyd's naked body. Floyd is shaking like he is freezing from the inside out, he shakes and shivers, with chattering teeth, as the warmth of Linda's body warms his troubled and scared being.

Linda kisses Floyd full of passion on his lips, Floyd slowly at first kisses Linda back only gently. The want for Linda takes over Floyd's body as he grabs a hold of Linda and moves her off him so he can lay down on top of her. The two lovers make love strongly, Floyd in the back of his mind thinks about blood and war. Linda in the back of her minds thinks and fears how to keep Floyd in sound of enough mind, long enough so he can be the leader their people need to win this war. The two lovers are just about to finish making love for the second time of this night.

"Give me your love Floyd, give me your love. Make me feel that you love me and only me."

"I can't hold it anymore, here's my love, take it baby," Floyd finishes and lays down flat on top of Linda. Linda rubs both of Floyd's sides with her hands lovingly.

Floyd is about to get up when Linda grabs his ass and pulls him back down saying to him, "One more time, make love to me like only a leader can make love."

"You got it baby, just give me fifteen minutes and I'll..."

"No, no fifteen minutes, make love to me now."

"But baby, I'm drained I need time."

"I don't want to hear it. Make love to me now, I don't care how you do it, just do it. Because baby you make me feel like a real woman. You don't want me to think, you can't please me fully?"

"No way is that happening baby. I'm all man, the man that will please you like no other before me."

"Well quit saying it and do it, my leader."

"Baby you won't be able to move after this time."

"Please my love, make that happen."

Floyd starts all over again but sadly his pecker is only half the size needed to make Linda purr. After hearing Linda say "Come on, give to me" over and over again, getting louder every time she has to complain to Floyd, he finally has it in him to carry forth, full in size and gesture. Linda loving her power, holds back her laughter as Floyd is tearing himself apart at the seams, trying his best to finish before he passes out from exhaustion.

Two lovers are through making love for the third time this night, one is passed out, the other is getting off the bed. Linda looks down at Floyd with an expression of no expression. She stares at him for a few minutes more, then she takes in a deep breath and sighs. She takes the blanket and places it over Floyd's throbbing body, as it fully covers him he moans quietly enjoying the warmth his now cold body is feeling.

Linda goes into the bathroom a few minutes later she is walking out of the bedroom wearing only a pair of pink panties, a thick black robe that comes to her ankles and a pair of pink, soft, comfortable house shoes, that make her feet feel like their walking on fluffy, silk. Linda walks into the kitchen to grab herself a beer. She drinks half of it down, catches her breath, she takes another drink and places the bottle on the counter. Linda chews on her lips as she picks up the phone to make a call, she doesn't want to make but knows for the better that she has to make.

Linda into the phone. "Hello it's me, yes I'll hold on." About two minutes later a very familiar voice comes through the phone. The voice asks about Floyd. "Don't worry he's out, Floyd won't be back on his feet until morning." The voice ask Linda if the plan is still a go? "Yes, everything is fine. Floyd does not suspect a thing, he loves me, he needs me." The voice asks Linda if she is sure she is still up for this? "Yes I am. I hate myself but I know I am doing all this for the betterment for my people. Many would not understand what I'm doing, they would think I am a traitor."

(Pause) The voice tells Linda to call them in two days and to make sure she keeps Floyd heading in the right direction. "I will. I'll call you in two days, I love you, goodbye." Linda hangs up the phone as some tears fall from her eyes. Linda says to herself, "Stay strong, don't follow your heart, lead with your mind."

The next morning Linda wakes up Floyd all loving, having him take a shower then for him to come down for a home cooked special breakfast. Floyd watches Linda walk away with an ass that deserves to be watched, thinking to himself "What would I do with out her? I love her and I need her, she takes my mind off my problems for awhile."

182

Floyd gets out of bed naked and dirty, on his way to take a piss, brush his teeth and take a shower, this is what goes on through his mind.

"Tonight is my last meeting with the President, then it will be two days and counting until the wormhole is destroyed. What brave men and women, my people are to volunteer for this mission. There is no guarantee, half way in, half the way to get back out of the wormhole before it collapses in on their ship. I want my people to survive but I know the answer, the truth it's a suicide mission. Rest in peace, my brave people, you will not be forgotten."

Floyd enters the shower. "Not many know this, not even Linda. Just a handful of my people know what will really happen when the atomic bombs ignites inside the wormhole. The wormhole with atomic speed will soar towards the planet Blicker. The wormhole will expand in size until it makes fatal contact with the planet. The planet known as Blicker will be struck by something that will break it apart and send its scattered pieces throughout the rest of the unknown galaxy."

Linda enters the bathroom saying to Floyd as he is standing in front of the mirror drying himself off with an over sized towel. "Breakfast is ready. I have made you eggs and bacon, along with pancakes. The coffee is hot and strong, just the way you like it."

"Thanks babe, sounds great, let me get dressed and I'll be right down to enjoy the great breakfast you cooked for me."

Linda watches Floyd dry himself off and comb his hair. She is about to walk away when Floyd says to her, "Tonight is the last time I go to the White House. My last time there was a nerve wrecking experience. We did it, we switched the President of the United States with one of our own. Great choice I made with your help of course."

"I'm glad that I could help you, but it was your decision."

183

"Yes I know, however it was your reason we chose him. A friend of yours no less. You even went to school together. I got to tell you, I think he has a crush on you. Poor fool, probably always had."

"Yes he has, that is why I'm sure he is the best candidate for the job. If nothing else he'll do it for me."

"Can't complain so far. Everything seems to be going fine, he is doing what I ordered him to do. He has ordered all the humans that are to be on the four star ships to an undisclosed location, where we have already switched them all with our people. It was a shame we had to kill all those soldiers. They were brave, I have a lot of respect for them, for what they stand for. They would have given their lives freely for their country."

"Yes they were brave my love, I know you would do the same thing. If it took your life to make sure our people would be safe forever, I know my love you would be glad to give up your life to see that happen."

"In a heartbeat baby doll. Let's just be glad that does not have to happen. I will survive, you will survive, Mike who is playing the role of the President of the United States will not. He will be our sacrificial lamb. My final triumph, for my people, making them forever follow me, as I uncover a plan led by Mike and the few others that we have chosen that know too much, to be the ones to plot against us. Choosing to become true allies with the humans, while making us their people, nothing but jailed slaves."

"Yes poor Mike, he served us well. He'll be missed, not by me, but I imagine someone will mourn him."

"Linda it's best just to think of him as a traitor in reality. That way when you look at our people, they believe in your eyes and voice that you truly believe this to be the truth."

"Yes my love, I have to believe this in my heart as well as in my mind. I feel cold."

"Good, then its already starting to work. Baby after all this is over with, you and me are going on vacation. From wherever we are at the the time, I can take a break now and then to give out further orders. We will rebuild this world to more of a liking for our people. Just think about it, we, all of our people will get to sit back and watch the humans tear apart and rebuild this world for us."

"My love all of this makes me want to go hide until this is all over with. I'm scared but I'm also excited for my people. This is our chance to finally live in peace, too bad it was not on Blicker, however I feel Earth is always the best answer for our freedom, away from evil, power hungry and uncaring of others lives, tyrants."

"This is our first and last chance, babe. In my bones, in my blood I feel that victory will be ours."

'Yes all ours my love, now hurry up before breakfast gets too cold to enjoy."

For the next couple of days Floyd and Linda make love and have a great time, doing their best to calm themselves for what lies ahead of them. As the sun rises on the last day for Earth and Blicker to be as they are, Floyd's mind is on overdrive trying to make sure that he has not forgotten about anything. Linda watches Floyd in distress, she turns her back to him to wipe tears away from her eyes. She turns back around with a fake smile on her lips and takes off her clothes.

"Hey big man, you interested? Do you have the time?", Linda asks Floyd, standing there naked and sexy.

Floyd turns his worried eyes toward Linda, when they see her as she is, they almost pop out of his head.

"Damn Linda, you always know how to make me feel better, I would love to make love to you one more time before we win the war."

"I don't want to make love with you Floyd. I want to have the hot kind of sex with you that I will never forget. The kind of hot sex that will always make me remember you. I love you Floyd, always remember this."

"I do Linda, I will always love you as well."

Floyd and Linda make love. Floyd is about to finish, when Linda begs him not to stop. Floyd contains himself for a few more minutes. As he is holding on, he watches Linda enjoying herself. To his eyes she has never looked more beautiful than she does right now. Floyd's calmness of mind lasts for only about two more minutes after that he has no choice but to finish for his ending is so powerful feeling that if he doesn't get it out fast, he feels like he will explode from the intense passion of it all.

The countdown has ended, it is time to finish what has been started. Three star ships are ready to travel to Earth to destroy its vast armies and navies. The people on these three ships watch as star ship number one flies towards the wormhole that has just opened up and will be in place for the next ten hours and twenty-two minutes.

This amount of time is not needed for in thirty minutes this wormhole will be gone, cutting these two planes off from the other forever. The wormhole does as expected when the nuclear bombs are set off. Star ship number one is destroyed instantly as the wormhole heads towards the planet Blicker. The people of Blicker have no warning as their planet is ripped apart to pieces and dispersed across the galaxy.

The three star ships reach Earth's orbit and start firing missiles that destroy armies across it. The plagues on blood types were dispersed yesterday.

186

In three days the first major signs of their effect will start to blossom to spread its reaches all around the planet. In under one day, Earth is pretty much under control of the outcasts. As final victory is upon them, Floyd sets out to implement his final plan.

Floyd walks in the front doors of the White House, with many guards in toll. The protectors of the White House are taken down quickly. With a swagger in his step Floyd walks to the oval office, where Mike is to be ready and waiting for him to make his big entrance. As Floyd walks into the room, he is grabbed up by ten of his fellow soldiers. In the back of the room are Linda and Mike standing there making out, like they are the only two people in the room. The ten soldiers that have a hold of Floyd are all overdosing on sugar. This is the only thing that is preventing Floyd from tearing them apart to get to Linda and Mike.

Floyd has had enough and shouts out. "What the fuck is going on Linda? How could you do this to me, I thought you loved me? I guess I am the fool?"

Linda takes her arms away from around Mike and walks towards Floyd, she stops at the President's desk and picks up a knife with an ten inch blade. She walks closer to Floyd and tells him this, "I do love you Floyd but you are a tyrant that has to be stopped. Your death is what's best for our people if we are to live in peace and harmony."

"That knife looks real mean Linda but it will do you no good, I will heal from whatever wound it will give me. I am high on Sugar."

Linda looks at Floyd with cold eyes and says to him. "Yes Floyd this is true however this knife's blade is covered in salt, just enough to counteract all the sugar flowing through your veins, making you feel so low."

"Linda no, don't do this to me."

Mike watches in expectation. Linda slows her steps to Floyd, Mike will have none of this, "Linda hurry, stab the bad guy. You don't love him, you never did. It was all in your mind. All you loved from this monster was sex. You're a Doctor, you're special. Do not be weak now. Stab Steinly, (Floyd's real name.) stab him now."

Steinly looks into Linda's eyes, he sees in them that she is having doubts. "Don't listen to the traitor Linda. I love you, it's too late for Mike, he's gone too far already. Linda listen to me, there is still time, it's not too late for you. Take that knife and stab Mike. Kill Mike now and all will be forgiven."

Linda looks back and forth between Steinly and Mike, she doesn't know what to do. She loves Steinly, she wants him to kiss her and hug her, she wants him to make love to her. With a heavy heart Linda is just about to drop the knife on the floor, when she looks at Steinly one more time and sees deep within in his eyes that he is lying. He is only saying what she wants to hear him say.

Steinly is smiling, knowing that he's suckered Linda into believing him. As soon as he gets free he's going to kill everyone in the room and make himself look like the President of the United States.

Linda screams out in a rage as she grabs a tighter grip around the handle of the knife that's blade is covered with salt and runs towards a still helpless Steinly. Steinly closes his eyes and prepares himself for a bloody painful death.

Linda to Steinly, "You lying bastard, you have to die." Linda stabs Steinly in his heart. The knife slides smoothly and deeply into Steinly's heart. Linda pulls the knife out of Steinly's heart and grabs him by his hair with her free left hand and with her right knife wielding hand she slices his throat from ear to ear saying a final, "Remember me doing this before?" Steinly lies dead on the floor as Mike takes the knife out of Linda's shaking hand.

"That was great Linda. You should be proud of yourself for what you just did for your people." Mike stops talking and looks at Linda who is looking at Mike without fully paying attention to what he is saying to her, "I'm sorry Linda it's now my turn to do something very big for my people as well." Mike takes the blood soaked knife and stabs Linda in her heart with it. Linda looks at Mike and spits in his face, which makes Mike mad and makes him push the knife even deeper into her heart.

Mike to his people, "Take these two pieces of garbage out of here and burn their bodies to ash. I have a world to rule as their president until the day I die."

All accounts of this story are true besides the fact that Floyd (Steinly) lied to the Real Agent Tate when he told him his people needed help to retrieve the tool that inserts and retracts the device that is surgically placed next to his people's hearts. The truth is Floyd and his people have already had this tool for months and have used it without the jailers finding out. They replaced the person that they stole the tool from with one of their own people. The reason Floyd told Agent Tate that they needed help to retrieve this tool was to make him and his people seem more vulnerable.

Speaking of replacing jailers. After the battle between Floyd and his team mates against the alien Agent Tate and his team of Alien Agents, Floyd had his people replace them and go back to their headquarters as spies. This fact was not told by Floyd to the real President of the United States and his cabinet members. Floyd also did not inform the President that many Aliens have been replaced around the United States as well as many Humans in high places of authority.

If only Steinly would have made himself the President instead of Mike, this story would have had a different ending. But the truth is the truth, so this sad ending is the one that unfolded and came to be as the truth, I think?

Two Lovers And Killer John
Chapter One:

The summer of 1987. Jimmy and Jamie are making love in the back of their truck in the dark of night. They parked behind a billboard for the night to crash out, one thing led to another. Jamie was mad about being broke and having to take jobs as a stripper. They're traveling across the highways from Florida to California, as of now they are in Texas. Jamie was walking around their truck yelling away as traffic rolled by on the other side of the billboard. Jimmy walked over to her, he kissed her neck, Jamie told him to stop, then she told him not to stop, minutes later they were making love in the back of their truck, on top of all their Earthly possessions.

"Hell yeah baby, that was great. Damn you are lucky to have a man like me that can rock your world like I can."

"Yes I am so blessed. You know what would be better? I tell you what would be better right now than your loving Jimmy and that is food. I'm so hungry."

"Relax baby tomorrow you'll get a job stripping for a few days just long enough for us to make it to California. I tell you I can't wait. California is where all our dreams will come true for us Jamie."

Jamie looks at Jimmy with his after sex smaller pecker shining in the moon light and she can't help it, she has to get her point through to the rock hard head of Jimmy. So Jamie picks up her sexy little cowgirl boot and smacks Jimmy across his rock hard head and yells at him.

"California, fuck California Jimmy! That is all you can talk about, is when we get to California, everything is going to be so much better. Well Jimmy, I'm tired of shaking my tits and ass to a bunch of horny drunks. You know what all of these drunks want to do to me Jimmy?

They want to fuck me, that is what they want to do. You should hear how much they are willing to pay me..."

Jamie stops talking and looks like she is in a world of her own thoughts. "Jamie baby, what is it? What's wrong?"

"Nothing. Nothing is wrong Jimmy, something is right."

"Like what?"

"Johns. We'll call them Johns."

"We'll call who Johns baby?"

"Shut up Jimmy and let me think. I will tell you a plan that is going to make us a lot of money."

"Sounds great Jamie."

"I said to shut up Jimmy, now let me think."

Jimmy gets up and walks away to take a piss, making Jamie have to take one herself. When they are through Jamie tells Jimmy to get his ass dressed and to shut up for what she is about to tell him is very important. "Listen carefully Jimmy. You and I go to a strip club, here is the great part, I don't get a job stripping, you do."

"Fuck that, no way. Besides it won't work. The places we go to for you to strip are full of men that want to watch naked woman. If I take my clothes off, they'll kill me."

"Yeah wouldn't that be great, ha,ha,ha. Don't get snakes in your boots, I'm only kidding. I swear I just don't know about you sometimes, if you didn't have such a big pecker and the fact you're loyal like a dog, I would've dumped your sorry ass on the side of the road by now."

"Right past the bitch and straight to being a ball buster."

191

"I'll bust your balls, I'll stomp on them. Now shut the Hell up and stop interrupting me."

"You shut up."

"Is that all you have to say? Good, now shut up and listen to the one that has the brains between us."

"I have brains, damn it."

"Yeah, but its like they've been fried on one side. You can talk, you can eat, you can fuck and you can drive a truck but that's about it. Don't worry darling, I know you love me, very, very much."

"Yes I do Jamie but you're being an ass crack that smells of crap, if you know what I'm saying?"

"That was so funny, after that you better pull down your pants and give your brains some air."

"You know what I'm going to do for you Jamie? You wonderful, good for only fucking, girlfriend of mine."

"I hope it's shutting the fuck up!"

"Close. I'm going to walk this field beside us looking for the largest turd I can find. Then I'm going to bring it back to you so you can eat it."

"You eat it, you sick bastard."

"No I mean it, I'm trying to do you a favor."

"A Favor? How can bringing me a turd to eat, help me in anyway possible but making me sick?"

"Well the way I see it baby, is like this. You've been talking so much shit, you have to be running low on it by now, so I'm trying to give you a refill."

Jamie wants to smack Jimmy across his hateful face but instead she yells to him, "I should make you lay on the ground so I can run you over with our truck. You hateful bastard, I can't believe you talk like this to me!" Jamie puts her hands to her eyes, like she is about to cry.

Jimmy feels bad and gets closer to Jamie so he can give her a hug and say to her, "I'm sorry baby."

Jamie takes her hands away from her eyes and then she quickly smacks Jimmy across his face making a loud smacking sound. "Fooled you dumb ass. How did that feel? Damn you, you made me hurt my hand, look it's all red. Oh well it was worth it. I don't know about you but I feel a lot better. I think we should do this once a day from now on. It would make me feel better and keep you in your place. So it's a win, win."

"Damn it Jamie, you're such a bitch, I'm out of here," Jimmy gets out of the back of their truck and starts to walk away. Jamie watches his ass move, then she sighs to herself and says softly as she can.

"I'm sorry baby, please forgive me. You know deep down I didn't mean it. You know me, you know how I get when I'm hungry and tired. I tell you what, why don't you come back over here to me. You can rub my feet, while I tell you my great plan, that's going to make us a lot of money."

Jimmy walks back slowly to Jamie. When he gets back in their truck Jamie rubs him gently on his face where she smacked him, really hard, hard enough to leave a mark. Inside Jamie is laughing as she kisses the pain away from Jimmy's face.

"I'm sorry you big sexy strong man of mine, now kiss me."

Jimmy kisses Jamie and instantly wants to make love to her again. Jamie feels this and lets it happen as Jimmy wants it.

While Jimmy is laying on top of Jamie trying his best to make love to her the best he has ever done, Jamie keeps going through her plan over and over again in her mind until Jimmy is finished with her.

"How was that baby? I know I made you feel it."

"Yes Jimmy, I can hardly hold still. You definitely made me feel like a woman should feel. You put me back in my place, you are the man."

"Are you messing with me? After all that and you..."

"No my love, I am serious. You really rocked my world. Give me a minute and I'll be able to walk again."

"That's more like it baby. I have to take another piss."

"Damn it, me too, hang on, wait for me."

Let's skip the pissing and getting back into the back of the truck and on to Jamie's plan.

"You see Jimmy my love, we go to a strip club and I do not strip, I pick up a John.

"What the fuck, are you crazy?"

"No I'm not Jimmy listen to me and don't get mad. I get all dolled up and we watch outside in the parking lot right before nightfall for the John with the best car. I follow him in, I'll walk by him shaking my ass so fine, then I'll turn back around and give him a smile, that says here I am."

Jimmy interrupts Jamie. "Like Hell you are Jamie, you will strip like a decent lady and let no man pick you up."

"Jimmy, Jimmy, small minded Jimmy. I'm not going to have sex with this John, stupid."

"But I thought you meant..."

Jamie interrupts Jimmy, "What did I tell you about that Jimmy, you and thinking? Nothing good ever comes from it. Don't worry Jimmy that is why I'm here for you. You are the strong loving man and I am the sexy smart woman by your side. Me and you against the world baby."

"Yes baby, me and you against the world."

"Good. Now then, I let this handsome rich..."

"What do you mean handsome?"

"Damn it Jimmy, you're pissing me off. Every time I try to talk you keep on interrupting me. Just listen and when I ask you a question, then you talk."

Jimmy gives Jamie a mean look as she sticks her tongue out at him while rubbing her breast, like she's the woman.

"You love me baby, I can bring you or any man to his knees. Just tell me you're sorry and I'll let you make love to me right before I pick up this handsome, rich John."

"I love you..."

"Say nothing else Jimmy, you are just to listen from now on until I'm done talking."

Jimmy just looks at Jamie without saying a word. "That's more like it. Now when me and this handsome, rich John walks out of the strip club, we will get into his car and you will follow us in this truck wherever we drive to. When we stop and get out of his car and walk into a hotel room, you pay attention to what room we go into. You will give us five minutes and then you will come through the unlocked door like a big bad, mean man and knock him the Hell out."

"I like the sound of this Jamie."

195

"I knew you would baby. See I think about you, I know how much you hate all those men watching me when I strip. They say all kinds of things to me while you have to sit there and let it happen. Now baby no more stripping, the only one who will ever see me naked again is you baby."

"I love you Jamie, this is perfect."

"I know, I'm a genius. Now after you knock him out, we will tie him up and take all his money. And best of all Jimmy this John will even pay for the room for the night for us. I can just imagine his face when he is all tied up and gagged. He will watch us make love on top of all the money we just stole from him. In the early morning we will leave and just go on our way, leaving him tied up for the maid to find. You know what Jimmy this is turning me on."

"Me too baby. Hold on a second, this John will see you naked when we make love in front of him?"

"So what Jimmy? Don't ruin my plan."

"Okay, okay, I'm sorry. I just thought..."

"There you go again, you stupid man of mine. You do not need to think just flex your muscles and like I said I will do all the thinking. How much money do you think we can make off our first John?"

"I don't know Jamie, maybe a hundred or so."

"A hundred or so? No way Jimmy. My first John is going to be rich, so rich that he will have a briefcase full of money with him. We're going to make thousands Jimmy, I can just see it now. You and me baby, we've hit the big time."

Jimmy and Jamie's first attempt didn't go as planned. In fact they made a mess out of things pretty good.

"I can't believe you Jimmy, you dumb ass.

You came into the room running like a fool and tripped. What the Hell did you trip over anyway?"

"I don't know."

"You don't know, how typical of you. Well after you tripped, my John grabbed a lamp and busted it over your stupid head. You know what I had to do Jimmy to keep him from calling the cops? What I had to do for free, twice!"

"I'm sorry Jamie, I really am. I didn't mean to trip."

"Yeah you're sorry alright. Just think of it like this Jimmy, you dumb ass. He was going to give me two hundred dollars to let him have sex with me. But instead I had to let him fuck me twice for free. He got everything and all I get is to leave limping with you."

"I don't want to think about it, stop mentioning it."

"Well you better think about it and what you should not to do the next time.

"Next time? No there will be no next time!"

"My ass! Let me tell you something Jimmy, there is no way that I am going to leave things like this. I want money for what I just had to go through. This first John will be the first and the last John who will fuck me for free, I tell you this, you hear me Jimmy, never again."

"Yes baby, I hear you, can't we just go back to stripping, it's much safer and honest."

"I could give a shit less about honest. I want money Jimmy, lots of it. Either you are with me or I will find someone else to take your place. Oh yeah and by the way, you can forget about getting you some tonight because I'm too damn sore and tired. That John was like a sex machine."

"Stop it, stop it, I don't want to hear about it."

"Well suffer Jimmy because I feel like telling you about it. Besides for the first hour or so you were knocked out. Don't you want to know what happened? Don't you want to know what he made me do to him?"

"No, no, no. I don't want to know, now shut up about it."

"Why is that Jimmy? Is it because it is all your fault?"

"Yes it's my fault, I told you this already Jamie. Now drop it and let's go find some place for you to strip so you can make us some money, so we can get the Hell out of this piece of shit town."

"Oh we are leaving this town alright but not before we find another John first."

Some people just don't learn their lesson. The second attempt of rolling a John didn't go quite like the first one but it went just as bad.

Jamie screaming at Jimmy in between smacking him in the face. "You dumb ass Jimmy, you ran into the room, this time not tripping but what happened next? Well Jimmy I'm waiting. Nothing, you have nothing to say? Well I have plenty to say. You ran into the room and got your ass kicked that is what you did, my hero. Step back ladies he's all mine."

"Shut up Jamie, that John knew karate or something."

"No I won't shut up Jimmy. He kicked your ass and you didn't even hit him back once. After he got done kicking your ass he looked at me and told me he was going to call the cops. You know what I had to do again twice Jimmy for free? That's right, I let a total stranger fuck me twice again while you laid on the floor bleeding like a weakling."

"Shut up Jamie, I mean it."

"What are you going to do bleed all over me and then pass out. You are pathetic Jimmy, I should have listened to my mother. She always told me to find a doctor or a lawyer to fall in love with and marry. But no dumb ass me I had to fall in love with the likes of you."

"I'm sorry Baby. Can we try stripping now?"

"No fucking way. And don't call me baby."

"But why? I always call you baby?"

"Well that stops now, I'm Jamie or ma'am to you. From now only my Johns can call me baby. I tell you Jimmy if you fuck up one more time, we are through."

"Yes Jamie, I understand."

"You better, I meant it. Damn I'm so sore. That first John was something like I've never had before but that second John. Damn for such a small man his pecker was that of a giant man's. He just kept going on and on. When he finally finished, I was shaking and praising him. He looked at me and smiled and then he started with me all over again. I still can't believe it. I think that small man fucked me for over two hours. I might never be the same. Next time we are going to find a nice safe old man John. I'm giving you one more chance if you fuck up again, I'll kick you in your pecker."

"Listen Jamie I was thinking why don't I just get a normal job. Between that and you stripping we can make a nice living for ourselves."

"Shut the Hell up. I have to ask you something Jimmy. I know he knocked you out with that last kick to your head and all but didn't you wake back up before he was done with me?"

"Yes I did, I woke back up before the first time was over with. I didn't know what to do so I just stayed quiet and watched the two of you have sex."

"You didn't know what to do? How about grabbing a lamp and bashing him over the head like the first John did to you? You could have done that."

"I didn't want to cause anymore trouble for us."

"You didn't say anything? All that time and you said nothing to this man that was using me like he owned me?"

"Well during your second time, I asked him if I could join in. He told me no, so I just sat there and watched."

"Is that what I heard? I thought I heard someone else talking but it was so soft I couldn't make out the words. Wait a minute you asked him if you could join in? You damn pig you. That's it you don't get to make love to me for a month, maybe longer. Now come over closer to me I have to give you something."

"What is it Jamie?"

"First turn around Jimmy the love of my life." Jimmy turns around nervously and Jamie kicks him in his ass as hard as she can. "Take that you pig, I hope it hurts really bad."

Jimmy grabs a hold of his ass and runs around saying, "My ass, my ass."

"Shut up Jimmy and quit being a wimp. I didn't kick you that hard and besides you had that coming."

"But Jamie you kicked me in the middle of my ass, it really hurts bad."

"Good, now remember this pain and you will understand how much pain you have caused me."

With the third John everything went as planned. Jimmy came into the room and knocked out the third John. He and Jamie tied him up, the both of them were so happy, until they checked out his wallet. The third John was practically broke, all he had in his wallet was a twenty dollar bill and a rubber. Nowhere even close to the two hundred dollars that he and Jamie agreed on. Jamie of course blamed Jimmy for this.

Then came the fourth John, then came the fifth John. In between both of these Johns, Jimmy and Jamie made a cool eight hundred dollars. Since the second John, Jamie has stayed untouched, she hasn't even let Jimmy touch her.

Now it is time for John number six. What a big mistake they made with picking John number six. John six was a really sick kind of man. Before Jimmy could bust through the door, John six had Jamie tied up naked sitting in a chair and was sucking on her toes.

Jimmy came running into the hotel room and could not believe what he was seeing. At first Jimmy thought he broke into the wrong room and apologized, then he recognized Jamie's moaning. Before Jimmy could do anything a gun was put in his face compliments of John six.

John six speaks. "Well, well what do we have here. Stranger are you trying to take my delicious date's toes away from me. Well guess what stranger you can't have her toes but you can have her shoes. So why don't you sit down on the floor like a good stranger and lick her shoes clean before I put a bullet in your head."

Jimmy and Jamie look at each other like they can't believe what they got themselves into this time. John six licked Jamie's toes very carefully with one eye on Jimmy at all times, as Jimmy licked Jamie's shoes.

After John six had his fun, he tied up Jimmy in the other chair that was provided. John six then untied Jamie and made her pay to have sex with him. After Jamie and John six were done having sex, John six tied Jamie back up naked in the chair. He licked all ten of Jamie's toes once again and then he got dressed.

John six was not done having fun yet. He took all of Jimmy's and Jamie's money, he cut up their credit card and then he put Jamie's shoes inside the bag he was carrying with him. Now John six had one more thing to say to Jimmy and Jamie.

"You two are very bad people. I don't really want to but I have to shoot the both of you now." Jimmy and Jamie moan for their lives as John six lifts up his gun towards their heads. He yells out to them, "Take this you pigs!" Then John six pulls the trigger and water sprays all over Jimmy's and Jamie's faces. John six laughs out loud and says, "So long suckers, it's been real." And then he walked out the door leaving them both tied up for the maid to find the next morning.

In the bright morning sunlight Jimmy and Jamie are giving their accounting of the events of the previous night to the police. Jimmy and Jamie wanted to haul ass but the maid didn't untie them first, she instead went running to the manager, who called the police and left Jimmy and Jamie tied up so the crime scene wouldn't be disturbed.

The highlight of the interview was when Jamie described John six as a tall, brown haired, brown eyed, good looking, toe sucking weirdo. The police asked them which way they thought John six went after he left them, Jamie simply replied, "I hope straight to Hell."

Chapter Two:

(The end of the summer of 1987. Darkness has crept inside Jamie, Jimmy has noticed this but doesn't know what to do about it. Deep inside Jamie the thought of having sex with the first two Johns, turned her on more than she wants to admit to herself. John six was very different thoughts to her fragile mind.

In her dreams, John six always comes to her with his arms reaching out to her as if to comfort her. Jamie always tries to talk to John six but she never gets a word out. Jamie walks closer to John six, when she reaches him he takes her by the hand and leads her to a chair. She sits there calmly as he ties her up. In her dreams John six does not gag her, as he sucks on her toes. He never stops, he just keeps on sucking and licking her toes. The sounds from John six's sucking and licking makes Jamie's mind slip into a sickening calmness.

It's been two months since the night with John six. Jamie is finally ready to start over with hers and Jimmy's scheme of rolling Johns. The reason is because Jamie had a breakthrough in her dreams last night. John six was sucking and licking her toes as usual but this time in her dream the ropes that bound her fell off and onto the floor. Happily Jamie slapped John six across his face and told him to stop. He listened to her, with fear in his eyes.

Jamie then had John six lay on the floor and open up his mouth as wide as he could. Without mercy Jamie put her right foot inside John six's mouth. Her foot wouldn't fit at first inside his mouth so Jamie kept on shoving her foot harder and harder into John six's mouth until he choked to death. Jamie woke up all sweaty and smiling.

The past month Jamie's been stripping at the same place every night, Roy's Hot Ladies Club. The money is good and her striptease fills the room with horny drunk men, wanting to fuck her.

Roy loves her talent and pays her extra for their daily sex date. Three days ago Jimmy confronted Jamie about her having sex with Roy so many times. Jamie took the money she received from Roy for their sex date out of her pocket and gave it to Jimmy, telling him to go buy himself some beer and weed. Jimmy looked into the cold eyes of Jamie and took the money from her steady hand. Jimmy as he walked away wondered to himself where all this pain inside his heart would lead him to next.

They were going to California, somewhere, somehow their road took a detour to Hell. Jimmy wanted Heaven and he knows now that his life with Jamie has never been close to it. Fun under sun, fun under the moon and stars, life with Jamie could be fun and exciting. When Jamie stripped in front of all those men she always went home with him but now it is starting to seem to Jimmy like he has to wait in line. Jimmy to himself, "I don't do lines. It's time for me get out before it can get any worse.

That was three nights ago and this is the afternoon after Jamie had her foot in John six's mouth dream. Jamie's mind is clear, she is walking to Roy's office the owner of the strip club, and she feels mean inside herself for the world. Jamie knows she's changed, she really doesn't love Jimmy anymore, she stops to wonder if she ever did. It does not matter right now for what's going on next is too important to waste thoughts on Jimmy.

Jimmy is parked behind Roy's Hot Ladies Club. He is telling himself that this is it, the last time he's going to help Jamie with another of her crazy plans. He understands the importance of what Jamie is doing, he also worries for her, she has almost gone over the deep end. Jimmy shakes a cold chill away from inside himself and sighs.

Jimmy kicks back in his truck and opens up a can of beer. He takes a few drinks, it's kinda warm. Jimmy pulls a joint out from behind his ear and fires it up. Jimmy tokes and tokes and then he chokes.

Smoke fills the cap of the truck as Jimmy laughs from the sudden head rush he feels. Jimmy rolls down his window and smoke rolls out of it thick and funky smelling. He looks around for anybody and everything is cool so he tokes and tokes some more but this time he does not choke. The joint is a roach and Jimmy is taking the last drink from his beer. He feels really good and would very much right now like to fuck Jamie. Jimmy burps and says, "But she's always has something else to do besides fucking me."

Jimmy gets out of his truck and walks over to the Roy's building and takes a long piss on it. "This is your face Roy, you fat pig bastard, one day I will for real piss on your face." Jimmy laughs and zips up his pants. Back to his truck he goes with a nice buzz going on inside him.

Jimmy is kicking back in his truck already bored and wanting to split. He yawns and rubs his eyes. In his mind is the day he and Jamie met. Two years ago in a nightclub in Florida is where it all started. Jimmy was twenty one and Jamie was twenty three. Jimmy had ten dollars in his pocket, when he noticed Jamie dancing all by herself. He walked over to her and said, "Hello beautiful can I buy you a drink." (Jamie was dressed like she had money.) When they were alone drinking their drinks and talking, Jimmy took the advantage of not being able to hear Jamie as a way to scoot closer to her.

A few minutes later Jimmy is kissing Jamie's neck, while going through her purse with his free hand. Jimmy feels five bills between his fingers, he hopes they're at least twenty dollar bills. Unseen Jimmy takes his new money and shoves it deep into the right front pocket of his pants.

Jimmy remembers how good Jamie's lips felt and it's a shame that he had to give her the excuse in a minute so he could take off. Jimmy was about to give it to Jamie, when she said to him, "Would you like to make love with me Jimmy? I'm lonely and it's been a long time."

In the car he used to have, Jimmy drove Jamie to her house. On the way there, Jimmy kept on thinking to himself that he should not have sex with one of his marks. Jamie was hot and sexy looking and it had been awhile for him as well and Lord knows he could stand to get laid. Jimmy said, "Fuck it, who knows maybe she'll be the one that will make me settle down."

When they pulled into Jamie's driveway, she had Jimmy turn off his lights before they did. "Do me a favor Jimmy turn off your car." Jimmy did what he was told. "Good now I need you to do me another favor."

Jimmy smiled and said, "Sure baby just take off your clothes and I will rock and roll your whole wide world."

Jamie laughed and giggled and then she gave Jimmy a great big loving kiss. She pulled away from him a moment later and laughed again, then she got serious. "That comes later Jimmy, right now I need you to walk up to my door and ring the door bell."

"Why would you need me to do that for you?"

"Because silly, I share this house with two other roommates, both girls. We're not suppose to bring guys over unless the other two know about it first. It's a dumb rule but it works."

"What do I do if one of your roommates answers the door?"

"Just ask for me, they will tell you I'm not there and then you and I can go find some place to park and have some sexy fun."

"Seems simple enough to me, I'll be right back."

Jimmy laughs to himself saying out loud, "Women."

206

Jimmy rings the doorbell, a few moments later a man answers the door saying to Jimmy, "Yeah what do you want?" Jimmy doesn't know what to do so he follows the plan and asks if Jamie is there.

The man behind the door gets all pissed off and starts yelling at Jimmy, "What the fuck! That bitch don't live here. What are you doing here you ugly punk, looking for that bitch anyway?"

Jimmy in shock yells back to the pissed off stranger, "Fuck you man!"

"Fuck me, no fuck you, you ugly bastard. I'm going to kick your ass!"

Todd Brown is a simple man, whose life was turned upside down because of the lady he just broke up with a little over a six months ago. That lady was Jamie, who turned out to be no lady at all unless you count her as a crazy lady.

Todd was having lunch with his sister when Jamie came up to them thinking Todd was cheating on her. Before Todd could saying anything Jamie had already grabbed his plate with half of his dinner still on it and busted it over his head. Jamie then started on Todd's sister Libby, Libby stood up and Jamie punched her in her eye.

The restaurant called the cops and they arrested her. Jamie understood this but what made her blood really boil was when Todd and his slut sister also pressed charges on her. To Jamie this meant in the coming future Todd had a great big payback coming to him.

Back to Todd getting ready to kick Jimmy's ass. Todd in a rage came flying out from behind the safety of his front door and lunged himself at Jimmy. Jimmy faster and thinner moved out of the way. Todd going too fast to slow down went right passed Jimmy and head first straight off his porch.

Jamie ran up to a fallen Todd and kicked him in his ribs several times. "Take that you horrible bastard. Do you know what I had to go through the last six months Todd? I tell you what Todd. People treating me like I'm crazy."

Todd, coughing and choking says, "You are crazy Jamie, you are the craziest bitch I've ever met. You better get out of here because I'm calling the cops."

"Like fuck you are, you dirty bastard, take this," Jamie with all her strength kicked Todd in his face, knocking him out.

Jimmy looked back and forth between Jamie and Todd and asked Jamie, "What the fuck is going on Jamie? What is the problem between you to?"

Jamie looked pissed off at Jimmy and asked him, "Didn't you hear what I said? This bastard made me go to jail. Now that I kicked his ass I feel a lot better. Let's get out of here and find someplace to spend the night together. I'm really turned on and I could use a shower before we make love for the rest of the night. I have about a hundred dollars in my purse that should be more than enough for a cheap room and some beer and weed."

Jimmy looked at Jamie and shook his head no, then he pulled the bills out of his pocket and said, "You mean this hundred dollars right here Jamie?" and then he laughed.

Jamie looked at him all shocked and then she found the humor in it all and then she joined Jimmy in laughing. "You are a bad man Jimmy. Can I trust you with my heart or are you going to steal that as well?"

"No way Jamie, I might break your heart but I will never steal it from you."

"That's good to know Jimmy. Now give me back my money or I will have to kick your ass just like I kicked Todd's ass."

Jimmy gave Jamie back her ninety dollars and they have been a happy and unhappy couple ever since. Jimmy comes out of his daydream when a crow lands on the hood of his truck and takes a crap on it as it flies away. "That right there Jimmy is your life," Jimmy says to himself.

Back to the present day. Jamie walks into Roy's office dressed like she could seduce the world. Roy gets up from his chair and walks to her looking like a fool in lust to Jamie. Roy with a big o' smile on his lips says to Jamie, "There you are Red, I've been waiting for you with balls on." (Jamie's hair was blond, she dyed it red before she asked Roy for a job.)

Jamie smiles and puts her left hand on Roy's junk and squeezes it hard enough to make him bend over from the pain. Roy likes it rough. "Shut you big mouth Roy and take off your clothes," Jamie says to Roy as his Mistress of pain and lust.

"Yes Mistress..."

"Shut up Roy, did I say you could talk to me? No I did not you dog. Fall to the floor, like a good dog Roy and roll around like you have fleas."

"Yes Mistress."

"That's it dog, you fucked up, lick my shoe." Roy falls to his knees and licks the tip of Jamie's shoe, moaning while he's doing it.

"No you stupid dog, lick its heel," Jamie says to Roy as she slaps him hard across his back, making a smacking sound that rivals the pain from it.

"Come with me dog," Jamie says to Roy as she grabs a hold of him by the hair on his head. "You are a bad and stupid dog Roy, for that I'm going to walk all over your body with my high heels.

I'm going to dig them deep into your body Roy. I will make you love the pain I give to you."

Roy a man that likes his lust differently, begs Jamie to dig her heels deeper into him as she walks up and down his back making his spine painfully crack in the process.

Jamie steps off Roy with one last hard press downwards causing her heel to poke a hole in Roy's shirt all the way to piercing his skin, making him bleed.

Jamie in total control yells at Roy, "Look what you did dog, you got your dirty blood on my heel, lick it off now." Roy raises up and licks his blood off Jamie's heel.

"It is time to tie you up dog. Put your hands behind your bleeding back."

Roy does what he is ordered to do. "No ropes this time, no this time Roy, I'm going to tape you all up so you can never get away from me," Jamie says to Roy as she takes heavy moving tape and wraps it eight times around his wrists. Then she takes the tape and wraps it around his ankles taping them together ten times. "Here dog, here is a piece for your big fat mouth."

Jamie looks down at Roy like he is a piece of meat and kicks him three times in his fat belly. "I know who you are Roy, but you don't know me. My name is not Rose in case you're wondering. I need something from you Roy. I need a name. There is a weirdo that comes in here sometimes, I have only seen him once. This weirdo makes you seem normal Roy. The name of this man I am looking for is a toe sucking piece of shit, that has a very big payback coming to him."

Jamie walks over to Roy's desk and picks up a letter opener and places it on Roy's face. "I owe you Roy for your constant rutting on me like a pig.

All the lust I gave you would make it worth it to me if I got my name. Roy if you don't give me my name when I pull the tape from your mouth... Well Roy you will have to receive the pain I was saving for toe sucking man. Do you understand me Roy? Nod your head yes if you do."

Roy nods his head yes. "So you are telling me Roy, with no words that you will tell me the name I want to know?"

"The name of the toe sucker?" Roy nods his head yes so fast that he makes himself dizzy. In Roy's mind he's thinking, if I get this tape off this bitch is dead.

Jamie smiles and taps the letter opener on top of Roy's head five times, each time harder than the time before. "You like this pain don't you Roy, you sick fat man? Well to each their own I guess."

Jamie rubs Roy's face with the letter opener, making sure to stop over each eye for a moment or two.

Jamie takes a few steps away from Roy, then she kicks him three more time in his belly, "You like that Roy don't you? Yes you do Roy, you good dog you."

Jamie looks down at Roy and shakes her finger at him, like he better do as she wants him to do. "Okay Roy here is your one and only chance, make it count. Remember Roy all I want is my name, nothing else. If you say anything else, I will put the tape back on your mouth, then I will kick you in your balls three times. Be smart Roy, I don't mind kicking you in your balls until you tell me my name, even if it takes all day. I know I could handle it, could you Roy?"

Roy shakes his head no. "That's good to know but I don't know," Jamie pauses to ponder.

"I would love to believe you Roy. But I think maybe I better dig one of your eyes out with this letter opener before I take off your gag.

211

That way you will understand how serious I am. Do I really have to do that to you Roy?"

Roy shakes his head so hard that he tips himself over. "Roy, Roy you clumsy dog you. Get yourself back up, this is no time for laying on the floor," Jamie says to Roy, like she is having the time of her life.

Jamie helps Roy back up, then she removes the tape from his mouth really fast.

She puts her left hand over Roy's mouth before he can say anything, "Remember Roy the only thing you better say is a name."

With Jamie's hand removed away from his mouth, Roy swallows deeply and says the name Jamie has been wanting to know for two long months, "Bobby Goodman."

Jamie gasps out loud loving the name she was told. "That's your last name Roy?"

"Yes Rose, Bobby's my Cousin."

Jamie laughs so hard she snorts, "This is perfect. Let me look at you. No, you don't look alike, he's better looking. You are doing great Roy, keep this up when you give me his address and his phone number."

"I can do better for you Rose."

"My name is not Rose, Roy, call me Lady. Now, how can you do better for me Roy?"

"I can bring Bobby to you Lady."

"Why would you do this, he's your cousin?"

"If it's between him and me, it's him. Besides he's a freak."

"Yes, he's a toe sucking weirdo. Great family you have Roy, you like to be stepped on while being punished and your cousin sucks toes."

"How did he get to your toes Lady?"

"What? Shut up Roy! Never you mind how your freaky ass cousin got his mouth on my toes. It is all about the fact that he did this to me."

"You didn't like it Lady?"

"Hell no I didn't, it was disgusting. The sound of him sucking my toes made me so sick feeling."

"So Lady, you just meant to have sex with him. Bobby sucking your toes crossed the line for you?"

"That is not the way it happen, he forced me."

"That's not the Bobby I know. As far as I know, he's into free toe sucking loving women."

"Well Roy, you are dead wrong. He, he... Just shut up Roy, I know what you're trying to do."

"What am I trying to do Lady?"

"You trying to make me loosen my grasp on this. It's not going to happen Roy."

"Are you sure Lady? To me you look like you want to untape me and then enjoy my body. This time Lady I will be the one in control. I'll be the one to punish you."

Jamie makes herself look ashamed. Roy is counting the seconds until he is free. Jamie is about to give Roy this whole drama filled breakdown to amuse herself but instead she laughs out a short evil filled laugh that chills Roy all the way to his dirty bones.

"You've had your moment Roy, it is over with. I want Bobby, I'll settle for both of you. Bobby is a dead man, do you want to be dead like him Roy?"

"No I don't Lady, I want to live. I'm sorry I made you mad Lady. I know how much you enjoyed my body in the past, so I figured I'd give it a shot."

"You are a very stupid man Roy. I hate your body, the only reason I let you have sex with me is because of your toe sucking cousin. I spotted him, I'll never forget his face. You and him were talking, I knew there was something between you two, I had no idea he was your cousin. I waited for Bobby to come from out of the back but he never did. He went out your back door."

"Yes I always make him go out my back door, he's bad for business. He knows a lot of ladies, ladies that want nothing to do with him again."

"I believe that. Too bad I didn't step in dog shit before Bobby sucked on my toes."

"Booby would have just wiped them off and started sucking away on your toes."

"You're probably right Roy," Jamie puts a fresh piece of tape across Roy's mouth.

"Nice and soft is the way you want things to play. Not in the cards Roy. You may not die today but you will pay a price." Jamie kicks Roy in his belly twice, then she kicks him in both of his legs. Roy is whimpering when Jamie rolls him over and kicks him in the middle of his ass.

"Go ahead and cry Roy, I won't think any worse of you. Maybe a good cry will do you some good. Roy you are a freak, you should be ashamed of yourself, you should want better for yourself. The world has made me cold. Your cousin, you, many others have used me."

Jamie walks away from Roy so she won't hurt him more. Roy thanks God that the crazy bitch is further away from him. Jamie has her back to Roy as she talks to herself. "His name is Bobby, I never thought Bobby was his name. I'm so close, if I can get through this, I'll be alright. My nightmare is going to die in life, just like he did in my dream. Play this cool."

Jamie turns around and walks slowly back to Roy. "Okay Roy, I'm going to give it to you. Don't smile underneath that tape because I'm not talking about my body. No Roy I'm talking about the way things played out."

Jamie rolls Roy back over so she doesn't have to look at his fat ass anymore. "I found the toe sucker right here at your place. If you would have let him go out the front door I would have got him that night. This wouldn't be happening now to you Roy, you stupid man. I had no choice I had to work for you, so I changed my hair from blond to red so toe sucker would not recognize me. I have never seen him again in here. Enough is enough, you will take me to Bobby's house or shack or wherever the fuck he lives. This is what I want Roy, don't disappoint me."

Jamie walks over to the door in back of Roy's office that leads to the parking lot. She opens it up and looks out of it searching for Jimmy. She spots him, he's not parked where he's suppose to be parked, he's too far back and too far to the left. "Bud (Jimmy) Bud? Don't go away Roy I'll be back in a moment."

Jamie sees that Jimmy is sleeping, this makes her blood boil. "Dumb ass, I can't believe him."

Jamie speeds herself to Jimmy. Jimmy is all kicked back, the sound of Jamie pounding on his window out of nowhere, scares him confused. Jamie has to tell him to unroll the window so she can scream at him.

"What the fuck is wrong with you Jimmy?"

215

Jimmy shakes his head hard and says "What?"

"Wake up you dumb ass!"

"I am awake Jamie, stop yelling at me, you're fucking my head up."

"I'll fuck up your head for you alright."

"Okay, okay, I'm alright now. What do you want?"

"What the fuck do you think I want Jimmy? What you think? I want to have a nice conversation with you in this parking lot like nothing is going on, huh Jimmy?"

"Oh yeah, I forgot for a moment. Well did you get this sicko's name?"

"Damn you Jimmy, you make me so mad! Yes I got his name. He's Roy's cousin Bobby."

"Bobby, I didn't figure it was Bobby."

"Who cares, you were sleeping on the job. Now the plan has changed."

"Like how? What kind of change?"

"Well get your sorry ass out of the truck and I'll show you. Remember my name is Rose and your name is Bud."

"I like that, Rose-Bud."

"Yes it nice, that's why I thought it up. The new plan is that we are going to take Roy with us. He's going to take us to where Bobby lives."

"Is he going to ride in the cab with us?"

"No he's going to ride in the back of the truck, all alone."

"Cool, more room for us baby."

"Jimmy if Roy rides in the back of the truck, how is he going to tell us which way to drive? Don't answer."

"Hell Jamie I don't know, this plan of yours is getting crazier and crazier."

"Don't say crazy. I don't want anymore people thinking and saying I'm crazy. Remember Jimmy we talked about this?"

"Yes I remember, I'm sorry Jamie. It's just that I don't think this is a good idea."

"You're right Jimmy this is not a good idea, it's a great one. We get two freaks at the same time now."

"What do you mean?"

"Don't worry about it, it's a surprise. Now get your sexy, strong ass in there and bring Roy out here and put him in the front of the truck."

"Okay Jamie, after this is over with, we need to have a talk about things."

"Fine with me Jimmy. After this is all over, you can talk to me about anything. Hell I might even listen to you."

Jimmy looks at Jamie, thinking to himself, "Even when I get what I want, I don't get it the way I wanted it. This woman will be the death of me, I just know it."

With Jamie's help and complaining, she and Jimmy gets Roy out of his office and into their truck unseen by all. Jimmy starts the truck and looks over at Jamie. Jamie looks back at him but she looks straight through him, like he's not even there. Jamie happily says, "Well Roy, point the way to the toe sucker."

The rest of the afternoon is spent down the road from Bobby Goodman's house. Jamie made Jimmy show Roy their gun. Threats of shooting him in various body parts of his was made by Jamie, while Jimmy mostly stayed silent. The night has fallen and Jamie is about to scream in frustration. About an hour after the three of them were parked in the truck, Roy got gas. He farted sixteen times or more, to Jamie they smelled like burnt cheese and rotten eggs.

Jamie told Roy that if he farted one more time she was going to make Jimmy (Bud) shoot him in his ass. Roy held and held a fart for so long that it festered inside his ass. Roy tried his best but to no avail this last fart had to make its way out. Roy tried to let it out slowly but once he let go this last fart lasted for twelve seconds. Worst than that was the smell of it, it was so bad that Jamie made Roy get out of the truck and sit down on the ground beside the passenger's back tire all taped up. Damn the consequences.

Jamie swears that she can still smell Roy's nasty ass fart on her clothes. She puts it out of her mind and goes over it one more time with two stupid men. (Jamie's quote.) Jamie makes Jimmy untie Roy and the three of them walk to Bobby's house.

"Get us in the house Roy, that's all you have do and your part is over with. I promise you this Roy, get us in and stay out of the way and you will make it out alive," Jamie tries her best to sound sincere.

Jimmy asks, "Jamie are you sure you don't want me to knock out, what's his name with the tire iron?"

"It's Bobby, damn it, how many times do I have to tell you? No baby, I want to be the one to crack his head open with this tire iron," Jamie replies waving the tire iron around, then poking Roy in his back with it.

Roy looks like crap when he rings the door of Bobby's house. He collects himself, he looks over at Jamie and Jimmy who are in hiding five feet down the porch. The door opens up and there is Bobby with Roy's very own wife standing behind him wearing a robe.

Jimmy and Jamie are waiting for their cue when Roy decides to skip the plan all together and go completely crazy and yell out loud. "What the fuck is going on here?" Agnes you slut! Bobby! You are cheating on me with sick ass Bobby?"

Bobby tries his best to slam the door closed. But Roy is already making himself inside the door before he does, causing Bobby to be slammed against the inside wall. Roy is on top of Bobby punching him in his face within seconds. Bobby bleeds and pleads for his life as Roy hits him harder. Roy stops punching Bobby and gets off him and stands up. Roy looks at Agnes and says, "You're next, you lousy cheating bitch."

Agnes runs away as Roy takes his attention from her and back to Bobby. "You sucked her toes, you sucked my wife's toes didn't you Bobby?" About this time Jimmy and Jamie walk through the door to see what the Hell is going on. "Answer me you sorry bastard, you sucked Agnes's toes didn't you?"

Bobby tries to talk but Roy has his foot on his throat and is pressing down really hard with it. "Okay don't answer me you sick fucking freak, it doesn't matter, you're going to die anyway." Roy takes his foot away from Bobby's throat and stomps it down hard on his mouth. Bobby's mouth opens up and Roy decides to cram his foot down it, shoe and all. "You like to suck toes, here suck my shoe!" Roy screams out in the rage of victory.

Jamie starts to cry, so Jimmy puts his arm around her and hugs her. "Jimmy he's going to die, my monster is going to die, just like he did in my dream."

Jimmy confused even more, feeling to himself that this whole thing is nothing but a bad dreams ask, "What dream Jamie?"

"Oh forget it and watch, we're getting to the the best part."

Bobby is choking to death as Roy keeps on screaming at him, "Suck it, suck my shoe, suck the soul off my shoe, you sorry ass bastard."

Bobby dies and Jamie laughs out tears of joy. Roy takes his foot out of Bobby's mouth and says, "Shut up you crazy bitch, here give me that." Roy reaches over and snags the gun out of Jimmy's hand. "This is much better, you two are dead, I'm going to shoot both of you in your heads, but first I have to shoot my cheating slut wife Agnes."

Roy motions Jimmy and Jamie into the house further by using his new gun. "That's it you crazy ass people into the house, don't stop walking until I tell you to. You two crazy fucks ever heard the term, cannon fodder? Shut up!"

Roy closes the front door and follows Jimmy and Jamie into living room, "Stop there and sit down on the couch and stay shutting up. Agnes, where the Hell you at? Come to me my cheating wife, maybe I'll show you some mercy."

Agnes comes into the living room from the other side of it. "No mercy for you Roy, you hateful pig!" Agnes screams out to Roy with a gun in her hand.

"Stupid bitch, put that damn gun down, I know you'll never use it on me."

"Yes I will Roy, I hate you. All these years married to a pig like you has made me lonely enough to fuck Bobby."

"Shut up you slut, how could you do this to me? I who gave you everything. I loved you Agnes."

"Of course you love me Roy, I'm beautiful and I let you have me when you want me. I'm the perfect wife."

"Perfect? Perfect wives don't cheat on their husbands. Now drop that gun before you hurt yourself."

"No Roy you drop your gun and step away from those scared looking people."

"These people right here Agnes?" Roy says pointing the gun at Jimmy and Jamie. "I tell you what Agnes if you don't drop your gun, I'll shoot them both. I swear it. Do you want these innocent people's blood and lives on your conscious? I know you Agnes, you couldn't live with yourself if innocent people got shot all because of you."

"You inhuman pig! Alright, don't hurt them and I'll put my gun down."

"That's my Agnes. Hurry up, my finger is getting tired, I might not be able to hold it still for much longer."

"So fucking what Roy! Go ahead and shoot us, shoot us dead, you lousy lay you," Jamie says to Roy, smiling as she gets off the couch. "Come on Jimmy get up," Jimmy gets off the couch like he is told to do, smiling as well.

"Are you two stupid or something? Sit your asses back down on that couch!" Roy says aggravatingly.

"No, fuck you Roy, shoot us, I dare you," Jamie says like she knows a secret. Jamie grabs Jimmy by the hand and they walk over to where Agnes is standing.

"Get back over here, you crazy ass freaks!" Roy yells out nervously, not knowing what is going on.

Jimmy and Jamie stop about six feet from Agnes. "Agnes is it? It's nice to meet you, I'm Jamie and this is the love of my life, Jimmy."

221

Agnes, in shock says, "Hello."

"Don't worry Agnes, Roy doesn't even have a real gun."
Jamie tells Agnes with humor in her voice.

"You crazy bitch, I do too!" Roy yells out, with a not
knowing tone very present in his voice.

"No Roy, you dumb ass, you have a water pistol in your
shaking hand."

"You lie, you are lying you crazy bitch!"

"Believe me Agnes, you can shoot Roy, all he has is a
water pistol. Take the your monster of your nightmares out
of your life. Set yourself free Agnes," Jamie says hardly
containing the excitement inside herself.

Agnes steady's herself and says, "Okay, here I go Jamie."
Agnes squeezes the trigger of the gun that is in her hands
and it goes off, making her heart stop. She smiles seeing
that Roy has been shot so she shoots him three more
times, making sure that he is completely dead.

"Thank you Agnes."

"You're welcome Jamie. Was Roy's gun really a water
pistol, like you said it was?""

"No I'm sorry Agnes, his gun was real."

"That's okay Jamie. Your lie made it easier for me to shoot
Roy. And that's all that matters, Thank you."

"You're welcome. Are you going to be alright Agnes?"

"Yes I'll be fine, I'm free remember. Now you two better get
out of here before the police get here"

Agnes and Jamie hug the other goodbye.

Chapter Three:

Trial and error has made Jamie change the way they do things. Jimmy is very unhappy about this change.

"Come on Jamie no more. No more men. I can't take this anymore. Please let's just stop."

"Stop? You are so simple Jimmy. We have made over eighty thousand dollars in two months."

"I know, that's what I'm saying, we've made enough."

"Not even close Jimmy, half of this is yours. That means I have only forty thousand."

"You can have a bigger share."

"That's sweet of you Jimmy. Sometimes I love you so much, like I do now. But no Jimmy I want, I need at least a hundred thousand dollars. Even more would be better. You can't have enough free money."

"The money is great Jamie... I can't do this anymore. I'm done, I guess that means we're through."

"What the Hell are you talking about? Are you telling me that you're breaking up with me?"

"Yes. I love you Jamie but you have changed. This life you have now, you love it, it gets you off."

"Shut your damn mouth Jimmy! Don't you dare say that to me again. I'm innocent, you hear me Jimmy? I'm innocent?"

"No you are not Jamie. You are guilty, I am guilty, we are criminals. We've damned ourselves."

"Save that shit for church Jimmy."

"Listen to yourself Jamie. When we got together, you were so happy and full of life and love."

"No baby I wasn't. My life has always been Hell. You made me happy Jimmy. The look of a brighter future was in your eyes, I wanted that in my life."

"We were so happy at first, when we first left Florida."

"Yes the first few days were great, we drove all day and made love all night. Then what happened to our perfect road trip of love?"

"I know baby, we went through Hell but together we got out of it alive."

"Alive with nothing, even the police did nothing for us."

"They could not find them, they had no leads."

"Leads? The Hell with leads. We took them to the woods where they kept us."

"Yes, but we couldn't lead them to the house. It's like it disappeared. I could swear we took them to the dirt road that led to the house. No house, no car."

"Not just you car Jimmy, but also all my stuff."

"All my stuff also Jamie."

"Yeah so what? It's all your fault. From that day until right now, everything is your fault Jimmy."

"I've made up for that, I've paid my price. I can no longer do for you what you need from me."

"You promised Jimmy. You promised you would make it up to me for what happened to me."

"I have Jamie, over and over again."

"Wrong Jimmy! You are not even close to making it up to me. What I went through and it is all your fault."

"I know Jamie but I..."

"You what Jimmy? You have something better to do than keep your promise to me?"

Jimmy says nothing as he closes his eyes in frustration.

"That's good Jimmy. Just in case you need to be reminded what happened, I'll remind you now."

"You don't have to I remember."

"Too damn bad, I think you need it."

(Flashback)

Jimmy and Jamie were driving down a back road. They had seen a sign that read that there was a Farmer's Market ten miles down it. (Jamie really wanted some strawberries.) It was a pretty day, everything was going great. The night before they ate pizza, drank beer, smoked some weed and made love twice. Jimmy was thinking about having sex with Jamie when they drove up on a man that was laying in the middle of the road.

Fast forward a little bit:

Jimmy and Jamie were sitting on the ground with a gun pointed at them. The man that was laying on the ground was holding it as he and his three freaky friends were laughing about the score they just made. They made Jimmy get in the trunk of the car after they cleaned it out first. All of Jimmy's and Jamie's stuff was thrown in the back of the truck that the gunman's friends pulled up in, while he was holding them at bay.

Two friends drove Jimmy to the lonely old house in the woods, while the third friend followed slowly driving the truck with Jamie and the gunman riding along in the back.

Jamie said please no as she took off her clothes. The gunman made her lay down naked on the bed of the truck. With his clothes on the man with the gun laid down on top of Jamie. He told her how much he loved her and missed her loving. Jamie just laid there confused and silent as this even more confused weird looking man cried on her bare chest of the lost love he never had with Jamie.

He kissed Jamie's frozen lips and sweet smelling neck. He told her to close her eyes as he began to make love to her with his clothes on. When he finished he whispered in Jamie's ear that very soon, he would be allowed to make love to her with his clothes off. He beat on the window of the truck, his friend pulled over and they switched places.

Friend of the crazy gunman was now holding the very same gun on a naked and scared Jamie. His friend laughed at the craziness of his friend as he took off his clothes. He told Jamie that he did not love her, like his friend does. He made Jamie's confusion lighten as he told her that his friend thought that every woman like Jamie was the same woman as the very first one, the one he loves with all his heart. To the gunman it makes no difference that their faces and bodies change.

The friend laughed out loud as he laid on top of Jamie. He asked Jamie as he was finishing what she thought the gunman would think if he knew about what happened to all the women like Jamie. That all of them were dead and laying together in one big pit of a grave. Jamie cried and begged for her life as the friend enjoyed her a second time. After they got to the house the gunman went into the woods to pray, as his second and third friend had their fun and turns, with an out of her mind Jamie.

Night fell as Jimmy wished for more air. Having to take very slow breaths for eight hours had put Jimmy in a slight trance. His body was numb, his mind it tried to make itself come to the understanding that it and its body may very well die inside this dark trunk. A noise outside the car, the stars of the night shone brightly in Jimmy's eyes as the trunk's lid opened up. The gunman, who's name was Donny, stared down at Jimmy with eyes of rage and fire.

A very disturbed about finding out the truth Donny, did his I'm out of my mind routine, for a coming out of his slight trance Jimmy.

Donny said, "They lied, they lied to me! All my Mary Lou's dead. Now I know that only one was truly my Mary Lou. All that came after her were only vessels with her soul inside them. My friends don't want me to be with the soul of the woman that I love more than my life itself. My friends are Demons from Hell. I hate them but I fear for my soul, I cannot be the one to send them back to Hell."

Donny walked around, trying to calm himself down. Donny decided that he didn't want to talk to Jimmy while he was laying in a trunk anymore so he pulled him out halfheartedly, just enough so that Jimmy fell to the ground softly instead of hard.

"You, man from the trunk of a car, you will have to send these Demons back to Hell. I will give you my gun, I will run away. I have sinned, while I was trying to re-find my love, my Mary Lou. My Mary Lou's soul is not inside your woman's body and mind anymore. I am sorry to tell you that your woman has been tainted by three Demons. It is not her fault, kill the Demons, give her your love. She will be damaged in the mind for quite sometime. Good luck. By the way, I'm Donny."

Donny reached down to Jimmy and handed him his gun. Donny looked up at the stars in the night sky and asked them, "Where is the soul of my love?"

Jimmy gathered his strength and pulled up his gun. He thought about shooting Donny in his balls but instead he let Donny run away into the darkness of the cool night.

Jimmy stood up slowly and then he fell back down on the ground. He was about to yell at himself, when from out the house came the aroma of delicious cooking beef stew. Jimmy's belly rumbled as he stood up again. He looked at the house, he wanted to walk to it but his legs would not let him yet. Fifteen minutes later, after Jimmy has taken a piss, he walked to the house, wondering to himself if there would be any beef stew left for him to eat.

When Jimmy reached the door, and was about to open it and rush in, gun waving when Donny's last words came to his mind. "Give her your love. She will be damaged in the mind for quite sometime." Jimmy stood back, cleared his mind and kicked the door open.

(This flashback now changes to Jamie's perspective.)

"Jimmy what I went through was the start of my down fall. Those three men used me to get off, then they made me start dinner. After the beef stew was on the stove top they made me clean their house. All while I was wearing a sexy mail order maid's outfit."

Jamie takes Jimmy's hand into hers and squeezes it hard. She gets out of her chair and sets herself down on Jimmy's lap and gives him a hug and a loving kiss.

"Jimmy my love, I know I'm a mean bitch to you. I can't help myself. I hate you and I blame you Jimmy for what happened to me. But Jimmy, oh my Jimmy, you saved me. What you did for me, what you did to them. I love you Jimmy. I still blame you but you killed those monsters for me, for our love. I will always remember this and this is the reason I have stayed with you and not killed you that same night, when I finally got my hands on that gun."

"It is all my fault Jamie. If only I would have kept driving and not stopped, where would our lives be now?"

"Much better now. We wouldn't have been without our car, all our stuff and all our money. I wouldn't have had to strip for money. All those eyes wanting to do the same thing to me as those three monsters did to me. So many times I wished I could have been allowed to pull out a gun and shoot all those sick horny men in their eyes. I've changed, damn have I changed. There's a sickness inside me Jimmy I never want to be touched again by a man. Yet inside me I want their sex wanting bodies on mine. I want to hear their lustful talks and moans as I out sex them."

"Which leads us to here Jamie. All those men, all these men you let have sex with you until you make them pass out. I can't take this anymore."

Jamie gets off Jimmy's lap and walks about five feet away from him. "Too bad Jimmy, it's the perfect plan. This is how we have made eighty thousand dollars so far and safely I might add. Besides it feeds the dirty beast inside me, you know I can't go without my dirty sex having."

"I love you Jamie but your touch and your heart is cold. It is all my fault I know but please give me back my life. I promised I would never leave your side. I owed you maybe I still owe you more still now. I don't know but I do know that life, my life almost feels as cold as your touch. Please release me from my promise. Let me heal my heart and soul, let me find some peace."

"While I think about this Jimmy, I have a question I need answered first."

"What answer can I give you that would do you and your troubled mind any good?"

"That night you came busting in the door of that house in the woods."

"What about it Jamie?"

"You are like that right now as you were then. Your eyes are different, in them I see clarity. Now and again since we've been together, I have seen this same clarity in them but mostly I have seen confusion, you pass off as being incompetent."

"What are you asking me Jamie?"

"You came into that house in the woods like my hero. You saw what I was wearing, you looked at me, in your eyes I knew you knew what they did to me, what they were planning on doing to me still. With cold steel eyes, you shot all three monsters to their deaths. You walked up to me, and in passing you put the gun on the dinner table right next to a steaming bowl of beef stew. You hugged and hugged me telling me you that you loved me and that you were sorry and everything was your fault."

"I remember. You hugged me so hard you made my back crack. Then you told me to go wash up, while you got me a fresh bowl of beef stew. We ate our stew together both of us crying and trying to make the other smile and laugh. Then we heard an explosion and our car driving off, we walked to the door and saw that the truck was on fire."

"Yes my love, I remember that as if it were yesterday. Why the incompetence my love?"

"To save my soul. I killed for you. I can never go back to not being a killer again. My incompetence made me safe, for you would not ask me to kill again if you thought I would fuck it all up."

"Too true my love. Yes the time is close, very close to end the hold of your promise to me. Too true as well, my love for you has depleted inside my heart. Too true I'm cold inside. I need a lover that is just as cold to the world, one that's been used and is searching for payback."

"Sounds romantic Jamie, I wish you the best. Well I guess that's that, see you around. You can have all the money but one thousand dollars, how's that to you?"

"Sounds romantic! Fuck you Jimmy. Today is not the day you leave me. I want you for one more, I'll fuck them 'til they drop, then you come in and tie them up. I got a date tomorrow night with a ugly rich man, that has a house on the hill, that looks down at everybody else's houses."

"What do you mean, that you have a date?"

"For the last time we do this, I've changed things up. Instead of meeting a man and letting him take me to his home to have sex with me until I make him pass out, I made a date with the big fish, the biggest of them all. This is my nest egg Jimmy, don't fuck it up."

"One more and that's it?"

"No, Jimmy my love, tomorrow night is the last one. The one after that, is the one for the road."

"One for the road? I don't like the sound of that. Sounds to me like the end after the end."

"I don't care what it sounds like to you Jimmy dear. Hee, hee, hee. I'm so wicked. To be honest Jimmy, I can't wait for our end, it will be one for the books, whatever that means. Hee, hee, hee."

The next night Jamie dolls herself up. She walks up to Jimmy to show herself off. Jimmy can't help himself, it's been awhile and Jamie looks hot and ready. Jamie grabs Jimmy by his ear and pulls him over to their hotel room's bed. She makes him take off his clothes and then lay down on the bed. Jamie gives Jimmy her sweet talks, while kissing his lips, neck and chest, she stops going down when she reaches Jimmy's belly button.

Jimmy is begging for Jamie to keep kissing him downwards. Jamie with a sexy, evil little laugh tells Jimmy to suffer as she pulls up her skirt and sits down on top of him, wearing no panties. Hot passion of two of the craziest lovers that has ever been on Earth continues on. Jamie in charge keeps on talking to Jimmy, like the sun rises and sets in his pants. Jimmy tries to take over and is scolded by Jamie. When Jamie knows that Jimmy can't take anymore, she stops what she is doing and looks down at him and tells him to suffer.

Laughing at a begging Jimmy, Jamie makes Jimmy wait until he is almost not ready to go on. Jimmy is in pain as Jamie starts all over again, including stopping just in time once again. Jimmy can't control himself and begs Jamie to let him finish.

"For the love we shared together Jimmy my love I will let you finish. I just wanted to show you what I do to all the men when I out sex them every time. You Jimmy, just like all of them, are weak. So strong on the outside, you men are but on the inside... The tougher on the outside the more they beg me to let them finish, while I always go unsatisfied. No man is my equal. Here you go my love finish like the strongest of them all."

Jimmy is so happy when he is finished but then realization comes to his mind and he can't help but to feel ashamed of himself for his weakness. Jamie laughs at Jimmy as she gets off of him. She walks over to the dresser opens up the top drawer and pulls out a pair of panties and puts them on. She tells Jimmy he has twenty minutes to be ready to leave with her for her date.

Jamie and the rich man's date starts with dinner. After dinner Jamie is charming the rich man on the ride to his home. He feels like the man as Jamie makes him drive faster. Two drinks and the rich man is all over Jamie, telling her everything he thinks she wants to hear. Jamie laughs to herself as she readies herself for sexual battle.

The rich man, basically a puppet, tries his best to be the one in control. Jamie puts him in his place as he begs for their love making to continue on. Jamie with such a big heart tells him yes and takes off her clothes. The rich man looks at Jamie's body like he's in love with it. Jamie knows this rich man does not stand a chance.

The rich man makes love to an already just made love to Jamie. He is passionate and caring at first as Jamie kisses him back with half the passion he is giving her. The rich man looks down at Jamie, who looks like she is going with the flow. Never before has he seen eyes like this when it comes to love making. His wealth alone makes then pull his hair and bite his chest.

Jamie counts to herself, she feels that the rich man can maybe make it to thirty five maybe forty seconds before his maleness takes over and he gives to her like she has never had it before. Jamie smiles and thinks, do it rich man, make yourself weak by out doing yourself. The rich man at thirty six seconds grabs a hold of Jamie and gives her whats she wants, what she needs so bad.

The rich man smiles as he finishes and Jamie asks him, "Is that it, you have no more loving to give to me?"

The rich man always a winner and never loses, is out of his element. He does not know that he is being played by a sexy lady that can turn off what she feels sexually at the taking off of her clothes. The rich man tries to take a moment to gather himself but Jamie will not let him, as she begs him for more of his one of a kind passion, of the like she's never felt before.

One hour later the rich man is shaking and dirty talking, like he'll never go to church again. Jamie is moaning so loud that she is making the rich man lose concentration and making this second time of love making go on as long as possible. The second love making is always for Jamie.

She allows herself this present for her lustful soul that she can't help to feed hot sex to it as much as possible.

The rich man looks down at Jamie and sees tears falling from her eyes. "Way to go man," he tells himself as Jamie moves around on the bed like she has no control of her body. Proud of himself, the rich man flaunts himself off his bed and to the bathroom that adjoins it. When he closes the door, Jamie stops moving around and sits up in the bed. She shivers and grabs the covers and covers herself.

Jamie stares at the bathroom door, listening to the rich man take his long after sex piss. Jamie says to herself, "Not bad rich man, not bad at all. I'll give you a pillow for your sore head after your knocked out for getting me off. Still I'm ready to go and you're almost limp. It's time to make you pass out rich man, it's time to take all your gold and silver. Hurry rich man, I'm getting cold and bored and I need to pee really bad."

The two lovers of the night switch places in the bathroom. Rich man has to stop Jamie from closing the door to give her a victory kiss first. The rich man puts on his robe and looks into his bedroom mirror. He thinks back to all the years it took him to get to where he is right now. He smiles at the much older man that he is and says, "I think I might just marry this woman."

Jamie hears this and closes back the bathroom door very quietly. "What the Hell!? How can he want to marry me, he loves me? Have I made so many mistakes that I can't feel love when it's for real?"

Jamie looks into the bathroom mirror and sees a woman that she does not know. "How far have you fallen? Jimmy used to love you, you still love him but his heart is so cold to love and it is all your fault. Why couldn't you just let it be, go on with your life with Jimmy. No those monsters used me, they abused my soul and my mind." Jamie looks away from the mirror and starts to cry.

When she looks back into the mirror, she sees that her tears are only an illusion. A flicker in her eyes makes her smile. "No the rich man does not love me, he only wants to own me. I will never be a fool in love with a man again."

The tears dry up and Jamie's smile returns to her. "They fall in love with me, I break their hearts and take all the money I can from them when I leave bloody and broken. Damn you world, damn you men of Earth, all of you are sick and horny tainted monsters that truly only want a woman for one reason. Sex. And no men can out sex me. Time for round number three rich man, you almost fooled me but now it's time I show you no mercy."

A sexy, made love to really good three times, Jamie pounces out of the bathroom ready to strike the beast. "Come to me man of my eternal passion, you will make love to me again. You will make me your sex slave. Take me. Own me as you want to own me. I only want to please you."

The rich man cannot even blink before Jamie is tearing off his robe. The rich man steadies himself and then he picks up Jamie and carries her to his bed of pleasure. "You are the woman for me. After I own you sexually one more time, I will make you my wife. You will have anything you have ever wanted. While I, your husband, will own your body and your soul."

The rich man puts his hand on Jamie's face to hold it still so he can look her in her eyes when he tells her. "Hot love, your mind will also belong to me. You will obey me and please me everyday for the rest of your life. Do you understand me future wife?"

Jamie in the thrall of sexual desire and future triumph says, "Give me your long loving future husband, make me your love slave that never tells you no."

"Let it begin then."

Jamie tries her best to push the passion she feels into the back of her mind so she can take control. The rich man's loving is too powerful. All Jamie can do is hold on and take the loving pain that she feels. The rich man out does his first two times making love to Jamie. He is out of control making love to Jamie as hard and as fast as he can.

"Baby,I'm about to explode, hold still, feel my love," the rich man says full of confidence, he finishes and looks down at Jamie with a weird look on his face.

"Whats wrong my love?" Jamie asks the rich man and does not receive an answer. "Are you okay my love? You don't look so good."

The rich man has a heart attack, while leaning over Jamie. He is about to fall on top of her when Jamie puts up her foot and shoves him backwards. Jamie shoves the rich man so hard that she sends him flying off the bed and onto the cold hard floor.

Jamie to herself, "Well this has never happened before. I didn't even need Jimmy this time. I guess I can call for him two pair of hands can carry more away than only one."

Jimmy walks into the bedroom where Jamie killed the rich man with her body. He looks down at the rich man lying ugly on the floor, he stinks he has shit himself. Jimmy looks at his face and sees his own face, dead to the world. Jimmy gasps and shakes his head no and closes his eyes. When Jimmy opens his eyes back up, his face no longer belongs to the dead rich man. Jamie walks angrily up behind him and asks him, "What the Hell you doing Jimmy? Stop looking at the dead man and help me find all his gold and silver."

Jimmy walks away from the dead man to do as he was commanded to do. He says to himself, "Just one more time man and you're free."

It is a week later. During this past week Jamie has enjoyed Jimmy's body like never before. Jimmy swears Jamie is trying to kill him with her body. "Practice makes perfect Jimmy, I'll take it easy on you but the next man I pick to be our last job together, I will kill with my loving. Now hurry up for after you finish, we're going out to find him together."

Jamie goes all out, making herself look more beautiful than she has ever before. She wears the most expensive diamond rings she has and her most expensive pearl necklace. Jimmy looks at Jamie and says, "Wow Jamie you look prettier than an Angel."

It's a few hours later, Jimmy and Jamie are sitting in their truck parked outside a lonely out of the place bar filled with rough looking men. Jamie is just about to pull away so they can find another spot for their last John together, when a red Corvette pulls into the parking lot.

Jamie smiles as a good looking, well dressed man gets out of his Corvette. "That's him, that is the John I'm going to kill with my body."

Jamie gets out of the truck not waiting for an answer from Jimmy. Jimmy watches as Jamie sexily walks herself to this last John like she owns the world. Jamie like a predator makes her move right away. The two lovers in the night lean against the red Corvette and make out. When they stop making out the well dressed man takes Jamie by her hand and leads her away from Jimmy's sight.

Jimmy is thinking about tomorrow, when out of the night he hears two gun shots that snap him out of his deep thoughts. He looks over and sees the well dressed John running towards his car, he gets in it and pulls away out of the parking lot as fast as he can. Minutes later tears fall from Jimmy's eyes as he is looking at the robbed and dead body of Jamie. Jimmy gathers himself and walks back to his truck and drives away to his freedom.

Cannibal Butcher

(The Eaten)

This Cannibal Butcher Is A Master Maniac. I Moan For
Limbs That Are No Longer There. With My Last Thought
I Laugh Hoping This Cannibal Butcher,
Chokes To Death On The Last Of My Meat.

(The Eater)

I Slice Your Meat Off Your Bones So Smooth And Deep.
I Fry Them Quick And Rare. Your Blood Flows
From My Mouth With Each Delicious Bite.

2016, November 14[th,] five days ago, the night of the
Supermoon. Chris a twenty three year old college student
is walking out in the night, trying his best to let things go.
His girl friend of two years Katie dumped him last night and
tonight the sack of weed he bought was full of seeds.
Chris rolled up a joint to smoke his sadness away. During
his toking Chris's mind remembers how Katie looked when
her clothes were off, how she could never smile when she
was on top making love to him. Making love to Katie was
always so serious but it was also so fine as well.

Katie knew what Chris liked and like the great girlfriend she
was she provided Chris with what he liked every night they
had the time. This last thought was what was on Chris's
mind when a seed in his joint popped in his face. Chris
said fuck and moved the joint away from his face. Good
move but Chris did not pay attention to the seed to where it
fell and that was on his lap. Chris looked at his joint then
he started to toke it up some more. While Chris was toking
the seed was doing its best to burn itself through his pants.
Chris was high and feeling better when all of a sudden the
seed made itself through his pants and burned the tip of
his pecker.

(Quote by Chris.) "Fuck! My dick, my dick is burning!"

Chris is high and his pecker is in pain and the only thing he could think to do after he dipped his pecker in a glass of cold water, was to take a walk to take his mind off his pain.

Let's step into Chris's mind five days ago.

"Stupid damn seedy weed!" Chris stops talking to himself.

Ten college students walk by. As they walk by Chris every one of them marching in a row stared Chris in his eyes and told him their name and their age.

"What was that? That was crazy, they must be on mushrooms. The seventh one, she was fine, her name is Kris. That would be weird to say my name to my lover when I was making love to her. That was weird, they were messing with me, they had to be."

Chris comes out of his thoughts and looks at the direction the ten students walked by him. Forty feet further up they have stopped walking and have turned around standing side by side to stare at Chris. Chris feels a cold wind strike his back as the ten students start chanting to him, "You're doomed, you're damned, you're going to die."

Chris yells back at them, "Shut the fuck up!" They stop chanting and then they walk away like nothing happened. Except for Kris who gave Chris her middle finger and said in reply, "Chris, you have always been destined to die very bloodily and painfully. I'm sorry, see you on the other side." Then Kris vanished from out of sight while Chris was blinking.

"Maybe I'm on mushrooms? What is this night all about? My mind, my deep thoughts are telling me that the ten people I have just seen, all ten of them are already dead to this world. What I saw, was their spirits, their tormented spirits that are damned to walk the Earth instead of crossing over to the other side. They are waiting on me to die for I will be the one that will help them to cross over."

239

Chris looks up at the giant sized Supermoon, the amazing Supermoon that has not been this close and bright in almost seventy years. Words fail Chris, so he looks up at the Supermoon until he makes himself a little dizzy. Chris says fuck this night out loud to himself and walks back to his dorm room to drink a few beers and smoke another joint then hopefully fall into a deep and peaceful sleep.

2016, November **15**th, four days ago, it's the second night of the Supermoon and Chris is trying his best to insert himself into the night's plans for two sexy lady friends.

"What do you say ladies, beer, weed and my body?"

"We would Chris, but we already promised to lick each others bodies from head to toe, stopping half way through for a long time, of course" Janet replies sexy like.

"Sounds like fun, can I at least watch?"

"Goodnight Chris, tomorrow we will want male, be around and you can be our male," Jennifer replies even sexier.

Chris watches Janet's and Jennifer's asses as they walk away slowly and so fine, he would bite them both. A voice says his name from behind him very low, a voice that Chris knows so very well.

"Hello Chris, how are you doing?"

Without turning around Chris responds back cool and cold, "Hello Katie, I'm fine, how are you doing on this night of Supermoon's awareness and splendor?"

"Oh Chris, look at me. Don't be so cold."

"How can I not be cold Katie, when your coldness two nights ago out of nowhere, froze my heart."

"Really Chris? You're really going to lay it all on me?"

"Not my fault Katie. You're the one that left me for you didn't love me anymore."

"In my heart I felt this Chris. Now my heart misses you, I think I made a mistake."

"You Think you made a mistake, not that you made a mistake Katie?"

"Yes Chris, I need one more night with you before I think can become I know."

"One more night doing what Katie?"

"Well not talking Chris. I want your body. I'm going to act like it's our first time. I want to see if your body turns on my body and mind out of passion instead of having the love for you in my heart making me feel love instead of hot hard great sex."

Chris closes his eyes in disgust as he realizes his pecker hurts more when it becomes hard. He opens his eyes as he turns around knowing what he is already going to say to Katie. In truth the burnt tip of Chris's pecker has made him realize that he no longer loves Katie. It has only been great sex for the past year or so.

"Thank you Katie but my answer is no."

"Thank you? No? What the fuck is wrong with you? I give myself to you and you don't want me? You bastard, I hate you. I'm going to fuck the first sexy guy I see. I'll make you pay for saying no to me. I'm going to give it better to him than I ever gave it to you. You bastard, how could you tell me no? I was going to take you back."

"And I was just to jump into your arms like nothing has happened? I think not. You don't love me Katie you just wanted your last time with me so our ending would seem more final to you."

"You don't know what you are talking about Chris. My heart has missed you more than my body."

"Maybe so Katie. In my heart I feel you are fooling yourself. As I look at you, in my heart I know I don't love you anymore. Sex would be a mistake to the memory of the past love we shared."

"Well maybe so Chris but from my heart you can go fuck yourself. Don't call me, we're through."

Katie walks away more mad then she is sad. She looks around for a hot sexy guy to have sex with for the rest of the night. In her mind is one word, payback.

Chris watches Katie's ass as she walks away. He thinks to himself, "What an ass Katie has, I'll miss it."

Not caring who sees, Chris reaches down and pushes his hard on down flat so it doesn't stick out straight anymore. Once again Chris has had enough this night and his plans become beer, weed and sleep.

2016, November **16**th, three days ago, Chris heads to the spot he was in last night to meet up with Janet and Jennifer. He is only twenty feet away when he spots them leaving with another guy.

"Damn! I could have used two ladies loving tonight." Not paying attention Chris bumps into a stranger as he is walking by, while talking to himself lowly.

"Watch it man," Voiced with anger and frustration.

"Fuck off, you bumped into me, watch where you're going."

Two strangers stare at the other, then they simply walk away without saying a word. Chris is out of weed so beer will be his only buzz tonight.

242

The afternoon of 2016, November **17**th, two days ago, Katie calls Chris, she wants to talk to him later tonight in the spot they talked two nights ago. The night Chris said no thank you to Katie, when she asked him if he wanted to make love to her. Here is the conversation.

"Come on baby, come on Chris, meet me tonight. We need to talk."

"What's there to talk about Katie? We're through."

"I still want my one more time with you. I don't know why, I just need this. If you have sex with me, I will be all that and you will rue the day you let me get away. Then I'll walk away from you, leaving you all alone knowing you made the biggest mistake of your life."

"Katie let me have some of what you're smoking. I didn't let you get away, you got yourself away from me." Chris's pecker is back to normal so is his confidence. "I tell you what Katie. Come to my room, don't say a word and let me fuck you anyway I want to and then yes, I'll let you have sex with me for your one last time."

"What? That's stupid."

"Well so are you Katie, too bad you don't know this."

"No Chris, you are stupider than a stupid. How's that for stupid, huh Chris?"

"How's what Katie? I didn't understand what you said."

"I said..." Katie repeats to Chris what she just told him.

"I still don't understand what you're saying Katie, tell me one more time."

A getting pissed now Katie repeats herself.

"I'm sorry Katie, what you're trying to tell me must be so stupid that I'll never be able to understand it."

"You are stupid, you asshole!" Katie hangs up on Chris.

Ring, Ring. "Hello Katie this is Chris."

"I know you are Chris, stupid. Are we meeting in the spot or not tonight?"

"Why the fuck not? Bring a girlfriend with you."

"I will not. Why are you going to try to have sex with her instead of me?"

"Of course not Katie. I'll have sex with the both of you."

"Find your own lady to screw Chris. Are we on tonight?"

"Yes come over and screw me Katie."

"No! We meet in the spot first."

"The spot it is then Katie, see you tonight at nine."

"See you then Chris, goodbye."

Chris to himself, "Damn I bet Katie is going to be the hottest she has ever been with me tonight. Nothing like fast and hard break up sex, three times in one night to bring out the best sex inside yourself."

It's eight o'clock and Chris is fresh out of the shower. His tummy is rumbling, he needs a burger and fries really fast. Out the door half dried and dressed, Chris hurries to fill his belly. Chris likes taking the back way, between silent, dark alleys with plenty of large shadows in the corners.

Chris is humming a song to himself, with the rest of his mind behind locked doors.

244

Half way down the second alley, out of the darkness, the stranger from last night steps in front of Chris's path, making Chris walk straight into him.

"Watch it man," Voiced as cold as ice.

"You again. What's your problem man?"

"You. You are my problem, man."

"What the fuck are you going to do about me then man?"

"This." The stranger holds up a can of mace and sprays it into Chris's eyes. Chris screams out for only a moment. A moment is all Chris is allowed to have before the stranger knocks him down with one mighty unexpected punch to his right temple. On the ground, Chris in confusion, tries to gather himself as the stranger stomps down on his body very fast and very hard.

Silence is what Chris hears as the silent stranger ties his hands together behind his back. Tape, sticky, cool tape is wrapped around Chris's mouth and head, as his eyes are too blurry to see if the stranger is frowning or smiling.

"On your feet meat, on your feet now!"

Chris does not move, so the now talking, crazy stranger helps Chris up by using the hair on the top of his head. "Up meat. I said, up meat. You will listen to me when I talk to you meat. You will do as I order you to do."

The stranger pulls a knife out of his right jean pocket and opens it up, then he takes the blade and presses it against Chris's throat. "Feel this blade meat. Feel it against your throat, one quick slice and you will bleed to death. Or I can have some fun and slice off your dick. It's up to you meat, get up and live for now or lay there and die now."

Chris wanting to scream for his life, gets on his feet.

245

"Walk meat, walk to my van. You had to bump into me last night. You had to be rude to me. I was going to stop. No more human meat I would eat. But no, you had to make me hate you, you had to make me want to eat you."

Inside Chris's mind he knows that this can't be for real. Nobody would be sick enough to eat him. This crazy stranger has to be fucking with him really bad.

"Three days ago I snatched up this pretty, little, young lady of twenty two years of age. It was the night of the Supermoon. The Supermoon made me do something I have never done before and that is to eat the meat of the one I picked that night. I always wait two days so the skin slices off the meat easier. Stop walking and get down, somebody is watching us."

Chris can see a little bit. He looks around to see if anybody is really there before he is helped to the ground with one hard push downwards. Inside Chris's mind "Please somebody help me, save me from this crazy, evil bastard. I don't want to die."

The stranger laughs out loud a crazy sounding asshole laugh, making Chris's heart stop beating for a moment. "You stupid meat, look at you all please help somebody, anybody help me in your eyes. You're so stupid, there's nobody there to save you and capture the monster. This is real life buddy, not TV, not a movie. But the really bad news for you is my bike is only twenty feet away from us."

Inside Chris's mind, "Bike, this crazy fucker has a bike? I thought he said he had a van?"

Laughter, "I bet I can read your feeble mind right now meat. Yes I have a van, I was just messing with your mind to give you something else to think about, besides me eating you. Now meat on you feet and march to your death."

Once again the stranger grabs Chris up on his feet by using the hair on his head.

"Now where was I? That's right. Three days ago I snatched up this pretty, little, young lady of twenty two years of age. It was the night of the Supermoon. The Supermoon made me do something I have never done before and that is to eat the meat of the one I picked that night. I always wait two days so the skin slices off the meat easier. Calm down meat, yes I'm repeating myself and we have made it to my van. You try to run while I'm opening the doors, I'll slice your nose off."

The stranger opens up the back door to his 1970's van. He smacks Chris upside his head and throws him inside the back of his van like he has no worth to him.

"Don't worry meat you will be able to hear the rest of my story when I drive you to my human slaughterhouse. I have speakers hooked up and I have a microphone to speak to you with. Enjoy your last ride, ha,ha,ha," the stranger tells Chris before he slams the doors shut.

Out of the parking lot and down the road the old van drives until it meets up with the highway. Bypass taken too fast sends Chris rolling around the floor of the van without any means for him to stop himself. With a roar of its engine the van makes it up to seventy miles an hour.

"Hello meat, how was the rolling around back there? I hope hard, fast and very painful. Okay I picked up this lady three days ago and drove her home just like I'm doing to you now. When we got to my home, I got out of this van and walked to the back of it. The moon, the Supermoon shined down on me so big and bright, I could not take my eyes off it. I stood outside my van, must have been twenty minutes or more before it came to me to eat fresh that night. I licked my hungry lips and opened up the door. I dragged out my dinner very hard throwing her head first to the ground."

The stranger stopped talking and sped up a little bit. "The Supermoon, damn that Supermoon..."

"When I picked my dinner off the ground and on to her feet the Supermoon shined down on her so bright... So bright that it made her look like an Angel. I should have known better but I was hungry and I wanted to find out how sweet the meat of an Angel would taste to my lips and tongue."

The van slows down to take a bypass off the highway. Silence fills the darkness of the back off the van like a eerie warning of imminent death.

Going down a back road at forty five miles an hour, Chris is enjoying the quiet. The voice of the stranger, is a voice that talks to Chris like he has already been eaten.

"Wake up asshole!!! Alright on with the show meat. I with mercy sliced the Angel's throat. I drained her blood, I closed her eyes. She no longer looked like an Angel so I open her eyes back up. I sliced into the flesh of her chest and removed a nice bloody thick piece. I seasoned it and fried it rare...

The stranger pauses to clear his throat, "The taste of an Angel's meat made me sick. I gave it four chews and then I spit it out. Her meat was so nasty, it tasted like death. I had the taste of death in my mouth. Beer after beer I drank them down. I never want to taste death again. Meat you are different, you are no Angel."

The van slows down and takes a right turn down a lonely quiet road. "I was going to quit, you hear me meat? I was going to quit. Two days after I tasted death, I walked the grounds of my past hunts trying my best to call away the beast of human blood and meat from within me. I figured if I walked around and felt forgiveness for what I did, I could free myself of the beast. I tried my best but all I could feel was a pounding in my brain at every spot I stopped at."

The van slows down and this time it takes a left down a rough feeling back road.

"I had enough, the pain in my head was driving me crazy, it was making me feel weak inside. The memories of the ten people I killed and eaten made tears come to my eyes. How could I have done this I said to myself. I closed my eyes feeling outside forces tear at my brain. When I opened my eyes back up, everything, everything was covered in thick red blood. It was everywhere but not one drop touched me, I was clean on the outside..."

The stranger pauses, he calms himself down to push back his rage.

"On the inside, Hell was inside me. I fell to my knees and puked. I puked out blood! I couldn't stop, blood just kept pouring out of my mouth and onto the ground. My heart and brain pounded, they tried their best to out do the other. I felt like I was going to die when outside my madness I heard a voice say to me, Are you all right man?"

The stranger stops speaking as he pulls his van into his driveway. The van drives for about a minute before it comes to a stop. "We're home."

"Are you all right man? The voice asked me. I looked around after I was snapped out of my madness, to my surprise there was no blood anywhere. I told the voice to fuck off and I got up on my feet and walked away slowly, still feeling a little bit sick."

The stranger turns off his van and sits back into his seat.

"You out of nowhere. Yes you meat, you had to bump into me. I was never going to kill and eat another human again in my life. Then you bumped into me and I looked into your eyes and I saw blood inside them. So much blood flowed out of your eyes."

The stranger opens up his door. "You are no Angel meat, no you are a Demon from Hell. I have to know, if Angel's meat is bitter, will your Demon's meat taste sweet?"

The stranger hangs up his microphone and steps out of his van. Chris waits in terror for the stranger to open up the doors of his safety zone. Chris does not have to wait long.

"Hello again Demon meat so nice to see you. Time to get out, stand up and get out of my van by yourself or I will come up in there and throw you out head first."

Chris decides to skip the pain so he gets out of the back of the van by himself.

"You are weak on Earth, are you not Demon meat? Yes you are. You are weak and I am strong. I am the God and Devil of my domain. My home, my slaughterhouse, here I have all the power. Look around, look up at the night sky. Take in all you can Demon meat, for you will never see any of this again."

Chris looks at the stranger and fear slips from his mind and rage comes forth. Chris to himself, "This stranger is nothing, he is weak. He is sick and he is fucking crazy."

Chris makes himself charge the stranger, he kicks at him and kicks at him hitting nothing but air.

"That's the spirit Demon meat. Yes fight for your life, fight to kill me. You can do it, you can kill the beast."

Chris keeps on charging and kicking at the stranger until he tires out and cannot kick anymore. Chris stands there staring at the smiling stranger, knowing his one shot has come to him and passed him by doing nothing for him but making him feel and look like a desperate fool.

"You feel better Demon meat?"

The stranger walks over to Chris and grabs him by his tied up hands and walks him to the front door of his house.

"Come on Demon meat, time to put you on ice for two days. Then I'm going to fry you up all nice and rare."

Through the front door and down into the dark and cold basement, the stranger and Chris walk.

"Here we are, your room Demon meat. Let me look into your eyes, yes, they are still full of blood.

Chris walks into his room after the stranger opens up the door and gestures Chris to walk in. Chris looks around there is no bed, there is a chain chained to the floor with a pair of handcuffs included. Chris has his back to the stranger and is just about to turn around to him to beg for his life by using his eyes only. Whop! Chris is struck hard in the the middle of his back by a sledgehammer, knocking him to the floor. The pain is unreal and Chris cannot yell out, he has to take his pain silently.

"Take this Demon meat, take your tenderizing," the stranger says as he brings his sledgehammer down hard on Chris's left leg, right below the knee. Then the stranger does the same thing to Chris's right leg. With mercy? The stranger brings his sledgehammer down on Chris's back about half as hard as the time before. This time the strike is across the lower part of Chris's back.

"Did you hear that snap Demon meat? You're never walking again. Hold still I'm going to untie your arms. When they are free, I want you to hold them very still so I can hit them both in the perfect spot."

Chris holds still as both of his arms are broken one right after the other. Pain, the pain Chris feels is too much for his brain to register. So his mind shuts down to a nice, safe, dark place for him to hide inside.

The stranger whops Chris here and there a few more times with his sledgehammer. He puts his sledgehammer back into its corner. The stranger drags Chris to the middle of the room and handcuffs him to the chain on the floor.

"See you in two nights Demon meat. Try your best not to die, don't take your kill away from me."

2016, November **18**[th,] one day ago, Chris is still alive, he has been left alone. The stranger has not even checked on him once. Chris thinks about Katie, Chris thinks about all the ladies he has had sex with. About every hour or so Chris says to himself that he is a dead man in waiting to die, then his mind drifts back to all the ladies he had sex with. Peace, sex and death is what is on Chris's mind for the next twenty four hours as he is left alone dying slowly from his tormenting pain.

2016, November **19**[th,] today, the door to Chris's room opens up. "You still alive in there Demon meat?" The stranger says jokingly to Chris.

The stranger walks over to Chris and then he kicks him in his side hard enough to make Chris moan out loud.

"Very good Demon meat, you're one tough Hellish bastard. Now it's time to see how long you can still hold on to life as I slice your meat off your bones."

The stranger grabs Chris by his broken legs and drags him out of his room and further down the hall. Chris prays to God to take his life but he gets no answer as he feels the pain of being dragged down the hall to his very soul. In the washroom is where Chris's journey ends.

"Demon meat, look at the drain hole, see all the blood stains. Make yourself comfortable, I have to the get the skillet hot," the stranger walks over to the small stove in the corner and places a skillet on the burner, he adds some oil and turns the dial to six.

Chris hangs on for three hours as the stranger slices off his meat until he finally dies from loss of blood. The stranger did his best to keep Chris alive as long as possible. By the time Chris died the stranger had already cut forty seven pounds of his meat from his body.

After Chris's death the stranger kept on slicing all the good meat from Chris's body until he felt he had enough. The stranger stuffed himself with four pounds of Chris's meat before his hunger subsided.

Wrapped tightly, Chris's meat is put in a freezer for safe keeping. The rest of his body is chop up into small pieces and burned to ash in a burning spot about a acre away from the stranger's house.

Three AM the night of 2016, November 30th, A burglar breaks into the Cannibal Butcher's house. Cannibal Butcher hears someone in his house. He walks out of his bedroom with his favorite human slicing knife in his hand.

In his living room is the burglar, when Cannibal Butcher comes around the corner of his living room he is shot in his face twice.

"Stupid bastard, never bring a knife to a gun fight," the burglar laughs at the Cannibal Butcher.

The burglar looks around Cannibal Butcher's house and puts anything worth money in a bag. He makes his way into the kitchen, for some reason he opens up the freezer and pulls out frozen packages of meat. On the freezer bag there is a name written, Chris and a date, November 19th .

The burglar throws the bag on the floor in disgust and on the way out of Cannibal Butcher's house he sets it on fire. The burglar watches the house fall then he gets into his car and drives away, saying to himself, "What a sick fuck."

Flashback to November **19**th. Chris is a Spirit, he is standing seven feet away while and is watching the Cannibal Butcher slice meat from his dead body. The Spirit that is or was Chris still feels that it should feel the pain from its Earthly dead body. It remembers hate but it feels no hate within itself. Confusion is replaced with calmness, which turns into happiness as the Spirit that is Chris looks for the white light.

No white light is present as Spirit Chris starts to feel more like he did when he was still alive. Chris senses a flash of light appear behind him. Chris turns around to see and out of nowhere the ten collage student Spirits have appeared, "Hello once again Chris."

"Hello Kris, you're looking sexy. I'm dead, I guess you already knew this even before I died. "

"Yes Chris, you are the last to die by the hands of the Cannibal Butcher."

"Yes I know but it would have been nice if you had told me more than I was going to die the first time we met. Like hey watch out, that man is going to kill and eat you."

"It was not in our place to inform how you were to die. Our task, until this is to end, is to warn the next victim. What the next victim does or does not do is entirely up to them."

"Well that sucks. Seems to me it's a little like Heaven stepping out of the way as Hell attacks a mortal who does not stand a chance at the odds that are stacked against them from the beginning."

"Chris is does not matter what you think. Your need to know why does not apply anymore. You are number eleven, you are the last. Your death completes the chain, get in line and let's fly to Heaven together."

"I don't know Kris, something's off, something's not right."

254

"Yes Chris, it is you that is off. You are thinking too much. Do not think for yourself, you are only one of eleven. You are no more special because you are last than the rest of us. Now stop deciding and step in line, like a good Spirit... Chris, we are giving you one more chance to step in line before we make you. Please don't make us do this to you. We love you Chris. Don't we Spirits?" Nine Spirits say, "Yes Chris, we love you."

Chris looks at ten Spirits and knows they are the ones that are doomed and damned to burn in Hell. Chris also knows that if he steps in line he will also be doomed and damned to burn in Hell, "No thank you Damned Spirits, I will not be joining your chain that is linked to Hell." Ten Spirits turn from victims to predators as they attack Chris, who is his own Spirit as nothing prevails from their attack. Ten Spirits cry and plead for forgiveness to Satan for failing in their task as their colors turn from clear to burning fire red.

Chris waits until the night of November 30th, the night of the death of the Cannibal Butcher. Ten on fire Spirits waited the same amount of time, all too much in pain to do anything but cry and sit on the floor. Chris watches as a stranger breaks into the Cannibal Butcher's house. Moments later Cannibal Butcher is shot by this stranger and he dies. Chris watches as the Spirit of the Cannibal Butcher steps out of its dead body.

Ten burning Spirits get off the floor still crying and make the Cannibal Butcher Spirit take its place at the end of the their line. A loud ripping sound, sounds out as a swirling hole rips open in the floor. Eleven damned Spirits fall to Hell and the hole closes up behind them. Chris sees a clearer light than his Spirit appear above it and he happily jumps up into it only to bounce off it. The damned Spirit of Chris stars to cry as the loud ripping sound, sounds out again. The damned Spirit of Chris gives Heaven its middle finger and jumps into the swirling hole in the floor that leads to Hell.

I'm Still Alive
Chapter One:

(June 1st 2017 New York City.) "Are you alright Doug?" Hazel asks a little bit annoyed.

"I think you better ask for the check, I feel it coming on."

"Not again, not tonight Doug. Try to stay alive at least until we get home. That way I can put you in bed and you can die more peacefully."

"That would be nice sweetheart. In a perfect world that would be great. Do you think I want to die and fall to the floor where many people have walked? Believe me when I I tell you this, I do not want to die in this overpriced, hip restaurant."

"This is getting old Doug. Every time it seems we finally have the time to get out and have some fun, you have to die and ruin the rest of the night."

"It's not my fault. Besides I'll be back alive, hopefully by the morning and we can go get some breakfast."

"Please Doug, reach deep inside your dying self and pull out a big portion of life for the night. You can do it Doug. I love you, you can and you will do this for me. Please Doug, pretty please baby."

"I love you Hazel, see you tomorrow sometime. Baby remember don't let them take me to the morgue. Show them my card, don't forget this time."

Doug looks at Hazel and he gives her a smile. Doug's smile fades away as the life seeps out of his body. Hazel takes her eyes off Doug and takes a bite from her getting too cold already dinner. Doug stops shaking and gurgles. He holds still for a moment then he falls face first into his dinner.

Doug bonces off his dinner and slides to the floor, banging his head hard with a whopping sound at the end for all the diners to take notice of.

Hazel out loud, "Damn it, I was having such a great time. Now here they come to do and say the same things to me like they always do."

Different diners say out loud. "My God, somebody help him!" "What happen to him?" "Is there a Doctor in the house?" "Somebody call 911!" "What did he order?"

"I'm a doctor." A well dressed man who is dining tonight with two very lovely and willing to to share ladies.

"Hooray," The diners say cheerfully.

The doctor wipes his mouth and gets up from his table with applause filling the room as he walks over to Doug's and Hazel's table. "I am Doctor Adams. What seems to be the problem ma'am?" Doctor Adams asks full of confidence.

Hazel swallows the bite of her dinner she had just taken. She wipes her mouth, then she reaches for her purse, while saying to the Doctor, "Hello Doctor Adams I am Hazel and that is Doug and he is dead. Here is his card that will explain everything to you Doctor Adams."

Doctor Adams looks at Hazel very confused and says out loud, "Quick she's is in shock, somebody get her a cold compress for her head."

Hazel laughs, "That is very kind of you Doctor Adams but I'm fine, I'm not dead and I'm not in shock. Waiter can I have our check?"

The owner of the restaurant motions for the waiter to stay where he is, "Ma'am please, don't worry about your check. Your date is dead. Your dinners are on the house."

257

Hazel looks at the owner of the restaurant and shakes her head no. "Doug is not my date. Yes we are on a date but Doug is my husband. Thank you for the free dinners, can I have a couple of to go boxes please?"

The owner looks around at everybody like he cannot believe what Hazel just said to him. Then a waiter says, "I'll get them," snapping the owner out of his confusion.

The owner very nervous and wanting this dead man out of his restaurant calls out to his already walking away from him waiter, "Get back over here. What is wrong with you? We don't get to go boxes for dead people."

The diners, silent and looking around at each other can't help themselves. It starts with one laugh then two, then three and within ten seconds the whole restaurant is laughing like they are watching a skit.

Doctor Adams has had enough with this crazy scene, "Please everybody be quiet. This man is dead, show some respect."

A man says out loud, "How do you know he is dead?"

Doctor Adams looks at the man angrily and says, "What?"

The man replies, like Doctor Adams is a fool, "How do you know that man is dead? You haven't check to see if he is dead or alive yet."

Doctor Adams looks at the man like he wants to smack him, "Well Mister I Know Everything, you want to take your best shot at it? Is this man dead or alive?"

The unnamed man nods his head up and down with a pissed off look on his face. "Okay Doctor Dumb Ass, I'll tell you." The unnamed man walks over to Doug and gives him a little kick. Doug does not move nor does he make a sound. "He looks dead to me Doc." Ha,ha,ha.

Doctor Adams in shock, "I cannot believe you just did that! You might just be responsible for this man's death."

"What the Hell you babbling about Doctor Wacko? That man is dead, he was already dead before I kicked him."

"Maybe so ass face, but I feel this is more of a case where if you didn't kick him, he would have had enough life in him for me to do one last ditch effort, which would have brought him miraculously back to life again."

"Fuck you Doc, you ain't laying that shit on me. I'm out of here. Baby grab our stuff, we're splitting."

Doctor Adams yells out to the unnamed man, "Don't let the door hit you in the ass on the way out." Doctor Adams laughs out loud then says to the crowd of diners, "What an asshole. Well I guess I can at least check for a pulse."

Hazel, in a bad mood is almost glad that Doug received that little kick to his side, responds to Doctor Adams, "Don't worry about it, Doug doesn't have a pulse. Doug is dead Doctor Adams."

"I'll be the Doctor shall I? I will tell you if he is dead Hazel," Doctor Adams says back really, smart ass like.

"Knock yourself out Doc," Hazel responds back coldly before she takes a drink of her glass of rose wine.

Doctor Adams say out loud, "What the Hell is wrong with everybody tonight?" Doctor Adams bends down on the floor and checks Doug's pulse, "Yup this man is dead."

"No shit Doctor Adams. Doug dies all the time. He's died so many times, I can't remember how many times he has died so far," Hazel stops talking and downs her glass of wine. She pours herself another glass and downs that as well. Hazel stands up and stretches her beautifully built and tired body.

259

"You want to know the really fucked up part about this Doctor Adams?"

Doctor Adams stands back up on his feet and looks into the pretty face of Hazel and quietly asks, "What is that Hazel, my dear?"

Hazel moves around like her whole body is itching her. She takes in a deep breath and slowly replies. "The really fucked up part about this Doctor Adams is that Doug has died so many times, his death means nothing to me anymore. In the back of my mind is this thought, what if this is his last death he has in him? What if he doesn't come back to life tomorrow?"

"I'm sorry Hazel you are so confused. I feel for you, I have to tell you this." Doctor Adams pauses to refocus himself. "I don't know why you seem to believe that Doug is coming back to life tomorrow. Please understand this Doug is dead, he is dead now, he will be dead tomorrow. I'm sorry for your loss. Now if you will excuse me I have to call this in." Doctor Adams does not wait for Hazel to respond back, he simply walks away from this as fast as he can.

Hazel watches Doctor Adams walk away. She looks around at the crowd of not understanding what is going on here diners and ask them. "Which one of you strong men will carry my dead husband outside so I can call a taxi?"

No one answers Hazel. Hazel sighs loudly. "Please will somebody help me? I cannot carry Doug by myself."

A little old lady named Betsy walks up to Hazel and gives her a hug. "There, there my dear, everything's going to be alright. Think of it this way, you are still here and you are a very beautiful still young enough woman. There are plenty of man out there for you to enjoy. Believe me my dear, I am seventy seven years young. In my life I have buried four husbands and I'm still dating, and I'm hoping to get married one more time before I die."

Hazel hugs Betsy back tightly. "I like you Betsy and good for you. Wow four husbands, really? Which one do you miss the most, if you don't mind me asking you?"

Betsy looks up at Hazel. "My first one dear. I loved them all but my first husband whose name was also Doug was my favorite, I loved him the most. I miss him the most."

"I understand. I don't know what I'd do without my Doug. I love him with all my heart."

"My poor confused dear, your Doug is dead. You have to understand this. For the rest of your life he will be dead to you. You will have to wait until you get to Heaven to see him again."

"Thank you Betsy, I really appreciate what you are telling me. But my circumstances are very different than yours or with anybody else's in fact. I know you don't believe me, I know no one here believes me. My Doug is dead this is true but as sure as I'm standing here, he will be alive once again tomorrow. My Doug dies all the time, here read his card, someone please just read his card."

Nobody will take the card out of Hazel's hand. Doctor Adams is through with his phone call and walks back over to Hazel and takes the card out of her hand and reads it out loud to the wanting to know diners.

Printed on Doug's card: Hello I'm Doug. I have this very rare medical condition. I die and I come back to life the next day. So don't cut me open or try to bury me for deep down on the inside of myself I'm still alive. Thank you.

Doctor Adams looks around in disbelief. "What kind of craziness is this? Is this some kind of weird joke I don't understand? What the Hell is going on tonight?"

Doug comes back to life early this time and reaches out from the clutches of death and grabs a hold of a leg.

The leg that belongs to Doctor Adams. "What is it now?" Doctor Adams looks down at who is touching him and sees a now back to life Doug holding on to his leg for support. "I can't believe this? Doug you are alive, man you are back from the dead, here let me help you up."

Doug reaches out his hand and takes a hold of Doctor Adams' stretched out hand and helps himself up. "Thanks Doc, it feels great to be back from the dead. It's the same night this time. Hazel how long was I dead this time?"

"Not even a hour, my love."

"That's my fastest time yet. Alright let's get out of here the night is still early, let's go home and make love baby doll."

"Sounds great baby, but when we get home you have to brush your teeth first. You know how I hate the smell of your death breath."

Doug and Hazel walk out of the restaurant hand in hand, leaving behind a very confused room of people and the rest of their dinners that are too cold to want anymore.

Chapter Two:

The wind that blows at Doug and Hazel is nice and warm as they step out of the restaurant and onto the sidewalk.

"Let's walk for a little while, I'd like to walk away the feeling of death I have inside me."

"It's a beautiful night, why not? That was weird Doug, you never came alive that fast before. It's more frightening. The next day is bad enough. Do you think that you will start dying for shorter amounts of time now?"

"I don't know. I like this better. I don't feel as groggy and out of sorts. Give me a kiss baby, I feel so alive."

"No way Doug. Death breath is awful. You might have been dead less than an hour but still... I don't want to make you feel bad... I just do not ever want to taste death again. Please understand. The first time when you came back to life, I kissed you and that was enough for me. I'm never going to kiss you again with death breath inside your mouth and on your tongue."

"Damn that was cold. Alright, let's find a store. I'll grab a tooth brush, some toothpaste and a bottle of water. After that I'm going to kiss you, I'm going to make out with you and I'm going to turn you on."

"That sounds hot and great my alive again lover of my life. Our life is out there Doug. You keep dying more while I become more jaded to death."

"Yeah I know Hazel, my lover, my sexy wife. Death has inserted itself into our lives. It's more than a bitch. It's a frigging drag, let's not let death cover our lives completely. Together we're better, we're stronger than death. We will survive. Someday I will not die again until it becomes my time to officially die."

"That would be wonderful. Doug my dear, you have it wrong about us and death."

"How so?"

"It's not us that is stronger than death, it is you that is stronger than death. How much stronger will you become Doug? Every death there seems to be more. Your pecker alone. Damn it's grown bigger. A lot bigger than it was before your first death."

"Are you complaining my Love?"

"No, I love it. It's just, I don't know. It's a miracle but I feel deep down that it might be a curse as well."

"My pecker's cursed?"

"Yes maybe just like you are. It's not normal to die more than once maybe twice, but thirty or more times like you have? Well that is really creepy. I'm sorry, you creep me out but damn do you still turn me on. I love you Doug."

"I love you Baby. Let's find this store."

"Forget it."

"Forget what?"

"Just kiss me. It's only been an hour, how bad could your breath be?"

"Come to me and find out. Also baby my pecker is rock hard like always. I thinks it's even bigger."

"Forget the kiss, let's get a taxi. I want to get home as fast as possible. I want to see how much more of a man you are after your shortest death."

"Damn what a woman I have."

264

"Don't forget it Baby. Who else would put up with you dying all the time?"

"Just you and every other big pecker loving lady."

"You better be careful Doug my love or I might just bite instead of suck tonight. Would you like that?"

"No, no I would not Hazel my love. No to biting and a very big yes to sucking. Hooray for you, hooray for Hazel."

"You smart ass, dumb brained, sex machine. I'm turned on, I want to bite you tonight. Not on your pecker but on your neck. For some reason I think right now if I would bite your neck, I would draw blood and taste it."

"I don't know how to answer that. Yes I do, Hell no crazy lady. Damn do you have a fine ass. I'm feeling like a beast myself right now. I would bite your ass, I would not draw blood but I would bite the Hell out of it right now."

"And I would let you. I would like that. I bite your neck and taste your blood, then you bite my ass as hard as you want and as many times."

"That sounds messed up. You bite my neck, I bite your ass. There's a joke there somewhere. Probably right in the center of it."

"Pervert, sicko. Hee,hee,hee."

Hazel stops laughing and looks over at the beautiful lady that is walking up to them. Doug is about to say something but says nothing after he looks over to see what Hazel is looking at. Hazel and Doug are both in a trance. Both feel a fever of sexuality in their minds and bodies. Both want this pale, sexy lady stranger to stop and talk to them. Both want more than that. Isidora smiles as her ice cold blood burns with the passion of having sex and drinking hot blood from a male and female human.

265

Isidora stops in front of a panting Hazel. Isidora then grabs Hazel by her hair and pulls her towards her lips. Hazel puts up no fight getting ready and willing to do something she has never done before. Doug watches without moving or saying a single word. Moans do not count.

"Come to me my child, let me taste you soft warm lips. Let me feel your life, let me feel your pulse," Isidora says as she is in kissing distance to Hazel. Isidora gives Hazel a kiss with over a thousand years experience. Hazel crumbles to Isidora's mighty grip, letting her do what she may to her.

"Your life tastes so sweet, like honey to my lips and tongue my beautiful living child. Let me feel your body, all its curves. Hazel your body is so sweet and sexy. Doug you are lucky to have such a fine and tasty lady to make love to and to be your wife."

"Yes I know, I like to make love to her all the time."

"I bet that's not all you like to do to Hazel? Come to me Doug, you can move once again."

Doug legs move as they are under Isidora's control. The back of Doug's mind is calling out to him for him to walk the other way. But his pecker is too much in control for Doug to pay attention to the back of his mind.

Doug is three steps away from the kissing the other so sexy, Isidora and Hazel. Isidora removes her right hand from between Hazel's legs. Isidora pushes a wanting more Hazel away from her. Isidora licks her lips and says, "Stand right there and don't move my sweet lady snack. I want you to watch me with your man. Watch how I turn him on more than he has ever been before. Men are so easy, are they not my living pet?"

"Yes... Yes they are."

Doug wants to take over as Isidora kisses him but he can't, he hasn't been commanded to. For the first time as Doug feels a kiss better than all, he feels like he's under the control of sexual dominance.

As Hazel watches still and silent, so do a few people that has stopped as they were walking by. Curiosity of strangers that just watched two sexy ladies kissing are now watching a man being kiss in front of them like none has seen done before. This pale sexy lady they cannot take their eyes off places her right hand between this lucky man legs.

Isidora does the same with Doug when she has had enough foreplay, she pushes him away from her and tells him to stay.

"Look here at what I will entertain myself with tonight onlookers. See an amazing female and male human of your species. I think I'll start with the female, she's sweeter. I can't wait to taste more of her especially her sweet hot spot." Hazel moans and shakes from want, as Doug's hard on stands out long and proud for all to see.

"Good night onlookers, you may walk away now. How many of you want to have sex with me? Yes I know all of you. I have to say, yuck. Some yes but most of you, dream on losers, I am way too far out of your league. I wouldn't even drink your blood. Well unless I had to of course. Blood is blood, however I am the Queen of the Vampires. I am Isidora, I am stronger than all. Weak you are with your living flesh hanging off your bones. I'd like to kill you all just to look at all the blood that would flow from your gaping wounds. But alas the night is growing on and I want to have some fun, so piss off you wretched not worthy of my greatness."

Hazel is gone, she wants hot and hotter. She wants to be in between Isidora and Doug.

Doug would not care if Isidora put a collar around his neck, with leash included and made him follow her.

The people that have stopped to watch now wonder to themselves why they are watching three strangers walk away. They also wonder even deeper why they are turned on and perhaps who was it of the three that are walking away is the one that turned them on.

Isidora leads Doug and Hazel to a near by alley. A flash goes off in front of the three about twenty feet away from them.

"What is this? Damn not again. I have had enough of you Betty, you and your damn Eternity's Diner. I told you to stay out of my way. My last warning to you was my last to you. So stupid are you Betty, I will feast on your magic blood. I hope it is the sweetest of all blood I have tasted."

A very changed Betty from where we left her in her story, steps out of a newly placed down Eternity's Diner. "Shut up you hag. Don't you ever get tired of giving me weak threats? You with all your undead power is null compared to us that is a we."

"One day you human pig woman that stinks of apple pies, I will sink my teeth into your flesh. I will save this world from your too dark of evil. Compared to you I am almost an Angel. Why you are simply what comes from beneath the bowels of Hell."

Betty is pissed as Isidora is laughing loud and scary. Betty in a rage screams out to Isidora, "Come on Vampire bitch jump into our void. We will strip you of your undead flesh and blood. We will shove your dark soul right in the middle of our void. There it will stay, like a cancer in the ready to infect the world."

"I tire of you Betty, what do you want?"

"Not what, you vampire hag. It is who we want. We want the male, we want Doug. Here Doug smell our apple pie. Let its scent snap you out of your mind control."

Betty opens up one of the doors to Eternity's Diner. The scent of apple pie rushes towards Doug's nose like a tornado. "That's it Doug, come to me, come eat some apple pie."

"No he is mine, so is the woman!" Isidora screams out in a rage of lost hope.

"Keep the woman, we only want the man. We will have the man without incident or we will unleash war on you. Isidora are you ready for that much hate and pain coming at you? I think not, you are not that foolish. Come to us now Doug."

Doug under a command from another more powerful force starts walking towards Betty and Eternity's Diner very slowly and calmly.

Isidora watches Doug walk away from her as a tear rolls down Hazel's cheek. Isidora notices the tear on Hazel's cheek, she quickly rushes over to her so she can lick up the tear before it falls to the ground.

"Not an Angel's tear but almost as delicious. For Betty that was the tear of a forgotten lover. So sad, so without hope. Its taste makes me crave what I love the most in this world."

"Go ahead and drink your woman, we could careless."

"Yes Betty that is the truth. I know this. How about I drink the blood of the one that you want. How does that sound to your evil ears Betty?"

Isidora rushes on the air to Doug and grabs him around his throat in a victory gesture.

269

"Don't you dare Isidora, he belongs to us."

"You want him so very much? What would you give me for his safe passage to you?"

"Please Isidora, you don't understand. Don't do this please, we will give you whatever your heart desires."

"Please? You are weak Betty. I piss on you and Eternity's Diner. Watch as I take your grand prize away right in front of you. I will be too quick for you to save him."

"Please Isidora, please don't do this, I beg you."

"Yes beg please to me you weak human hag, as I drink your prize free from all blood in his even weaker body."

Isidora stops talking and bites down deep into Doug's neck and pulls away a thick chunk of flesh. The wound is jagged and deep as blood comes pouring out of it with no intent to ever stop flowing out.

"Watch human bitch, watch me drink, watch me kill."

"No please," Betty screams as she falls down on her knees crying and sobbing.

"You weak human, watch the end of your dream. I can feel this. This human man is the most important to you of all that you have gathered inside you."

"Yes you Vampire monster, you have ruined everything, all is lost, there is no hope. How can we go on now?"

"You can't Betty, you have lost. Now watch what victory looks like."

Isidora with no more words, bites down deep into Doug's bleeding wound and drinks down as hard and as fast as she can.

Isidora is laughing while she is drinking blood. She is having the time of her undeath, then something starts to happen. How could she not notice, was it because of the scent of apple pies? Isidora does not know as she feels the undeath of her start to decay to final death.

Betty stands back up and laughs her dark heart out. "You stupid Vampire. Don't you know you're not suppose to drink a dead human's blood?"

Isidora has already stop drinking Doug. The immense strength inside her is fading away fast. Very soon Isidora will turn into ash. Isidora thinks to herself, "I was to live forever. How could I have been such a fool?"

"That man is living death, he has died hundreds of times throughout his life until now. It was not his life we wanted but his final death we needed."

Isidora is just about to start coming apart at the seams, as Doug falls down dead to the ground.

Betty opens up the second door to Eternity's Diner which allows a part of it to escape into the night of New York City. It wraps itself around the dead body of Doug and the almost dead body of Isidora's. In a instant both bodies are frozen in time.

A coming out of her trance Hazel watches in horror as her husband and the sexy vampire lady she wanted to have sex with, float up into the air and glide towards Eternity's Diner without making a sound as they pass by.

"Hello Hazel," Betty says.

"Hello Betty, what do you want with me?"

"Right to the point, I like that. Well Hazel, we have the disease and the death we need to end the world. There's not much we are in the need of now."

271

"What about me Betty?"

"What about you my dear?"

"Well since the world is going to end, I think I'd rather be all safe inside Eternity's Diner with you Betty."

"Would you now? Okay why not, there's always room for one more. Besides I just baked a fresh apple pie, if I'm right, I think it is time for it to come out of the oven this very moment. Come my dear, join me for a slice of apple pie for all eternity inside Eternity's Diner."

"Thank you Betty, I would love to."

Betty and Hazel step inside Eternity's Diner together. After they are through the doors close up behind them and Eternity's Diner vanishes from out of sight until it reappears for the last time on June 1st 2018.

Thus ends Dark Stories for the Mind. I want to thank you, I hope you enjoyed my first book. This is just the beginning, I can't wait to bring you more Dark Stories for the mind in the near future.

Peace and be true to yourself.

Keith Starblue